Lavinia

Shiloh
Rite of Passage
Trilogy

Book One

by

Nash Wilder

Ghost Writer Books

Published in Cincinnati, Ohio, U.S.A. by
Ghost Writer Books
http://www.GhostWriterBooks.com

ISBN: 978-0-615-24190-6

Library of Congress Control Number: 2007941857

First American Edition 2008

Non Profit Donation

A portion of this book sale is being donated to the following nonprofit organizations:

Parkinson's Disease cure research
In honor of my brother, Flavius Paris "Pete" Rhodes

The Michael J. Fox Foundation for Parkinson's Research
Grand Central Station
P.O. Box 4777
New York, NY 10163
http://www.michaeljfox.org

Humanitarian endeavors

Oprah's Angel Network
P.O. Box 96600
Chicago, Il 60693
http://www2.oprah.com

Plantation preservation

The Middleton Place Foundation
4300 Ashley River Road
Charleston, SC 29414
http://www.middletonplace.org

Acknowledgment

Numerous research sources were consulted to portray actual historical characters, places, times, events, and factual trivia. Any embellishment is purely a fictional interpretation of the author in whole or part.

The life account of Lavinia Fisher was derived from publications and documents provided or recommended by:

The South Carolina Historical Society.

The South Carolina Dept. of Archives and History.

Their information is gratefully acknowledged.

A special thanks to the manuscript editors for their professional critiques.

Dedication

My dearest loving daughter,
Elaine Anne "Lanie" Dellecave-Wedding,

In loving memory of my motherly aunt,
Edith (Aunt Edie) Martin,

The unwavering love and friendship of my soul mate,
Elaine Ann "Lane" Gruber, who passed into heaven.

All will live in my heart, thoughts, and prayers,
transcending with my last earthly breath into eternity.

Poem

We pass quickly through life
Leaving indelible marks of remembrance
On those so dearly loved
Only to look upon each face again
When death reunites our souls
On a field of clouds surrounding heaven

Michael J. Dellecave

Table of Contents

Lavinia

Shiloh
Rite of Passage
Trilogy

Book One

Prologue

September 23, 1792

A cockcrow signaled a new Virginia dawn, while agonizing cries filled the air. Window light graced the face of an expectant mother. She cringed as her back arched with each stabbing contraction.

"Hold me, Samuel!" she shouted.

Her skin reddened and her knuckles whitened while squeezing her husband's hand. Perspiration saturated her, and trickling sweat stung her sight. A midwife blotted her brow.

"You're doing fine, Anna," Samuel said.

She tried to smile, but her facial expression twisted from the piercing pain.

"Ahhhh. Ahhhh. Ohhhh my God!" she screamed panting.

"Push, Anna! Push!" encouraged the midwife.

After a climactic thrust she laid exhausted. Seconds later a baby's cry triggered smiles and laughter.

"She has the face of an angel, Anna!"

"Samuel, she's so beautiful!"

"Just like her mother. And already a full head of chestnut brown hair!"

He lightly rubs his hand across his daughter's slimy, matted scalp.

"Her name shall be Lavinia, after your mother."

"Yes, Samuel, Lavinia."

As Anna glowed with contentment she cradled their firstborn close to her bosom. A proud Samuel looked on and grinned. Then he leaned over and gently kissed his daughter's forehead. It would be the first of much affection Lavinia would receive from her parents.

Anna and Samuel were common folk. Their small farmhouse was humble but comfortable. She was a schoolmistress and he a hardworking farmer. Lavinia would be their only child. It was a family filled with love.

Anna started tutoring Lavinia when she was just a toddler. Lavinia's intelligence rivaled her inherent beauty. She was quick-witted and quite intuitive. As she grew in book knowledge she also matured physically. At the tender age of ten she blossomed early into adolescence.

Lavinia was especially close to her father. She was his pride and joy. In many ways she was the son he never had. He taught her to ride, shoot, hunt, and the craft of carpentry. She also mastered the task of sowing and harvesting crops, along with the proper care of horses and livestock. Her mother educated her in the art of homemaking, and tutored her in piano. Lavinia became an accomplished musician and a quite capable cook, seamstress, and housekeeper. She was a well-adjusted and happy child.

As their little girl matured, her facial features became more stunning. Her deep, dark brown eyes opened wide when she smiled. Oh yes, her smile was like no other. She beamed with perfect teeth and dainty dimples that accented her rosy cheeks. Her hair grew long on her tall, gangly frame.

By the time her teen years arrived, she developed into a shapely young lady. The neighboring farm boys had already started to pay visits. She always seemed to possess an innate ability to flatter and tease her male suitors.

Although she appeared to enjoy their attention, her interest was still rooted in family. However, on a hot fifth of August afternoon, just before turning the age of sixteen, events would channel a new direction for her life.

"Samuel! Lavinia! The stew is ready!" Anna hollered from their covered front porch.

The two of them had been trimming a fallen tree for firewood, but a storm was quickly brewing. Moments later a drenched Lavinia came running into the house.

"Mama, come quick!"

"What is it?"

"It's Papa!" she yelled out of breath.

Anna threw down her apron and ran frantically behind Lavinia.

"Samuel! Oh my God!"

"Lavinia, ride to Doc Crowley's place! Tell him to hurry!"

She rode hard. The town physician returned only to find Anna sitting in the rain and weeping. Samuel's head lied in her lap as she stroked lifeless cheeks.

"Papa! Papa!" Lavinia wailed, throwing herself upon him.

"I'm sorry. There's no healing from God's lightning strike," the physician told them.

"Why, Mama? Why?" Lavinia asked as rain-mixed tears streamed down her cheeks.

"We can't question the Lord's act," she whimpered.

"No Mama, but I can hate Him!"

"Lavinia, that's blasphemy. Don't say such things."

"I hate Him, Mama! I hate Him!"

She ran back to the house sobbing uncontrollably. Lavinia never could accept why Papa was taken from them.

As time passed, her mother became more distraught and to herself. Anna attended church each Sabbath seeking solace. She insisted her daughter accompany her, but Lavinia never regained faith in the Almighty.

Anna continued to teach down the road at the one-room schoolhouse. Lavinia tried to keep up with the farm chores and repairs. She did all possible that her father had taught her. During the evening she comforted herself playing Mama's piano. It was a difficult time for both of them.

The following year Anna remarried a laborer named Frank Pierce who was a widower. Lavinia empathized with her mother's loneliness, and they could use help operating the farm. Frank moved into the only house Lavinia knew as home.

At first, all seemed well between the newlyweds, although Lavinia never took to him. He wasn't the considerate, hardworking man she was accustomed to know. He always had a tendency to be controlling, and soon demonstrated his true colors.

"Anna, where's my dinner?"

"It'll be awhile, Frank."

"I want it now!"

"I'm sorry, but I started it late."

"No! Please don't!"

"Mama!"

Anna was lying on the floor. Lavinia rushed to her mother's side.

"Get out of my way!"

"Leave Mama alone!"

He raised his hand to strike Lavinia.

"Frank, let her be. You're drunk!"

"Shut up, you poor excuse of a woman!"

Lavinia grabbed hold of her mother crying.

"It's okay, honey. I'm fine."

Lavinia rushed out of the room.

"No, Frank! No!" Anna screamed, as he kicked her over and over again.

Ka Bang!

A rifle shot penetrated the ceiling.

"Leave Mama alone, or I'll kill you!" Lavinia shouted, pointing the long barrel his direction.

"Why, you little bitch!"

She cocked the gun hammer again.

"No, Lavinia! No!" her mother yelled.

Anna stood up and hugged Frank.

"Mama, why do you protect him?"

"Oh, my child," her mother sobbed.

Lavinia shook her head and walked outside.

Over the upcoming months the manhandling and mistreatment repeated. No matter what Lavinia said or did, Anna continued to endure the physical and mental abuse. Lavinia could not bear to watch her mother wither into a shell of a person any longer. Now sixteen, she knew she must prepare herself to leave.

Lavinia wanted to start a life with a kind, loving man, like she remembered her father to be. About that time, a tall and handsome lad drifted through town. He stopped by the now dilapidated farmhouse. Anna answered the door.

"Ma'am, good morning."

"Good morning, young man."

"I'm lookin' for work, ma'am."

"I'm sorry. We can't afford a hired hand."

"Excuse me, ma'am, but this house is in need of serious fixin'."

"I know. It'll just have to wait."

Lavinia appeared at the door.

"Hello, Miss."

She looked and smiled at him.

"I'll work for lodging and meals, ma'am," he told Anna.

Lavinia yanked on the back of her mother's apron strings.

"Very well. You can sleep in the barn. We'll drop off your meals. My husband is particular about who comes in the house."

"That will be fine, ma'am. Thank you."

"What is your name?"

"John. John Fisher, ma'am."

"I am Mistress Pierce. This is my daughter Lavinia."

"My pleasure ma'am, Miss Lavinia."

Lavinia flashed her unforgettable smile, and led John to the barn. He was very attracted to such a beautiful young damsel, but remained aloof. He was in dire need of work, and didn't want to jeopardize his newly found position. Over the next several months Lavinia found herself flattering him at every opportunity. For the first time she was the one in pursuit.

John and Lavinia soon found themselves in a heated romance. He could no longer rebuff her advances. She had never given herself to a man before, but a feeling of recklessness prevailed over her. She snuck into the barn nightly to receive his passionate affection. It had been a long time since Lavinia felt the caring from a man. She eventually confided in John about the relationship between her mother and stepfather.

"I worry about Mama constantly."

"Why doesn't she leave him, Lavinia?"

"I have spoken with her many times. I think she feels too old to find someone else, and is afraid to live her years alone. John, I can't live here any longer."

"Where will you go?"

"I don't know."

There was a pause as a serious look crossed his face.

"Come with me, Lavinia."

"What are you suggesting?"

"Let's start a new life together in the Carolinas."

"Are you proposing?"

He looked at her and grinned.

"Marry me, Lavinia!"

"I will, John! I Will!"

Lavinia talked with her mother about betrothing John and moving away. Anna was happy for her daughter's newfound relationship, but disheartened over her departure. However, she realized it was for the best.

"I will always love you, Lavinia," she expressed teary eyed.

"Oh, Mama, I love you so much. I am worried about you. Why don't you leave him? Come with us."

"No, dear. You and John must live your own lives. My time has passed. It's God's way. I'm getting older and have no one left except you and Frank. He really doesn't mean to hurt me."

"How can you love him?"

"Child, know that the only man I really ever loved was your father."

Anna paused and became upset. Lavinia placed her arm around her mother's shoulders.

"I love you, Mama."

"I know, honey. I love you too. I want you to have this. So would Papa."

Anna pulled off her cherished emerald ring, and slipped it on her daughter's finger. Lavinia's father had given it to her mother many years ago.

"I will wear it always, Mama. Thank you."

The two held a long embrace.

"Write me from the Carolinas. And visit when you can."

"I will, Mama."

Lavinia and John left with not much more than the clothes on their backs. After a short stay in podunk towns, they settled in the booming city of Charleston, South Carolina.

Upon arrival, she quickly found a job as a seamstress and he as a laborer. Before long, a winter chill brought unexpected news.

My Dear Lavinia,

I write this letter, hoping it was you telling me of this event. Just try to be happy for me and don't worry. I'll be fine.

I want to inform you of my untimely pregnancy. Although my emotions are conflicted, I must remain thankful for this blessing from God. His reasons must always be accepted unquestioned.

Although Frank is apathetic, this life growing inside has filled me with new purpose. I am into my third month, and my health is good.

*I hope you and John are doing well. Do write me
when your time permits.*

I love you always,
Mama

Lavinia soon came to have a baby sister. The child was named Olivia. Anna wrote of the newborn being the spitting image of Lavinia.

Life became quite busy for the Charleston couple, but she wrote her mother often and visited when possible. Although a huge age difference separated her from her only sibling, she vowed to remain close.

Lavinia continued to fret over the abusive conduct of Frank, but Anna assured her that things were better. Nevertheless, Lavinia always despised him.

As the fresh years of both marriages mellowed, ironically Lavinia and John started to drift apart. John seemed to most enjoy spending leisure time with his male friends. He became more interested in making a quick buck, opposed to an honest day's work. He also developed a heavy thirst for any alcoholic concoction. Eventually, he lost his job and converted their Charleston home into the Six Mile Wayfarer House.

1

Shiloh Plantation

Friday, February 18, 1821

I look at my timepiece. It reads one forty-five in the afternoon. I begin to climb the drafty stairway to my father's study. The candle flame flutters, and the loose wooden slats creak with each footstep. Flashes of silent lightning occasionally brighten the dismal area. I hear the winds stir, joined by rumbling roars of thunder.

Atop the landing, a once cheerful hallway is darkened from ominous skies. I walk down the lonely corridor, followed by my flickering shadow. I look up to the sound of raindrops pitter-pattering along the rooftop.

As I unlock the room entrance, the droplets intensify by the hundreds. I latch the door behind me and rush to close a window. I see the heavens engulfed into an abyss of darkness.

Howling winds are sweeping twigs and debris along the ground. Young tree branches bend, and leaves twirl through the air. Soon Mother Nature bursts out with a torrential downpour, cleansing all creations. The window sash vibrates as it whistles seeping air. Pelting rain penetrates beneath its sill and drips to the floor.

While I turn toward Father's desk chair, a cracking bolt of lightning strikes. The soft candlelit room illuminates. I sit and pause, listening to the deluge of pounding water. My eyes shift to the ironclad strongbox as I scoot it in front of me. Slowly, I open the hinged top, and unfold one of its tattered letters. Once more, I read the first paragraph. The dancing candle flame rekindles the sentiment of my words held so dear.

Dear Mother,

I have fallen into love with the beautiful woman, Lavinia, now in your company. Please care for her as a daughter until my return.

Leaning back in Father's chair, I gaze into space and reminisce life's journey. Before long, vivid memories consume the essence of my being. My story starts two years ago when I sat at this very desk.

*   *   *

Saturday, January 23, 1819

I dab a quill in the inkwell, while an intruding morning breeze quickly thumbs back the slave journal's pages of time. I smile fondly, seeing Grandfather's beginning inscription.

Shiloh Plantation
Savannah, Colony of Georgia
1756 Year of Our Lord

Rhythmic sounds of trotting horses and squeaking wagon wheels divert my attention. I pause from the journal, and step out onto the second-story portico. This secluded retreat offers relaxation and solitude, rejuvenating the mind and spirit. When Father is home, he calls me here for private conversation.

I walk across the alternating black and white sandstone tile squares to the decorative wrought-iron railings scrolling its outer perimeters. Each meticulous fitting and form demonstrates exquisite European craftsmanship. I look down to an identical structure below, each supported by four circular columns crafted of limestone. Mother favors the lower level, steps away from her secret garden.

The structures face the southwest rear of our plantation home, embracing the westerly winds in the heat of day. The serene Savannah River borders our home's front entrance, where visitors may also call by boat. Grandfather beamed with pride when recounting the architectural design of the main "big" house and porticos.

I lean slightly and grasp the front iron railing. Straight ahead is our mile long entranceway, graced on each side by hundreds of majestic live oaks. These stunning creations of nature are lined in straight rows, as if strong sentries standing guard. Their massive overhead branches, draped with Spanish moss, intertwine across the roadway. This canopy of nature camouflages all traveling beneath it from my vantage point. I only have occasional glimpses of an oncoming wagon.

Meanwhile, vocals of several songbirds in quick succession attract my interest. I turn to see a sole mockingbird perched on the side railing. The long streamlined gray and white feathered bird mimics well the calls of other species. He incessantly repeats assumed melodies and watches me, while cocking his head side to side.

Father told of this late morning ritual and the whereabouts of a rice filled reward. The prize container is hidden behind Mother's largest floral pot. I throw a handful of golden grain upon a white floor tile, and the beseeching bird ceases his melodic antics. He alertly swoops down to feast on another benevolent meal.

I understand why Father finds enjoyment interacting with such a simple creature. The mockingbird, although poorly gifted with intelligence, demonstrates a wealth of commonsense. Father values sound instinct and becomes annoyed when this trait escapes people.

I resume leaning against the railing. Nearing noon, the strengthening sun warms my face, and a pleasant breeze ruffles my hair. I inhale the sweet floral fragrances rising from Mother's secret garden. The scent of early blooming azaleas and camellias dominate, amid scores of lilies and daffodils. I tip my head backward and close my eyes to savor nature's simple pleasures. Meanwhile, I hear the clatter of horses drawing nearer.

The Lord bestows much life and many blessings upon our Shiloh Plantation, and I am eternally grateful. For generations these fertile grounds have nurtured and preserved our way of life. My name is Adam Shiloh, the third generation of rice planters.

Gazing to the horizon, I slowly look east to west upon thousands of Shiloh acres. This idyllic land appears to stretch without boundaries. The panoramic view never ceases to exhilarate me.

Plentiful fields of grains, vegetables, herbs, and groves of fruit-bearing trees thrive. The longleaf forest abounds with wildlife and game including deer, wild turkey, rabbit, and quail. The river, streams, and lakes spawn a myriad of delectable fish and mussels. Our domesticated livestock and fowl provide plentiful fresh meat, milk, and eggs.

The swamp forest supplies abundant cypress and tupelo trees for construction and furniture. A variety of intriguing wildflower, songbird, and reptile species flourish within the marshlands. Boggy areas give birth to spectacular spider lilies. Beautiful flora gardens landscape our home with vibrant seasonal colors and aromas. The abounding magnolia, crepe myrtle, and oleander blooms further enchant the senses.

As the squeaking wagon wheels become louder, I observe silhouettes working the distant rice fields. Although our climate supports a flourishing crop, the spread of tropical diseases also prevails. African slaves bring malaria and yellow fever that thrive on coastal marshland. Most slaves appear to have developed an inherent immunity to the illnesses, but European plantation owners are very susceptible. Throughout the rainy summer season the lethal epidemics spread rampantly. Grandfather intentionally located the rice fields and slave quarters a great distance from the big house.

During this peak sickness season our family resides inland. This summer home retreat is about four miles west of our Milledgeville state capital, near the Georgia frontier. While we are absent, we entrust freed black overseers to manage the day-to-day rice farming. These elder taskmasters, themselves products of Shiloh servitude, are assisted by the most trusted slaves. Father finds the Negroes respond well to these foremen, hoping themselves for freedom's reward. He believes a harmonious working environment yields more productivity.

I stand back from the railing and outstretch my arms. The approaching wagon appears beneath the final cluster of branches. It is Tamba, our most reliant house servant, arriving from the stables. He has harnessed two of our strongest steeds, Gabriel and Nicodemus. Preparation for our Charleston, South Carolina, journey is underway.

Tamba, now twenty-four years old, is a strapping man capable of the most challenging physical chore. Although a loyal, well-mannered soul and quick study, if riled he can be quite menacing. Upon Mother's insistence, he will accompany me on this trip. I will enjoy his companionship immensely.

I am exactly four months younger than Tamba. We grew up together on Shiloh. We share the same love, respect, and trust, as I do with my brothers, Wade and Jeremy. Father says these feelings are the *gold, frankincense,* and *myrrh* God conferred upon us. We should unwrap and share these precious gifts with all who reciprocate.

I step back into the study to complete my writing task. There is a light knock on the door leading to the hallway. I look over to see the knob turn, but the entry is locked to ensure privacy. Father always latches this entrance, especially to deter an inquisitive and playful Jeremy, and I do the same.

"Adam."

"Yes, Mother."

"Please join me on the downstairs portico before departing."

"I will momentarily. Let me first complete the journal entries."

"Very well. And just like I tell your father, there is no need to secure this door when you're in there."

"Yes, Mother," I acknowledge and sigh.

Neither a closed door nor other deterrent stops an interruption from Mother. She can be spirited and headstrong but always means well. Today her anxiety heightens as does mine. My older brother Wade departed for Charleston on horseback several weeks ago, and his return remains long overdue. He was to meet with potential buyers of our fall rice harvest and negotiate purchase and delivery terms. I must verify the transaction, and locate his whereabouts. Anticipating my undetermined absence from Shiloh, I am working to bring family business matters current.

I again dab a quill in the inkwell and smile, while inscribing the next newborn entry.

January 21, 1819 birth of Gumbu
Second son of Tamba and Fatu

Two days ago marked another proud birth for Tamba and his lawful lady Fatu. This child is the fourth generation to live on our plantation. Tamba and his father were also born here, but Tamba's grandfather Vandi is native to the West African country of Sierra Leone. He was purchased as a slave when Grandfather emigrated from England to start Shiloh. Although Grandfather has long passed, Vandi now in his eighties still resides here.

Looking at the journal entry documenting the purchase of Vandi, I vividly recall Grandfather's story.

Sierra Leone Negro Vandi
Estimated age twenty-five years
Giant man with strength of bull
Purchased in Charles Town

Colony of South Carolina
Tuesday, June 29, 1756
Henry Lauren slave broker
Bill of sale, Gazette maintained
Caleb Godfrey ship captain
Vessel sloop ship Hare
Port Colony of Rhode Island

When he told the tale, Charleston had not been called Charles Town for quite some time. However, Grandfather persisted saying the latter. He was very set in his ways and at times quite stubborn.

The slaves from Vandi's homeland have a centuries old reputation of rice-growing experience, making them extremely valuable and desirable for plantation rice planters. Their ten-week voyage to Charles Town was plagued with hunger, disease, vermin, and beatings. Grandfather also recalled that the slave ship captain touted the pleasure of ravaging the youngest and prettiest females. Any captives who died during the passage were discarded at sea without prayer or conscience. The captain, in an effort to justify these actions, characterized slavery as a way of African political life. Unfortunately, Grandfather indicated the captain was correct, regarding enslavement complicity of Africans by Africans.

However, Grandfather being a religious man, was infuriated and appalled by this account of barbaric conduct. He vowed to always treat his slaves with human decency and kindness. This was the creed of Shiloh Plantation honored to this day.

Since Vandi can no longer work planting or harvesting the rice fields, his last journal entry reads:

Vandi, 78 years of age, good for nothing

I always detested the good-for-nothing connotation, but this is a common notation for the old or infirm.

Nowadays, Vandi works for the Lord preaching the gospel each Sabbath. He converted to Christianity from native pagan worship many years ago. Although Christians, the slaves still embody ancestral rituals within their services. I observe them dancing in a circle amid the rhythmic pounding of sticks. As the crescendo of their fervor climaxes, experiencing possession by the Holy Spirit, they glorify the Lord with shouting praises. This dramatic ring-shout ceremony demonstrates religious excitement and human bonding lacking in our worship. Most certainly, a congregationalist would never catch heavy eyes from a sleepy pulpit.

Vandi also pleasures the children with ancestral anecdotes, crafts, music, and songs. With admiration, he always speaks gratefully of Grandfather's well-doings. Hopefully our families will continue to share in the history of Shiloh.

Vandi's servitude to Shiloh and his people is unequivocally worthy of positive mention. I pause and again smile, while my quill scores his journal entry.

Vandi, 78 years of age, good for ~~nothing~~ many things

The Sierra Leoneans, like other ethnic groups, are rich in culture and tradition, speaking a creole English language influenced by their African tribal dialects. Not only do they posssess expertise in rice-farming, but their other craft skills are incomparable. They are especially proficient in the art of basket weaving. Vandi and his people must be commended on their efforts to preserve their ancestral customs.

*   *   *

Soon my thoughts turn to Father and Wade, as I see their inscriptions in the slave journal.

Father, being the family patriarch, has managed and cared well for everyone on Shiloh. He has a strong reputation for his principles and faith, but is also known as a firm but compassionate disciplinarian. Likewise, he is well respected by all slave families for his kind concern and fair treatment. I frequently observe and practice the teachings of his wisdom.

He also endows me with many English traditions and philosophies. As a boy we would emulate the red fox hunt of his English ancestry. Although Georgia is a habitat for this species, Father prefers chasing our wily gray fox instead. He finds this four-legged foe far more formidable. Although we lack in stonewalls and fences to clear, the varying Georgia terrain offers credible challenge to all.

As he ages, Father favors the less strenuous sport of wing shooting, describing it as pleasurable exercise. Wildfowl such as geese and mallards are shot in flight. He finds this hunting method demanding far greater skill than a traditional stationary target. It also affords the prey greater latitude for escape. Father always reminds me that any task without challenge offers no satisfaction to the soul. With the advent of this preferred pastime, the old gray fox and my riding backside received a reprieve.

Father has an old English recipe for building a man's character. One notion of his is that hunting grooms well-bred boys into gentlemen. Although he thoroughly enjoys the sport, it is our time together I cherish most.

Recently, Father departed to England seeking diagnosis and treatment for an unknown malady. His condition is an enigma to the most prominent physicians, and he had exhausted the possibility for cure within the States. He last consulted with Doctor Tomlinson Fort near our summer home.

Doctor Fort, although unable to treat his deteriorating condition, did recognize the symptoms from an article he had read entitled, "An Essay on the Shaking Palsy." The reading of this account all too well described Father's progressing illness.

> *Involuntary tremulous motion, with lessened muscular power, in parts not in action and even when supported; with a propensity to bend the trunk forwards, and to pass from a walking to a running pace; the senses and intellect being uninjured.**

Father decided to seek medical attention from the physician author himself, Doctor James Parkinson of Huxton Square in London. Father is greatly missed, especially by Mother, and we pray for his wellness and speedy return. During his absence, my older brother Wade assumed the primary responsibilities for operation of the plantation.

Wade developed his business acumen under Father's mentoring, but is well educated in his own right. Mother being a past schoolmistress and accomplished artist, tutored Wade and myself during our adolescent years. We later attended Franklin College in Athens, Georgia.

* * *

An Essay on the Shaking Palsy, by James Parkinson, was originally published as a monograph by Sherwood, Neely, and Jones (London, 1817).

After completing the last entries of the slave journal, I unbolt the door and relock it from the corridor. Father maintains money and valuables within the study, and is keen on security because he is leery of transients. I walk down the hallway toting my rifle and knapsack of belongings.

Mother waits on the downstairs portico surely fretting and sipping hot tea. I believe her mind weighs with thoughts of Wade. She is deeply distressed from his unaccounted absence and fears for his safety. As I start down the stairs, I think of the additional barges needed for timely delivery of our rice crop. We normally export through our Savannah port, but it is severely lacking with trade ships. Last year's yellow fever epidemic resulted in a prolonged quarantine of our city, and many rerouted vessels never returned. This combined with today's ailing cotton market, Georgia's primary cash crop, has compounded our trade dilemma. The largest and closest port of Charleston proves the best export alternative.

The crafts will be rowed along four to six mile wide inland waterways. These meandering bodies of tidal-salt-water marshes separate the mainland from a chain of barrier islands extending the length of the coastline.

We receive many plantation shipments of domestic goods and equipment by vessel, but never have transported such a great distance for export. We can only hope for good weather with favorable wind and tidal currents.

Reaching the bottom landing, I continue through the entrance parlor and onto the portico.

"Good morning, Adam."

"Mother, good morning."

She sits smiling and fanning herself, but I sense a facade of contentment.

"I was in town yesterday and noticed the cute Gruber sisters. You know Elaine has eyes for you, and I think Julie is sweet on Wade. Elaine is such a lovable, petite girl. She comes from a respected family, and is so sophisticated and well-mannered."

"Mother, are you trying to get me hitched?"

"Well, it would do you and Wade well to be wed. Two brothers marrying two sisters, why your children would be kissing cousins. Besides, I do want grandchildren before I'm old and gray."

"Wade, married? That is wishful thinking."

"And you, Adam, what about you?"

"Someday, Mother, but not now."

"Well, you know Elaine won't wait forever. Join me with a cup of tea and baked cinnamon bread before leaving."

"Thank you, Mother. I ate earlier, but will partake in a cup of tea."

Although tea is my least favorite beverage, indulging Mother will hopefully soothe her uneasiness. I plop down my knapsack and lean the rifle against the railing, hanging my hat atop the barrel. Before sitting, I bend over and kiss her cheek.

"Tea for Adam, please," she summons, interrupting Fatu's sweeping of the far end portico.

"Yaas, ma'am, right away."

Fatu was born on Shiloh, and even as children a playful attraction existed between her and Tamba. She is a most dedicated house servant with a resilient constitution. Only two days earlier, she had given birth. Fatu's mother died bearing her, and Mother's fondness of Fatu has been most nurturing ever since. Mother's first child was a stillborn infant girl, and the breech delivery almost killed her. I believe this is why she cuddled Fatu as a child. Their surrogate relationship epitomizes true human bonding.

Although educating people of color to read and write is prohibited by state and local laws, Fatu and Tamba have been discretely tutored by Mother. However, word pronunciation is sometimes influenced by their native tongue. Last year, Savannah passed legislation subjecting such teaching offenses to a thirty dollar fine. Mother simply scoffs at the ordinance. She considers it needless oppression, stemming from the insecurity of ignorant whites.

Well mannered and dispositioned, Fatu very willingly tends to Mother's beck and calls. She even satisfied Mother's curiosity in the Sierra Leone craft of basket weaving. Fatu calls the interwoven work of pine straw, palmetto fronds, and sweetgrass a shukublay. The design of these coiled baskets is amazing, capable of holding water like a clay vessel. Mother made her first basket last winter under Fatu's guidance.

"Mother, have you word from Father?"

"Not recently. Pray for his cure."

She quavers and becomes teary-eyed while I gently pat her hand. Fatu returns with my steaming cup of tea.

"Very hot, Mass Adam."

"Thank you, Fatu. You and baby Gumbu are doing well?"

"Yaas, Mass Adam. We's doin' fine."

Her fortuitous interruption is well timed, prompting Mother to regain some composure. As Fatu walks away to resume sweeping, I pick up the piping hot beverage.

"Mother, you know Father is strong willed. If medicines do not cure the aliment, his mind will."

I gingerly sip the scorching hot water as my eyes shift upward. Looking through the rising steam, she is again on the verge of tears.

"Try not to fret, Mother. We must be strong. Father always teaches strength of character evolves through adversity."

Again I gently tap her hand, attempting to calm her fears.

"I know, Adam, but your father and Wade together overwhelm my soul."

"Worry not, Mother. Wade shall be found," I assure her.

I spot Tamba at the entrance road and yell out to him,

"Board plenty of supplies!"

"Yaas, Mass Adam," he responds, while checking the harnesses of Gabriel and Nicodemus.

Tamba is quite ingenious and loads the wagon with enough hay not only to feed the horses, but also to serve as our bedding along the way. Of course, as the destination grows closer, so do our backs to the hard floorboards. Nevertheless, the diminished comfort far exceeds the exposed ground. Barring inclement weather and with moderate pace, we should arrive in Charleston before next Sabbath.

After sipping half of the steaming tea, my forehead quickly hosts beads of perspiration. I fail to realize why Mother revels in this daily ritual. During the summer months it is pure punishment in advance of the sweltering afternoon heat.

"Well, Mother, we shall be on our way. Wish me luck."

"God's speed, Adam. Please be careful. I already fear for one son. Don't forget to send word on your safe arrival."

"Yes, I will, Mother."

I stand and wipe my brow.

Her eyes again swell with tears. She pulls me down and kisses my forehead, while placing a recent sketch of Wade in my shirt pocket.

"Take this so you may show his face. And don't forget to stop at the Middleton home. Perhaps Henry spoke with Wade. Convey my warmest regards to him and Mary Helen, and please send word on your safe arrival."

"I will, Mother," reassuring her.

Mister Middleton is a lifelong friend of Father, and family members respectfully call upon him when in Charleston.

Mother's deep torment can only be imagined. Not only does she agonize over Father's failing health and Wade's disappearance, but now is apprehensive to my departure.

Although she loves all of us deeply, it is our eight year old brother, Jeremy, who commands her utmost care and attention. He serves as a catalyst to her anguish. Jeremy was an unexpected pregnancy when Mother was thought to be barren. He realizes Father is ill and Wade is missing, but his youth prevents him from fully comprehending the gravity of our situation.

"Mother, where is Jeremy, the little general?" I inquire, donning my hat.

We call Jeremy that because he incessantly plays war. Wade and I whittled him a wooden rifle and pistol as gifts for his last birthday.

She smiles and nods toward the secret garden that spans the side of the house. I step off the portico and walk the cobblestone footpath.

Nearing the entrance, I observe Jeremy pretending to fight with Tamba's firstborn Sanie. Both are the same age. Each is hiding in Mother's circular gate temple, behind one of twelve round pillars. These limestone uprights brace a vaulted domed roof of copper. Lying on the floor between the supports are her prized pots of flora. This freestanding, open-air structure affords shade on sultry days. It also occasionally serves for afternoon tea or private dining for Mother and Father. Of course, it now accommodates a rip-roaring shootout with the toy guns.

"Ka bang! Ka bang! Ka bang!," each boy shouts across from one another, scampering behind their next column refuge.

Running beside them is an excited barking Colossus, our large black Newfoundland. Pray tell neither crush any of Mother's flowering blooms, as the consequences for their backsides will be severe. The smack of her hand will pain them far more than imaginary bullets.

Both boys have heard many War of 1812 stories from Wade and myself, but Mother discourages our fighting tales. She regards them as inappropriate for young ears. However, she reluctantly acknowledges future conflict may fall upon Jeremy for resolve.

"Bid me farewell!" I yell, trying to distract their attention from play.

"Coming!" Jeremy hollers, as both boys run to a side of me.

"Well, lads, who is winning your latest battle?"

"The Georgia militia!" Jeremy proclaims.

"Who are you fighting?"

"Sanie is the Massa-chu-setts militia," he struggles to say because his front teeth are missing.

I chuckle at his whistling pronunciation and comical smile.

"Silly boys, we cannot fight ourselves. One of you pretend to be an Indian or Tory enemy. Now bid me goodbye."

Each take hold of a side of me with a quick hug.

Looking up at me, Jeremy blurts, "Will you bring back sweets?"

He giggles, and Sanie grins ear to ear.

I hesitate, teasing them for a reply, as they squirm and tug on my shirt.

"Only if Mother confirms good behavior during my absence. Jeremy take good care of her. You are now the man of the house."

Jeremy outstretches his wooden rifle, crying out, "I will protect Mother like a real militiaman!"

"Me too, Mass Adam!" Sanie joins in.

"Good boys. Now wish Tamba farewell. Skedaddle!" I tell them, rubbing the top of their heads.

Both burst toward the rear of the house. A barking Colossus trails. When leaving the garden, Mother's crucifixion statue beckons my spiritual attention. I approach and kneel on one knee, removing my hat and bowing in prayer.

> *Dear God, heavenly Father, please care for Mother and Jeremy during my absence. Let us find Wade in good health, and please remedy Father's illness. God Bless Shiloh and all living*

upon it, man, woman, child, and beast. Thank you, sir. Amen.

Afterward, I grab my rifle and knapsack from the portico and climb onto the wagon. Tamba has already boarded and is patiently waiting. As we leave, Mother waves the handkerchief she had been using to dry her tears. Fatu tries to console her, while we nod and tip our hats. Tamba signals the horse team ahead with a whistle and yank on the reins. My last glance back pictures Jeremy and Sanie pretending to be horse soldiers at the expense of a howling Colossus.

We slowly ride out of our Shiloh sanctuary, passing under the magnificent oaks standing guard. Our wagon wheels creak along as trotting hoofs churn the earth beneath us.

My thoughts turn to Father as we approach the tallest tree of the lane. This particular gigantic oak serves as his place of solitude, just as the secret garden does Mother. During troubling times he is strangely consoled observing, "Even the strongest branches collapse from their own burdening weight, but always grow anew. Souls sometime shoulder shattering torment, but we must rejuvenate and stand strong like the resilient oak."

"Tamba, pull over."

"Yaas, Mass Adam."

He brings the wagon to an abrupt halt.

I walk beneath the humongous growth gazing upward, squinting from the glare of peeking sunlight. I circle the massive trunk and scrutinize a remnant of a huge bygone limb. I discover a tiny bud signaling new growth, promising to someday restore the grandeur of the branch.

The wisdom of Father's words suddenly becomes clear. I smile and pat the tree bark, thankful to have experienced my first epiphany. Confronted with unknown journeys ahead, my spirit must remain resolute with the resilience of Father's oak.

Tamba again whistles and snaps the reins. Gabriel and Nicodemus rear back their heads, snorting with flapping tails, and trot toward the main road.

I begin to ponder scenarios of Wade's whereabouts, hoping for his safe return. I slouch in the wagon seat and stretch out my crammed legs. I slide the hat brim to my brow to shade my face, and cross my arms. While closing my eyes, I take a slow deep breath. Although not bodily tired, I try to calm my restless mind. In short time, Tamba turns the wagon toward Charleston by way of the King's Highway.

2

Six Mile House

We continue traveling on the King's Highway, the only passable road leading to Charleston. Near the coastline, this countryside route is densely wooded with longleaf forest and marshland. Other than sparse travelers, mail delivery, and merchant wagons, there are few inhabitants within miles. Of course, wild beasts, renegade Indians, and dreaded highwaymen always require defense. We are well armed with pistols and rifles, should any two or four-legged foe confront us. Likewise, a small pistol I dubbed Equalizer is conveniently concealed in my boot. It was a belated Christmas gift from family, upon my return from the War of 1812.

The highwaymen are scraggly sorts, assaulting and robbing unsuspecting pilgrims. They earn a living through any dishonest deed imaginable. I once heard of these rogues stealing a cow ailing with fever and butchering it. They sold the tainted meat to an orphanage, and the children took ill for days. Only the Almighty could find redeeming value in such wretched beings. Although I am distrustful of the red savages, even they uphold honorable beliefs.

For six full days our rolling wagon wheels squeak and thud as we bump along the rocky dirt road. The only other sounds interrupting the still of day are birdcalls and communicating coyote howls. Of course, the silent welting of our skin by hungry mosquitoes gives rise to an occasional curse. Periodically, we spot deer, elk, and wild turkey amid the woodland thicket.

The evenings are even quieter, only bearing sounds of crickets and hoot owls. We break at nightfall on our last night of travel, and our dancing campfire flames shimmer against a cloak of darkness. After supper we sit near the crackling logs, warming ourselves from the chilly night air. Tamba tells ancestral stories handed down through Vandi. All are enjoyable as if hearing the first time. He ends the evening playing banjo while we sing negro spiritual songs. I find the entertainment nourishing to the soul.

We douse the dying embers, and I lie down in the wagon bed with rifle aside me. My back indicates the hay is well depleted from the appetite of Gabriel and Nicodemus. Always alert to danger, Tamba and I alternate guard duty every several hours, allowing each other to rest. I look up to a blanket of dazzling stars that quickly soothes me asleep.

At twilight, the who-who-who of a barred owl awakens me. Perched in safety and not beholding to a firearm, the unusal dark eyed species seems the wiser. Grandfather spoke of one Cherokee Indian myth revering these creatures of the night. The women would bathe children's eyes in water with owl feathers to help them remain awake longer. Thinking of Jeremy, I know Mother would scoff at this practice.

"Tamba, good morning. We should arrive in town before dark."

"Good mo'nin', Mass Adam, I'm glad."

"I know, Tamba, these days have passed slowly."

After watering and feeding the horses, we enjoy a breakfast of fruit and biscuits. Then we start the last leg of our journey to Charleston.

Following an uneventful day, the sun starts its final decent as we reach the Ashley River. A sign bears direction to the Middleton and Drayton Plantations, but we cross by ferry toward town. On the other side, we head eastward on Dorchester Road and turn southward onto Old State Road, only miles from our destination.

Out of nowhere, ominous clouds race across the sky and blanket the countryside. The playful chatter of nearby mockingbirds is hushed. An unidentifiable flock of waterfowl flies hurriedly from sight, as whirling wind crackles leaves along the ground. I take a deep breath, sensing a changing texture and fragrance within the air. The birth of a thunderstorm promises to curtail the tranquil day.

We batten down the wagon and wear our coats for Mother Nature's imminent drenching. So close to our destination, we forge ahead with a strong sense of urgency. Tamba and I are tired by the trip, wanting nothing more than a hot meal and soft bed.

Passing a cove area, the sun vanishes below the horizon as dim moonlight and stars barely penetrate eerie clouds. Moments later all heavenly bodies disappear into darkness. Rain slowly descends on us, and each droplet brings a chilling dampness intensified by the plummeting night temperature.

As the storm strengthens, thousands of raindrops loudly bombard the wagon. Their oncoming angle pelts my face. Stirring winds gain momentum, and we grab hold of our hats. All at once, the heavens unleash rumbles of thunder, followed by a violent downpour. The cloudburst severely impairs our vision, but we push onward.

Gale-force winds soon howl and violently sway the wagon, like a rocking cradle lullaby gone mad. Gabriel and Nicodemus forge the turbulence with snorting nostrils and water soaked heads. Amazingly, their footing remains stable. They trot ahead undaunted.

Suddenly, powerful roars of ground-shaking thunder and flashing lightning strike pure fear within the stallions. Each rear up on hind legs, sounding a cry of panic I never heard before. The startled steeds gallop full stride down the road, seemingly outrunning the wind. The racing wagon, turned four-wheeled chariot, jostles uncontrollably. Airborne wheels bounce and spin above the hole-pocked road.

Tamba desperately jerks on the reins, yelling,

"Whoa! Whoa!"

I also grab and pull the bridle straps, but to no avail.

Without notice, the horses' harnesses disengage, and they charge ahead in a frenzy. The freewheeling wagon careens from the road toward a formidable oak.

"Tamba, jump!" I cry out, leaping into the air.

Ironically, the waterlogged ground and mud puddles cushion my fall. I stand up dazed. A figure slowly emerges from the blinding rain.

"Mass Adam, you all right?" he hollers over the deafening storm.

"Yes, Tamba. I am wet and muddy but fine. And you?" I shout.

He nods as water gushes off his hat brim.

Together we struggle against the relentless elements, making our way to the wagon. Surprisingly, it withstood collision with the tree trunk. The only damage is a missing wheel.

"We must seek shelter from this horrid night. Let us collect our belongings," I yell, amid another outbreak of thunder and lightning.

"Yaas, Mass Adam!"

Our movements hasten as we bend our heads, fighting the unmerciful pounding of rain and blustery wind. We press forward hoping to find the runaway horses. After several minutes, there is still no sign of Gabriel or Nicodemus.

"Look, Mass Adam!"

He excitedly points to a distant fluttering light, and I grin.

As we approach, we realize the glimmer indeed signals refuge. A roadside sign reads Six Mile Wayfarer House and Tavern. We trudge toward the establishment, which sets back from the road a good distance.

When stepping onto the piazza, I hear muffled talking and laughter. I peer through a water-streaked glass pane and see a most welcoming fire ablaze. A man and woman are standing across the room, facing away from us. The lady is attired in a long, high-waist, tan dress. Her long dark hair extends midway down her slender back. The man is wearing a light-colored shirt and dark trousers.

Other men are seated at two round tables playing cards. Most of the cardplayers appear to be a scruffy bunch. For a brief second, Father comes to mind, because he possesses an innate ability to interact well with people of diverse backgrounds. He would be an excellent innkeeper for the likes of these patrons.

I step to the solid oak front door and rap hard using the bottom of my fist. After a moment and no answer, I return to the window and look inside again.

I start to talk as Tamba turns his ear toward me.

"Nobody hears over the raging storm!"

He gestures a massive fist. With the underside of this hand, he slams the hardwood three times. The entrance shimmies from his powerful blows, and clinging beads of water fall to the ground. Surely all inside heard his knocking. If not, they must be deaf.

Seconds later the door slowly cracks open, exposing the partial face of a woman.

"Good evening ma'am. We are seeking accommodations for this …," I holler, as another volley of thunder drowns out my ending words.

She looks at me expressionless, standing almost eye level, but slightly shorter than my six-foot frame. Turning toward Tamba, she slowly tilts her head backward. Her eyes roll to the top of his imposing stature. She also takes notice of our belongings and rifles in hand. When the door finally opens I see a shapely, buxom lass. She has the facial features of an angel.

"Welcome," she greets with a friendly voice and gorgeous smile.

I have never seen such cute dimples.

Her deep brown eyes sparkle, while she pushes back her long dark hair from her face. I feel mesmerized, staring at what must be the most beautiful woman in the Carolinas. I do not recall having such a powerful attraction to a grown woman. Although I had a casual relationship with an amorous girl during my college years, we went separate ways after graduation. Since then I have not had a lady on my arm. Of course, Mother encourages me to court the Gruber sister, Elaine. She is an attractive and reserved woman that undoubtedly would make a fine wife and mother. I plan to know her better upon my return home.

"Welcome," she repeats, breaking my trance.

She motions us inside with a sweeping gesture.

"Thank you, ma'am."

As we enter, Tamba stoops to clear the doorway, and we remove our soggy hats. An immediate silence falls upon the room. I only hear nature's fury and crackling of burning firewood. One man, somewhat disheveled and knock-kneed, walks toward me. He is a good-looking sort, tall with fair skin and dark hair.

Leaning over he whispers in my ear, "We don't allow Negroes in the house. He'll have to stay out back in the barn, if you're lodging."

Why does he not speak aloud? Perhaps he fears alienating Tamba, a gargantuan man holding a rifle. First sight of him can be extremely intimidating. Although I do not agree with many rules governing persons of color, the wishes of one's home must be honored. I tell Tamba to bunk in the barn and promise a warm evening meal. Being an obedient soul, he puts on his hat and leaves.

"My name is John Fisher, and this is my wife Lavinia."

"Pleased to meet both of you. I am Adam Shiloh of Savannah."

I shake his hand.

Turning to Lavinia, I gently hold her soft hand and bow my head.

"Ma'am, my pleasure."

I follow with a kiss atop her fingers as she lingers within my grasp. She flashes me an enticing smile, deemed most flattering. My thoughts again submit to her seductive beauty.

"Adam, where ya headed?" John interrupts.

"Charleston. My horses broke loose from the wagon down the road away," I respond, still distracted with Lavinia's presence.

Meanwhile, my wringing-wet clothes continue to drip onto the oak-timbered floor.

"We can put you up for the night," Lavinia cordially offers.

"Four bits includes bed, meal, and drink for you and the Negro. In advance," John states.

"Fair enough."

I shell out the coins, having my money pouch lightly filled to dissuade a would-be robber. The reserve money remains hidden under the wagon seat, well guarded by nature's wrath.

"Come sit by the fire and dry yourself," John suggests, signaling me to follow.

"Lavinia, bring the man hot tea and a bowl of stew to warm his stomach, and take some to the Negro."

My footsteps squish across the floor as the heat woos me closer.

"John, we have no more tea leaves," she responds.

He seems oddly perturbed over a trifle issue.

Only indulging in tea for politeness, I volunteer, "A mug of ale would be greatly appreciated instead."

"That we have plenty," Lavinia assures, projecting a lively voice and delightful smile.

"Thanks to you and Lavinia for your hospitality."

I plop down my knapsack and hat on the rock fireplace hearth. Leaning my rifle under the mantel, I hang my saturated coat over the barrel. I sit on the stone hearth and remove both boots from my rain-soaked socks. I am careful to reinsert Equalizer from my boot into my sock. The fire breathes well with crisscrossed logs and should dry my clothes quickly. Shooting flames and glowing embers also tame the dampness and chill of the night.

"So, Adam, haulin' goods to Charleston market, are ya?"

John follows with a swig of ale.

"No. I am in search of my brother Wade, who traveled this very road several weeks ago."

At that moment the lovely Lavinia reappears. She is carrying a drink in one hand and a wooden bowl of stew with bread in the other.

"Don't recollect a boarder called Wade. Do ya?" he asks her, while still looking at me.

"That would be my brother, Wade Shiloh of Savannah. I have a likeness of him."

I show them the sketch, and without hesitation he responds, "Nope."

Lavinia shakes her head no, and sets my meal on top of the hearth. Before turning away, she hesitates with a captivating glance. My appetite is momentarily satisfied by the hunger in her eyes. I sense a taboo attraction yet feel the euphoria of a giddy schoolboy.

"Lavinia, show the drawing to the others," John commands.

She takes the sketch from me, looking at him contemptuously before sauntering to the tables. This friendly merchant couple apparently bickers as any other. Smelling the steaming bowl of hot stew with thirst quenching ale quickly sets my motion to eating. Meanwhile, John joins the cardplayers in a hand of luck.

After finishing my meal, I stand and face the roaring flames to dry more thoroughly. Lavinia returns, positioning herself between the fire and me.

"Adam, no one recalls seeing your brother."

She looks toward the players, apparently to see if she is being watched. Folding the sketch, Lavinia places it in my shirt pocket and slowly zigzags her forefinger across my chest.

"Thank you, ma'am."

I am surprised, yet intrigued with such boldness. She cracks a mischievous smile and leaves without another word.

Turning to dry my backside, I take a longer look at the cardplayers across the room. From the laughter and conversation, these guests who I presumed to be customers are actually friends. Although all seated seem strongly opinionated, they do not hesitate to do whatever John Fisher requests. It is as if each were a laborer. As I observe the motley crew, I feel my clothes warm to the touch.

A burst of laughter echoes from across the room, as John rakes in a hand of winnings.

"Adam, come and meet everyone," he urges me.

Although extremely tired, I politely walk over.

"This is William Hayward, James McElroy, Seth Young, and John Andrews. Over there, is Joseph Roberts, James Sterritt, and John Smith," he introduces, pointing to each person.

I bid hello and nod, but do not sense the friendliness received from the Fishers. Of course, Lavinia's hospitality is extremely peculiar.

The person Roberts has a cropped, half-moon cut from his ear lobe. This is a mark of punishment for a crime. I feel somewhat leery of these individuals, but Mother has always taught me to give the benefit of doubt. However, she also espouses honoring suspicious feelings. For now, I will do both.

"Join us in a game of poker," Hayward slurs, appearing half inebriated.

"Not tonight. My journey tires me and dawn comes early."

Hayward grumbles and gulps down a mug of ale.

John summons Lavinia, who returns barefooted from another room. Her dark hair flows forward, covering her well-endowed bosom.

"Lavinia, show Adam to his quarters," he orders.

I collect my boots and belongings, while she lights a candle amid the hammering fury of nature's outburst. I walk behind her along a dark corridor, seeing our shadows trail from the flickering flame. At the end of the hallway, Lavinia stops, turns, and faces me. Her glistening hair clings to her gown. She raises the candle between us at chin level. I look into her hypnotic eyes and see my lustful reflection. Her flirtatious ways are unnerving yet excite my senses. I find her alluring and dangerously seductive. At this moment, my thoughts are not of sleep.

"Your room, Adam," she motions, with a sensual voice and devilish grin.

She opens the door, and I notice a damp musty smell, most likely harbored from the rain. I set my belongings down inside as she lights another wick atop a writer's bench. Suddenly, a strong storm breeze from a partially open window snuffs out both flames. I rush and close the sash, stepping by way of a small puddle. Although quick to move aside, my socks did not escape more wetness. The floorboard cracks apparently provide drainage to the cellar, preventing a much larger pool.

I turn around and bump into Lavinia. Instinctively, I reach out to balance myself. I feel the softness of her hand clinch mine, as my moist, sock-covered feet blanket the top of her bare toes.

"I am sorry, Lavinia. I did not mean to walk on you."

I take a step backward.

"There is nothing requiring apology, Adam. I never second guess fate."

I attempt to release my grip, but she holds onto my hand once more. When I start to talk, she instantly places two fingers over my lips. Then she pulls me into her voluptuous bosom, hugging me firmly. Her soft cheek rests against my stubby unshaved face, and I smell an enchanting fragrance embodying her hair. Thinking of what consequences hold, I pause briefly before embracing her.

We linger in each other's arms, as her bewitching beauty holds me spellbound. Ironically, her grip is likened to an innocent child seeking affection. I gently rub my hand up and down her back as if consoling a troubled mind, yet feel my heart racing from excitement.

"Adam, do not think of me as a scarlet woman," she whispers in my ear, as her lips brush against my lobe.

I feel goose bumps from the warmth of her breath, and pull back my head. Even in darkness, her loveliness radiates.

"Lavinia, are you not married to John?"

"He is a changed cruel man, making me party to regretful deeds. I no longer love him as a husband."

"Lavinia! Lavinia! Are you down there?"

She rushes to open the door.

"I'm here, John. The window was open and a gust of wind blew out the candles! Adam, I will be at the town market tomorrow morning. Look for me," she utters, nervously composing herself.

I nod yes, hearing his footsteps scamper down the corridor. I sit down on a chair and cross my legs.

Bolting into the room, he shines his light about, observing a wet floor beneath the window. Seemingly satisfied by her explanation, he lights both extinguished candlesticks. He hands one to each of us with a disgruntled look.

Lastly, he simply remarks, "We bid you good night."

Irritated from Lavinia's extended absence, he grabs her roughly by the arm, and they leave squabbling.

I sit and stare at the jittering flame, passing my palm over the melting wax. Feeling the bite of the fire, I concur this is no dream. My heart remains racing. Never before have I experienced such strong desire mixed with a feeling of compassion. Although I do not fully understand her predicament or intentions, her beauty and charm have captivated my soul.

By now my mind and body are exhausted. I need rest before the rooster crows. The room door has no lock, so I lodge a chair under the knob. I want no more surprises tonight, unless a dream. I blow out the candle and plop down on the goose feather bed. I place Equalizer under my pillow and the rifle aside me. My eyes drift asleep.

I awake early and step to the window, avoiding the rainwater residue. The harsh storm left telltale remnants that include dozens of puddles and scattered tree limbs. The sun peaks through the horizon, gradually penetrating the dense morning fog. A cockcrow beckons man and beast from sleep, as chirping songbirds welcome the new dawn. I open the sash and inhale the pleasant fragrance of oleander blooms.

I walk to the dry sink and splash my face several times to help fully awake. An adjacent towel is embroidered with a horse, and my thoughts immediately revert to Gabriel, Nicodemus, and Tamba. I hurriedly put on my boots, tugging at the stirrups. With all my possessions in hand, I scurry down the still dim corridor.

When I enter the tavern area, the man Hayward is stoking the fire with fresh wood.

"Good morning."

He looks at me, giving a grunt and nod. Judging by the smell of tobacco and stale ale, he must have one hell of a headache. This can only complement his gruff demeanor.

"Where might John or Lavinia be?"

"John's sleepin', I reckon. Lavinia rode to the town market to pick up fruits and vegetables," he struggles answering between coughs.

"Please tell them goodbye. I must be on my way."

As I open the front door, thinking he is unheard, Hayward mumbles, "Don't forget the dumb Negro. Don't wanna smell up the stalls."

I pause and turn, giving him a disgusting look. He just smirks and turns away, while I head toward the barn.

The rising sun is still burning off thick mist, hindering my vision as I walk. Finally, the silhouette of a wagon is visible and Tamba comes into sight.

"You found the horses and repaired the wagon!"

"Yaas, Mass Adam. Gabriel and Nicodemus was grazin' een dah field over yonder. I found dah wheel by dah oak."

Tamba's herculean strength is quite impressive. He once defeated six grown men in a tug of war. It is of no surprise he single-handedly lifted the wagon and reattached the wheel. As always, he displays resourcefulness and ingenuity along with brawn.

We board the wagon and Tamba tugs on the reins with a whistle and yell. Being only six miles from Charleston, we should arrive in short time, barring no more unforeseen circumstances.

"Tamba, did you rest?"

"Yaas, Mass Adam. Miss Lavinia brought me suppuh last night. This mo'nin' she ask me 'bout you."

"What did she ask?"

"She wanna know if you have a woman. I told her Mass Adam not hitched."

"Single I am, Tamba. That I am," I concur smiling.

"She rale pretty woman, Mass Adam."

"I know, but the price for pretty things can be costly."

I wink, and he just grins and chuckles.

Minutes later, we pass wayfarer houses advertising as the Five Mile House, and shortly thereafter the Four Mile House. Tamba concludes that traveling from either direction crosses the Four Mile and Six Mile houses first, leaving the Five Mile House short of trade. Recalling Hayward's ignorant departing comment, Tamba is not the one who is the veritable dimwit.

As we pass the Four Mile House, a man and woman wave from the yard. I flail my hat, returning the hospitable gesture. We continue traveling on Old State Road, and soon observe town directly ahead.

3

The Arrival

As we enter Charleston, Old State Road becomes Meeting Street Road. I traveled downtown only once as a young boy, following the 1804 September hurricane. Father, Wade, and I were visiting the Middletons and made a trip into the city. The monster squall had levied irreparable damage. Now I notice new buildings, a full seaport, and the city swarms with people. The liveliness of this town is worthy to capture with paint on canvas.

While crossing Market Street, the marketplace is bustling with customers and purveyors. I gaze across the crowd, but notice no sign of Lavinia. Continuing down Meeting Street Road, we pass many storefronts, housing upper-level living quarters. The businesses appear well patronized.

In the distance, I hear commotion echoing from the wharves. I see slaves loading and unloading precious trade goods from barges and sailing vessels. Most certainly the commodities include indigo, rice, and cotton.

This morning the horses acted somewhat skittish. No doubt they felt traumatized by last night's storm. Now the gentle ocean breeze creates a far more hospitable and relaxing air. Gabriel and Nicodemus trot almost dignified as if sensing the cultured atmosphere. Mother credits the French Huguenot influence for this worldly stage.

I promised to send Mother word of our safe arrival and to call upon Mister Middleton. After locating the post office and sheriff, we will venture to Middleton Barony Plantation. Of course, Hayward's mention of Lavinia's marketplace destination remains ingrained in my mind.

The dirt road eventually transitions to uneven cobblestone, and I am reminded of how these mismatched street pavers came to pass. Grandfather said the empty merchant ships sailing from Britain would ballast their hulls with these heavy rocks. When docking in Charleston, the stones would be exchanged with the weight of goods for the return voyage. As our jolty ride continues down Meeting Street Road, I take great pleasure to trounce upon the British cobblestone. My bitterness over the Redcoats during the War of 1812 remains an open wound.

I look up and down the crisscrossed bumpy streets to observe proper women adorned in long embroidered dresses. The loose garment is styled with a low neckline and high waist bunched just below the bosom. Many ladies are sporting complementing attire of bonnets, shawls, spencers, and parasols. As their leather slippers tiptoe over wet ground, the body skimming dresses are lifted to safety. While protecting the delicate fabric, the show of petticoats and flirtatious smiles garner the attention of passing men. Tamba and I look at one another and smile.

The front of their hair is parted in the middle, with tight ringlets covering each ear. Long hair, on the back of their head, is drawn up into a loose bun. I envision Lavinia in her humble farm dress, with free falling silky hair. She is a splendid portrait of natural beauty requiring no frills. Her image and touch have truly possessed me.

Approaching a trough, we stop momentarily to water the horses. A general store across the road catches my eye.

"Tamba, wait while I inquire for directions."

"Yaas, Mass Adam."

I sprint across the street, dodging an oncoming carriage. The jangling of a bell signals my entry into the shop. I immediately smell a strong tobacco aroma. Since I left my box of cigars at home, now is an opportune time to stock a few. Even though it is still morning, I have a weakness for the aromatic beauties. They remain one of my few but guilty pleasures. I especially relish a fine smoke while sitting on the portico accompanied by a cool evening breeze. Such activity is therapeutic for thinking and calms the soul.

Before long a rotund storekeeper enters from an adjoining room. He obviously responds just as well to the dinner bell.

"Good mornin' to ya," he greets.

Smoke swirls to the ceiling as he waves hello with his right hand. Catching a whiff of the unpleasant odor, I instantly know it is an inexpensive stogie.

"And good morning to you, sir."

Over the years I have been partial to several tobacco blends, but none as pleasing as Cuban grown. Father well knowing this addiction, thoughtfully gives me a box each Christmas. While I peruse the store selections, the long brown morsels are spotted on the darkest corner of the lowest shelf. They are seemingly hiding from their impending fate, as I snatch a handful.

"Will that be all for ya?" the storekeeper mumbles from one side of his mouth.

I look up and see his discolored teeth clinching the stinky stogie stub.

"That it will."

I hand him a silver dollar.

"Comin' or goin'?"

"I am just arriving, looking for my brother. Did you see him by chance?"

I show him the sketch, and he clears his throat while staring at the drawing.

"No, can't say I have. What's the problem?"

He returns a handful of change with an inquisitive look.

"He never returned home from Charleston and is long overdue."

"Check with the sheriff. There are rumors of people missing. It's those damn highwaymen, thieves and murderers they are."

"Where can I find him?"

"Sheriff Cleary, Colonel Nathaniel Green Cleary. His office is in the courthouse."

"Which way might that be?"

"The courthouse is easy. Just follow this street down to Broad. It sets right on the corner."

"Oh, and one more location, the post office?"

"In the Old Exchange building on Bay and Broad Streets. Just a hop and skip from the sheriff's office."

"Thank you kindly for your help."

"You're welcome. Come again."

The bell tings a farewell.

We proceed south toward the post office, and I observe many grand private homes. The residences are graced with colorful gardens and landscaping, surely belonging to the most successful merchants.

Tamba waits with the horses while I enter to mail a note. The premises are well organized, and I stand at a counter to write.

Dear Mother,

As promised, I am notifying you of our safe arrival in Charleston. It is Saturday, January 30. The town is cosmopolitan as you well described. I have begun the search for Wade and will call upon the Middleton residence this afternoon. I shall write again to inform you of progress and lodging.

Your loving son,
Adam

I step to the mailing window, and a distinguished gentleman greets me.

"Good morning, sir. A piece of mail?"

"Yes, sir. One en route to Savannah."

I hand him the letter, then unfold the sketch.

"Have you seen this person?"

"I have not. For what reason do you inquire?"

"He is my brother, Wade Shiloh. Several weeks ago he traveled to Charleston, never returning to Savannah."

"Do you have more drawings?"

"No, why do you ask?"

"We have a new printer in town, Morse, Samuel F.B. Morse. Perhaps he can replicate this picture. Many people pass through this building, and a posting could prove beneficial."

"That would be most appreciated. Thank you for the information and consideration. My name is Adam Shiloh."

"You are most welcome. I am Postmaster Thomas Bacot."

I engage his firm handshake and bid goodbye.

Tamba and I proceed to the huge, three-story structure that houses the courthouse. He remains with the wagon while I enter the building. I am overwhelmed by the detailed intricacy of the lobby. Most noticeably, it contains a grand marble split staircase and huge crystal chandelier. Sheriff Cleary's office comes into view, but I find the entrance locked. I peer through the door window, only seeing a sleeping dog curled up in a corner chair. I decide to return later.

We continue riding south to land's end at the tip of the peninsula. The ocean lies straight ahead, and we are bound on each side by rivers. The Ashley borders the west and to the east lays the Cooper. It appears the two rivers converge to fill the vast sea bay. Grandfather referred to this area as Oyster Point, describing it as a shell beach. The placement of cannons on this ground, during the War of 1812, has since labeled this location as the Battery. We loop around this landmark, and return to Market Street in quest of Lavinia.

The vibrant marketplace, with low building stalls, stretches from Meeting Street Road to the waterfront. When Father and Mother visit, they always speak of the fine selection of meat, fish, produce, and bakery goods.

"Tamba, pull over."

"Yaas, Mass Adam."

I begin walking among the horde of people.

Above the bartering noise, I hear tormented cries of cattle being slaughtered in makeshift street corrals. I watch as they are butchered into sections and chopped into salable cuts of beef. The unwanted remains are thrown onto the roadway.

Seconds later turkey buzzards draw my attention circling overhead. The hovering scavengers swoop down to feast on the discarded street scraps. Hundreds more roost on rooftops. They obviously eat well, judging their plumpness. I later discover they so well rid the city of garbage, that a ten-dollar fine is levied if anyone harms them.

On a nearby street corner, baskets similar to Fatu's are offered for sale. I cross over and pick up one of the many sizes and shapes, scrutinizing the craftsmanship. Indeed, the quality appears comparable.

"Are you a Sierra Leonean?"

An elderly negro artisan flashes a toothless smile.

"Yaas, suh."

She is wearing a freed negro badge for inspection. Grandfather told me about these City of Charleston branded emblems. Any free person of color, Negro, mulatto, or mestizo, over the age of fifteen years must register and purchase one. Should the identification ever be absent from sight, a fine is levied. If the penalty is not paid in a timely fashion, the person is committed to prison labor.

Although labeled as free people, this non-slave society is severely lacking in human rights. Nevertheless, they contribute to the city's economic growth. Many are skilled tradesmen earning a living as carpenters, coopers, shipwrights, bricklayers, blacksmiths, millwrights, and weavers.

When reading the badge, Tamba comes to mind. He always carries identifying papers should we become separated. Of course, anyone attempting harm to Tamba would be foolish.

I glance across the street and chance to see Lavinia shopping for fruit. Standing in the shade, her beauty seemingly outshines the sun.

"Sell me your best basket for carrying produce, quickly now," I implore the street vendor, as my heart palpitates.

"Yaas, suh."

She hurriedly provides me change.

I scurry across the roadway, meandering through a throng of patrons. After bumping into bystander shoulders and stepping on a few toes, I reach Lavinia. She is haggling with a merchant.

"But this fruit is not fresh like the morning dew. I will pay half the asking," she protests scowling.

"Sold! You barter well! I would fear to be your husband," concedes the chuckling street vendor.

"Rightfully so," she agrees, displaying a dimpled grin.

I sneak behind her and whisper, "Lavinia."

She twitches from startle.

"Ohhh, Adam. I so hoped you would come."

"Let us go and talk."

"I must return soon because John will look for me," she nervously answers.

Lavinia notices the empty basket I am carrying and appears puzzled.

"For you," I gesture.

"Thank you, Adam. You are more than kind."

She beams with delight.

"Come, Lavinia, we will not be long."

I gently nudge the small of her back, prompting her to leave and pay for the produce. After filling her basket, we walk down the street. I am very eager to talk with her.

"Lavinia, about your predicament with John. Why do you not leave him?"

"You don't understand. John will stop me if I try. Besides, there is nowhere to go here. I have no living family except Mama and an adolescent half sister living in Virginia. All of my acquaintances are only loyal to him."

We turn the corner, continuing down State Street. The market noise gradually subsides. She appears exasperated, and her dimples all but disappear.

"No, Lavinia, today's dawn brings a new friend, Adam Shiloh."

"Oh, Adam."

She sighs and her dazzling smile reappears.

I point to a low rock wall, only steps away.

"There is a place to sit."

She sets her basket down and scoots next to me, as I lay my hands on my crossed leg.

"Adam, do you like me?"

Slowly, like a shy schoolgirl, she strokes her forefinger atop my hand.

"Very much, but my mind is troubled."

"Because I'm married?"

"Yes."

"My marriage has been over for several years. I am but a piece of property to John, not unlike your servant."

"You no longer love him?"

"No. I can't tolerate his overbearing and abusive conduct. I want to have a life with a caring and loving man of respectable stature. John now follows a life of questionable character."

"Perhaps he can change."

"He wasn't always like this. I have tried to mend his ways, but to no avail. Now I only want a divorce and to wish him well. I have had opportunities to leave in the past, but rebuffed the advances of many men."

"Lavinia, I cannot deny my attraction to you."

"Oh, Adam, I like you so much. I don't know why, but I'm drawn to you also."

She lays her soft, warm hand on top of mine.

Looking down, I notice her lustrous fingernails and a simple emerald stone on her right ring finger.

"You wear no wedding band?"

"No. I only honor my mother with this family heirloom. Adam, I wish we could spend more time together."

I look up, and we smile at one another.

"Then we shall. When can we meet again?"

Although my conscience does not condone the words I just spoke, my fascination with her is overpowering.

"There is an abandoned farmhouse several hundred yards from Six Mile House, heading toward town. I can get away for a short time almost nightly."

"Then we shall rendezvous there. When is the best hour?"

"At dusk. John plays cards after eating and will be less inclined to notice me missing."

"And if he does?"

"I'll merely say I went for a walk. Whenever you are there, signal me by lighting a candle in the window."

"How will I know you are coming?"

"When you see a burning wick in my sill. I should be on my way now. We must not raise suspicion, fearing what John might do," she stresses, picking up the basket.

"Very well. I will see you soon."

"I will be waiting, Adam."

Our hands share a warm embrace.

We hurry back to the noisy marketplace. She boards her wagon and rides away, waving goodbye. An ocean breeze lifts her hair, while the prospect of seeing her again raises my spirit.

As I board our wagon, Tamba is gesturing farewell to a passerby.

"Someone you know?"

"No, Mass Adam, a Sierra Leonean worker. Told me where dah Methodist Church iz."

The Sabbath is quite important to Tamba, and I assure him he can attend tomorrow's service. He is a Methodist, and I am Episcopalian. He indicates the Old Bethel United Methodist Church is on the corner of Pitt and Calhoun Streets and is open to everyone, including freed blacks and slaves.

We return to the sheriff's office, but the entrance remains locked. Again I peer through the door window, and the mutt is still curled up in the same position. Its sleepy eyes flutter, but ignore my intrusion.

From here we head northward, arriving at the export wagon yards of King Street. I observe many pioneers dressed with coonskin caps, cowhide clothing, and moccasins. It is reminiscent of the wilderness I explored during the war. Their overloaded wagons lumber along the trails from the Carolinas and Georgia frontiers to barter mostly hides for supplies. I see teams of four to six horses or mules hauling farm wagons of cotton and tobacco crops.

These hunters and farmers infuse the economy with purchases of food, drink, lodging, and sundries. Following a brawling good time, they return to independent solitude. Their goods, purchased by the brokers, are resold to foreign buyers at profit. The Charleston commerce is a dichotomy of trade, fueled both by archaic and modern methods.

After pulling up to the export offices, I traipse building to building inquiring about Wade. So far no one recalls him. Many owners express goodwill for his safe return, and caution me about the dangerous highwaymen. I have been in town a matter of hours and hear foremost about these notorious characters. After canvassing the open establishments, I plod back to the wagon.

"We shall return on Monday to query more merchants. All will be closed on tomorrow's Sabbath."

Tamba, aware of my frustration, tries to console me.

"Mass Adam, we'll find Mass Wade."

His massive hand pats my shoulder. I give him a halfhearted positive nod.

By midafternoon, we begin to tire and ride toward Middleton Barony. This time we cross from town over the Ashley River bridge leading to the road of its namesake. The newer wooden bridge is a sizable structure. It is wide enough to accommodate wagons coming and going, and each side has a rail path for foot traffic. However, traveling the road on the other side is not without challenge. Some passages narrow to a wide bridle path.

After a tedious road journey, we arrive at the Middletons and ride down a long entrance lane. We pass slave herdsmen tending to grazing cattle and sheep. I also see horses and mules in a nearby meadow. Vegetable gardens and rice fields line the perimeter. We pass along a collage of out buildings that include workshops, barns, and stables. Behind these structures is a community of servant and slave quarters. I hear a cacaphony of sounds, emanating from stomping mules and cackling chickens, to a slamming blacksmith hammer and stroking carpenter saw.

Directly ahead stands three adjacent buildings, appearing most welcoming and magnificent in craftmanship. The extremely large center home, being the big house, is flanked by two smaller residential structures. The big house is conjoined with a three-story tower, serving as a sheltered entrance. Outside steps lead up to the tower's first-level doorway. The home is actually five stories, counting an apparent cellar and attic. The neighboring north and south flanker buildings are much smaller, being only two stories in height.

Tamba halts the horses, and I amble around to the front of the big house that faces the Ashley. Most visitors surely approach from this direction, arriving by barge or boat. Roadway travel is typically longer and more difficult, especially during wet weather. Wagons and animals can easily become entrapped in the pluff mud of the soggy saltmarsh.

The stately big house and flanker buildings are elevated on a bluff overlooking a terraced hillside. I see distant lakes and a myriad of trees and flora leading to the river below.

While I observe the breathtaking vista, the big house front door opens. I turn around to see a house servant.

"Good day, suh," she calls out.

"Good afternoon, ma'am. I am here to see Mister Henry Middleton."

She nods.

I walk toward her, and she ushers me inside.

"One moment, suh."

Leaving me standing in a grand entrance parlor, she walks away. Moments later, a distinguished gentleman with graying hair and receding hairline approaches me. He extends his hand.

"Hello, young man. How may I assist you?"

"Good afternoon, sir. Are you Mister Middleton, Mister Henry Middleton?"

I reciprocate his strong grip. Father always says strength of character is measured through the firmness of one's handshake.

"That I am, and who might you be?"

"I am Adam Shiloh, the middle son of William and Caroline Shiloh of Savannah."

"Adam, why of course, I remember you! You were only around ten when we last met. That's the age of my son Williams today. It's been a few years, and you've grown into a fine looking young man. You have the tallness of your father and good looks of your mother," he remarks chuckling.

"Mother sends her warmest regards to you and Mistress Middleton."

"Please express my gratitude, and tell Caroline I only wish your father and her were also here. You know he and I have much history together. I trust everyone is doing well?"

"Father is at this moment in London seeking treatment for an aliment. Mother and Jeremy are well. It is Wade that brings me to Charleston. He departed Savannah four weeks ago with no return, and I was hoping he may have stopped to pay respects."

"No, Adam. I'm sorry to say Wade has not called for quite some time. Please come to the study so we may further discuss these matters."

"Thank you, sir."

He places a hand on my shoulder, leading us to mahogany high-backed chairs, identical to Father's and equally comfortable.

On the way he summons a servant.

"Jessie, hot tea for our guest and me."

"Yaas, suh."

"So what ails your father that our physicians lack remedy? Is he experiencing failing faculties? We're aging you know, your father and I."

"Father's mind is keen and responsive, but his trembling hands and weakened voice are bothersome."

"I am grieved to hear such news. Please convey my best wishes for a timely recovery. Anything I may do for your family only requires asking. I will also seek a blessing from the Almighty this Sabbath."

"Thank you. Thank you very much."

"When did you arrive?"

"This morning. I would have been here last night, but was waylaid by a broken wagon from the storm. Tamba, my house servant, and I sought refuge at the Six Mile Wayfarer House."

"Oh yes, the turbulent winds uprooted some of our flora and seedling oaks. Have you made arrangements for continued lodging?"

"I will be staying in town, if you would be so kind to recommend a reputable hotel?"

"Nonsense, I have plenty of sleeping room. You can stay here at Middleton Barony. I insist. Your father would be disappointed if you lodged elsewhere. Besides, Mary Helen and the children are vacationing at our upstate Whitehall home in Greenville, and I welcome the company."

"You are right. Father always speaks fondly of your times together. It would please him greatly knowing my stay is with so close a friend."

"Surely I can help you find Wade. I know the politicians, judges, and lawmen of Charleston, actually the whole damn state. You know I used to be governor, and now I'm just ending a political term as congressman. Hell, I occasionally tip a few with President Monroe."

"Thank you. I gladly accept your offer."

"I'm happy to assist, Adam. You can sleep in the south flanker that partially serves as the gentlemen's guesthouse. One of the upper story bedrooms will afford you complete privacy throughout the evening. The first level operates as a business office for all the plantations, but only during the day. Your house servant can bunk in the servant quarters. He will be most welcomed there."

"You are very gracious, and I appreciate your hospitable invitation. My stay should be brief."

"Remain as long as you wish. Your family is always welcome in my home. Did you arrive by road or the Ashley?"

"By road. The trip from town after crossing the wooden bridge was tiresome."

"I know. Coming by way of the river can be less cumbersome and timelier. You can also cross by ferry to the outskirts of town down the road near Drayton

Plantation. Over there, the peninsula roadways are more traveled and better facilitated."

"We crossed the ferry route to town when arriving."

"Oh, well good, you're familiar with the terrain. Of course also feel free to commandeer one of the pleasure barges. With eight oarsmen and a favorable tidal flow, you can arrive in Charleston within several hours. Of course, our rice barges, being forty feet long and fourteen feet wide, can accommodate a whole wagon and team."

"Thank you again."

"Whatever I can do. Now tell me more about Wade. Was he traveling alone or in one's company? Where was his journey to end in Charleston?"

"He was traveling by himself on horseback. Wade was to conduct business with a King Street exporter for the fall rice harvest. I stopped there this morning, but no one remembers him. I plan to question more merchants on Monday."

Jessie enters the study serving our piping hot tea. I can already feel my forehead sweating.

"This is Adam Shiloh of Savannah. He will be our guest in the south flanker gentlemen's quarters. Do see his accommodations are ready."

"Yaas, suh," she acknowledges, glancing at me.

"Oh, and also arrange lodging for his house servant, Tamba."

"Yaas, suh," she assures while leaving.

Following the brief interruption, Mister Middleton sips his steaming tea.

"Did Wade have a sizable sum of money in his possession?"

"About twenty silver dollars."

He raises his brow, wrinkling his forehead.

"An amount certainly enticing to any highwaymen. We have grave problems with these lots, accosting unsuspecting souls and stealing anything imaginable. There has even been mention of persons disappearing. It's starting to affect our vendor trade and cast a stigma of fear on our great town. Sheriff Cleary will be summoned immediately so we may meet. I will notify you upon confirmation."

"I did call on Sheriff Cleary earlier, but no one was present."

"He was probably tracking down outlaws. I hear he has been quite busy with citizen and traveler complaints alike. I know how to find him. Meanwhile, Jessie will show you and your servant to your lodging."

"Thank you."

"Please join me for an eight o'clock supper, and you're welcome to accompany me for a garden constitutional before dinner. The flora is a continual effort of labor, becoming more beautiful each passing year. Your mother marvels at the progress with each visit."

"Undoubtedly, she will quiz me regarding the landscaping. I most certainly look forward to the walk. My legs beg for exercise after the wagon ride here. What time, sir?"

"Let's meet out front around seven o'clock."

"Very well. Thank you very much for your warm and gracious hospitality and likewise the influential assistance."

"You're welcome, Adam."

Mister Middleton again summons Jessie to escort Tamba and me to our rooms.

Outside, I inform Tamba of our stay and instruct him to meet me early each morning. I introduce Jessie, and she directs him to the nearby stables for boarding the horses. While leading me to quarters, she informs me Tamba's housing will be within her servant duplex structure.

The south flanker guest accommodations are most comfortable. As on Shiloh, the furniture is of mahogany, almost impervious to the clinging humidity. After bathing, I lie down for a short nap before putting on a fresh change of clothes. My thoughts drift to Lavinia, with anticipation of our farmhouse rendezvous.

Nearing seven o'clock, I saunter to the front of the big house to await Mister Middleton. I gaze toward the Ashley River, which borders a portion of the peaceful gardens. I remember Mother praising the formal French design, influenced by the architecture of the Garden of Versailles. She said the acres of land include lakes, ponds, and sculptures. The presence of ornamental accents also enhances the natural habitat of the flora and wildlife. Organized footpaths traverse throughout, staging visual effects to further enrapture the senses.

Mother recalled that creation of the grounds took approximately one hundred slaves ten years. Originally the landscape only provided for greenery of various shades, sometimes artificially induced through shadows. Henry integrated this straight-laced French discipline with colorful blooms, characteristic of English secret gardens.

She described individual garden areas as being geometrical, and displaying symmetrical collages of trees, shrubbery, and flowers. The plantings are protected from animals in the grazing fields by a deep ditch called a ha-ha. This ingenious barrier houses a fence below ground level, affording an unobstructed sweeping view of the grounds.

Mother also said each cultivated garden creation is personified with a usage theme. One manicured area is designed for sport, while another for tea, or yet romping children. If her description is only partially accurate, I am about to enter a paradise.

She has not been here in quite some time and would enjoy any unseen plant varieties. In the past, Mister Middleton has given her new species to transplant within her secret garden. This pleasurable pastime aids to relieve her anxieties.

Mister Middleton soon arrives, leading me down a terraced hillside toward the Ashley. Ahead, two distinctly shaped lakes come into view.

"These are the Butterfly Lakes. My mother had an affinity for these creatures as yours does flora," he comments fondly, while hesitating with an empty stare.

"I recollect Mother speaking of these precise formations. The creature itself could not possess wings of greater symmetry. It is as if these still waters could rise and fly."

Mister Middleton chuckles.

Returning up the sloping hillside, we stroll beyond the north flanker, and come upon an enormous live oak by the riverbed. The tree is breathtaking, certainly the largest of its species. None on Shiloh imitate its height or breadth, including Father's gigantic oak.

"Sir, the growth is like nothing comparable."

"Yes, it was a trail landmark used by the Indians for centuries. Estimates have this enormous feat of nature nearing eight hundred years of age. Your father always marvels at its formidable size and longevity."

Returning to a pathway, we approach a most magnificent alabaster marble statue. The form is of a sitting and partially draped wood nymph. Her leg is crossed as she laces her anklet. Her soft flattering face appears lost in deep thought. The sculptured detail of her pose and attire is exquisite. Graced with colorful blooms of surrounding flora, she exudes overwhelming beauty and serenity. My eyes behold a most delicate mating of man and nature. I am charmed from her loveliness, no less than that of Lavinia. I stand in awe at the setting.

I mull over her stoic smile, concluding her enigmatic expression projects a profound presence. Intentional or not, it stimulates a pondering mindset. As with da Vinci's Mona Lisa, interpretation is left to the beholder.

"Who crafted this beautiful figure? I find it pleasantly intriguing."

"It was sculpted as a gift by Rudolf Schadow, almost ten years ago. It is a glorious work of art."

"Most indeed, sir."

Resuming exploration of the property, we meander around a walkway surrounding another body of water. It is rectangular in shape.

"Adam, this is the reflection pool, home of the heavenly swans."

"Their graceful movements are seamless with the water like the arabesque of a ballerina."

"Yes, and equally entertaining to watch."

In addition to the astounding plant life color and sweet aromas, a multitude of songbirds fill the air with melodies. Egrets, herons, and waterfowl also complement the terrain. The only devilish creatures surfacing are occasional reptiles rippling the still waters.

Soon dusk approaches, reminding us of the time. We set our path to the big house for supper. Before entering the dining room, we stop by his study.

"Adam, I hope you are enjoying your stay."

"Absolutely. Very much, sir."

"Did you like the garden tour?"

"It was extremely pleasurable, and the incomparable grounds surely rival the Garden of Eden. Mother would be ecstatic."

He grins.

"Oh yes, I know well her love of flora, ever since giving her that first rose plant years ago."

"It is aside a trellis that is consumed by the vine growth."

"Fantastic, I am pleased it takes well to the Georgia soil. You know, the first tea plant in our nation was introduced here about seventeen years ago."

Foretelling my next question he chuckles volunteering, "Yes, that is how your mother began her tea garden."

"What other beautification plans do you have for the grounds?"

"Well, I am constantly adding new botany species and ornamental landscape. Only time will tell."

"This land is artfully sculpted, as Schadow did the wood nymph. The splendor of your plantation will serve well many generations to come."

"I can only hope my descendants see the beauty as do your eyes, Adam. Now let us see what Jessie has sculpted for dinner," he says jovially.

As we amble down the corridor, Mister Middleton comments on his magnificent display of paintings and collectibles.

"Adam, more artwork is displayed within the north flanker which is home to the music room and library."

"I look forward to seeing it all."

He observes my interest in a particular family portrait.

"A favorite of my father and mother, with me as a baby. It was painted by Benjamin West, as were several others."

"An exceptional artist."

"Top of his craft. He's the first American born artist to earn international recognition as a portrait painter."

All of the home furnishings are absolutely magnificent. When we reach the dining room, a huge mahogany table dwarfs the French china setting for two.

Jessie, assisted by another house servant, serves overflowing containers of food. I smile at the appetizing smell of fresh baked corn bread, fried chicken, and steaming vegetables. Although I am hungry, this nourishment would satisfy a half-dozen famished adults.

"Eat, Adam. We have plenty."

"Thank you. This is more than enough."

After indulging in a dessert of hot apple pie, Mister Middleton suggests convening in the north flanker. There we can chat and imbibe snifters of brandy.

We rise from the table, complementing Jessie on a delicious, well-prepared meal. Mister Middleton dismisses her for the evening and requests a six o'clock breakfast. We walk outside toward the third building.

"Adam, are you an avid reader?"

"Most certainly."

"You shall be pleasantly pleased."

We enter the north flanker into a grand library. I see shelves of literature towering to the ceiling. The reading material is well organized and categorized alphabetically by writer. I examine several rare author works.

"Your collection is most impressive."

"Thank you. These are some of my revered holdings. Only through the written teachings of the past, can we learn to base our future. The real wealth is here, not in the rice fields."

"Very well spoken, sir. How many publications exist?"

"It is in the thousands and growing every year. I honestly lost count. Perhaps a good project for Jessie."

We chuckle.

"Come, Adam, let's relax."

He leads me toward another room.

There we are greeted with two more high-backed mahogany chairs. They are positioned on each side of a fireplace. While we sit and enjoy a libation, I view several musical instruments including a piano.

"Do you play?"

"Not really, Adam. I leave entertainment to the talented. As a young man, I remember my father playing the flute exceptionally well. Mother played the harpsichord until her passing five years ago. My sister Septima is also well gifted with the harp, but I seem to do better as a botanist and politician."

"Mister Middleton you are a true measure of success, even if not a musician."

"Thank you for your kind comment, Adam."

"A Cuban?"

I present two of the delectables from my inside jacket pocket.

"Absolutely. Brandy without tobacco is no less than bread without butter."

We laugh and lick our outer tobacco wrappings to slow the burn. Picking up a flickering candle, he lights both brown beauties. He draws a few puffs and passes the burning aroma under his nose.

"This is a fine specimen."

"These Cuban imports are hard to better. Of course, this peach brandy is equally tasteful," I concur, after a sip of the flavorful spirits.

"I received word from Sheriff Cleary late this afternoon. We meet tomorrow at his courthouse office following church services."

"Very well. Thank you." I acknowledge, puffing on my cigar.

"Adam, knowing both of our families are Episcopalian, please join me in worship. We'll attend St. Michael's since it is catty-cornered from the courthouse, making it most convenient to Sheriff Cleary's office."

"It would please me greatly to join you in worship."

"Excellent! Jessie will see the carriage is ready for departure at seven o'clock."

"May I at least offer the carriage services of my house servant, Tamba?"

"Why of course, that will be fine. We'll ride to the ferry, weather permitting, and cross to the outskirts of town. Otherwise, we'll voyage down the Ashley by barge."

My mind instantly thinks of Lavinia. By way of the ferry would route us past Six Mile House. I could take note of the abandoned farmhouse.

"You said Saint Michael's?"

"Yes, the glorious church exudes the presence of heaven, but sometimes supports a dull sermon. Of course, with Mary Helen and the children being at Whitehall, we can doze without interruption."

I laugh.

Mister Middleton, a regarded and respected businessman and politician, demonstrates a lively sense of humor. Of course, an intoxicating beverage sometimes serves well as punch for entertainment. After we engage in a long conversation, I unsuccessfully hold back a yawn.

"Excuse me."

By now the snifters are empty several times over, and our cigars disintegrated into ashes.

"Adam, you seem tired. So am I. Rest and we shall convene in the morning. Please join me for a six o'clock breakfast."

"That I will. Thank you again for your gracious hospitality."

We bid each other good night.

Although I do not know Mister Middleton well, I am pleased to have his concern and best interest. Father would also be elated, knowing I have accepted the assistance of his lifelong friend. While walking to the south flanker, I recollect Father saying, "Friendship evolves like courtship, a prelude to a marriage of unconditional support and trust." He and Mister Middleton are certainly a testament to those words.

Early morning Tamba arrives to receive duties for the day. Being the Sabbath, he normally is excused from obligations following lunch and prior to dinner. Likewise, time is allotted for early morning church attendance. However, he understands there is now no normal schedule.

We walk to the big house, and Jessie greets us at the front door. She directs Tamba to the kitchen in the cellar and leads me toward the dining room.

Along the way, I notice a number of hanging fire buckets containing wet sand. Likewise, a substantial number was present in each flanker building. The stitched dark leather body is about one foot long, embossed with the Middleton coat of arms. Like Father, Mister Middleton obviously is very conscious of fire and safety. Mother, although cautious, would most appreciate the container decor.

Upon entering the dining room, Mister Middleton is sitting at the head of the table reading a newspaper. He looks up and lays down his reading material.

"Adam, good morning, I trust you slept well?"

"Good morning. Very well, thank you. The plump goose feather bed is most inviting."

"Excellent, now for a welcoming meal. Jessie, hot tea for Adam," he summons, gesturing his cup.

"Yaas, suh."

"I know you have not been in Charleston for many years. Perhaps, you would enjoy a small tour of town, following church and our meeting with Sheriff Cleary."

"That would be most appreciated. I may have need to call on other people and places during my search for Wade."

Moments later, Jessie enters, serving my least favorite steaming hot beverage. After a hearty breakfast, Mister Middleton again calls out for Jessie.

"Is the carriage ready?"

"Yaas, suh. It's out back with Tamba."

"Thank you, Jessie. We'll return for supper."

"Yaas, suh."

She smiles, while clearing the table.

We depart for church and our day of activities. Our carriage route leads southward, paralleling the winding

Ashley. A few miles down the road Tamba nears the river ferry turnoff, and Mister Middleton nods toward a spread of land.

"There is the Drayton Plantation. Charles Drayton attended school in England with my father, Arthur, and married father's sister, Hester. Unfortunately dear Aunt Hester passed many years ago, but not before bearing him eight children. Charles and I continue a friendly family rivalry with our botanical gardens. Adam, I hope my jabbering isn't boring you."

"I find the history of family and tradition quite interesting. The toil and fortitude of our forefathers seeded our existence. Their memory should be celebrated and preserved throughout generations."

"Adam, your youth reflects the wisdom of a matured man. Most certainly, your father is proud."

"Thank you, sir."

"Down the road further is Saint Andrews Episcopal where I frequently attend church services. It is the oldest church in South Carolina, dating to 1706. Being a quaint country church, it attracts a small but dedicated congregation."

"I do recollect passing the church en route here. Its close proximity to Middleton Barony does afford convenience."

In short time, we board the ferry and cross the Ashley River into rural Charleston. We travel the main roadways toward town, and I hear many church bells resonate throughout the countryside. I chance a glimpse of Lavinia, walking across the distant piazza, when approaching the Six Mile House. A moment later we pass the deserted farmhouse. My anticipation of seeing her heightens.

Eventually, the towering bell steeple of Saint Michael's comes into sight, summoning Charlestonians to the Almighty.

4

Charleston Tour

Soon the carriage wheels bounce along the uneven cobblestones of Meeting Street Road. As we approach Saint Michael's Church and Cemetery, the ringing of its church bells overpowers all others. I see the tower ropes sway to clang eight massive bells, and notice the steeple clock's lone hour hand. The reverent sounds awake the living to heaven's promise, while the graveyard souls slumber in death. Worshippers are making pilgrimage by foot, horseback, and carriage.

After we disembark from our carriage, Tamba proceeds uptown to worship at the Old Bethel United Methodist Church. He is instructed to return following his services and await our departure from Sheriff Cleary's meeting.

Mister Middleton and I enter the massive entrance doors of Saint Michael's and stand within a crowded vestibule. He exchanges nods, handshakes, and quiet hellos, as many people address him as Congressman. Some still call him Governor.

After brief pleasantries, we enter the sanctuary and walk down the center aisle beneath a grand candle-lit crystal chandelier. Cedar box pews fill the altar level and a three-sided seating gallery looms overhead. Mister

Middleton motions me to enter a long double-pew, number forty-three.

"This large pew is obviously of special significance."

"The Governor's Pew. Fortunately, Governor Geddes is Presbyterian," he answers grinning.

"Adam, President Washington attended service here during his Southern Tour of 1791. He worshipped from this very pew, which seems to have acquired celebrity status. I was but a young man at the time when my father introduced us. My father was a signer of our Declaration of Independence."

"Yes, I know. It's an historical event to certainly hold in high esteem."

"He idolized politics with a passion. And did you know he also designed a portion of our Great Seal of South Carolina?"

"No, sir, I did not. His contributions to the development of our nation are certainly the measure of a patriot. He will be revered, especially by South Carolinians, for years to come."

Mister Middleton beams with pride, while continuing to talk and point out recent church changes.

Momentarily, an organist commences the opening hymn, and the rector steps to the lectern. The striking tall pulpit, with a massive sounding board, is supported by two Corinthian columns. This crafted creation will certainly echo the sermon to the most distant ears.

The music is joined by a choir of young boys attired in white loose-fitting garments, best described as wide sleeved gowns draped over cassocks. The purity of their dress and falsetto voices grace the church with an angelic ambiance. Unfortunately, Mister Middleton's singing voice is by way of his musical instrument talent.

When sitting down at the close of the hymn, he leans over whispering, "The rector is Nathaniel Bowen, also the bishop of South Carolina."

The sermon is well delivered, but reserved and lacking in spirit. There seems to be an epidemic of fluttering and flapped eyelids. Having observed the exuberance of slave services, we are undoubtedly deprived of religious fervor. The uninhibited negro expression of praise unleashes the inner spirit. Their emotional awakening of the soul remedies any outbreak of bobbling heads.

Outside, Mister Middleton introduces me to several prominent Charlestonians, including Bishop Bowen. We converse briefly before crossing the street to Sheriff Cleary's courthouse office. Mister Middleton notes City Hall and the Guardhouse occupying the other two corners.

As we open the sheriff's door, Sheriff Cleary stands from his desk to greet us. The snoozing dog jumps from a chair to investigate. Standing on hind legs, she outstretches both front paws against my knee. I follow with a hearty rub atop her sleepy-eyed head. She wags her tail with delight.

"Daisy, down girl!"

The obedient pooch returns to lay down and squeals a big yawn.

"Daisy minds you well, Nathaniel."

"Henry, she knows I'll lock her up too."

They chuckle and greet with a spirited handshake.

From my past observation, this could have well been the animal's sole exercise for the day.

"I haven't seen you since last election, how are you?"

"I'm doin' fine, Henry, and yourself?"

"Very well, Nathaniel, thank you. Is matrimony yet on your horizon?"

"No, Henry. You know I want my sanity."

Everyone laughs.

"Henry, your message expressed urgency."

The sheriff glances toward me, obviously curious to my presence.

"Nathaniel, please meet Adam Shiloh of Savannah. Adam, this is Sheriff Nathaniel Cleary."

We exchange firm grips, and his smile reveals tobacco-stained teeth.

"Gentlemen, rest yourselves."

The sheriff gestures toward two chairs, and he resumes sitting behind his desk.

"Nathaniel, Adam arrived from Savannah yesterday in search of his brother Wade. He departed by horseback from Savannah toward Charleston four weeks past, and his whereabouts is unaccounted. His scheduled return is long overdue," Mister Middleton states matter-of-factly.

Sheriff Cleary picks up a tobacco pouch from the desk and looks my way.

"What route did your brother travel?"

"By way of the King's Highway."

Sheriff Cleary stuffs a clump of the shredded tobacco into his mouth. The chaw bulges one cheek to deformity, as if a goose egg fills his jaw. He begins chewing the wad while talking.

"Did your brother have a stop along the way?"

The clarity of his speech is amazing, considering how much foreign matter fills his mouth.

"I am aware of no stops other than Charleston. He was to meet with the King Street export merchants. I canvassed many yesterday with no results."

The sheriff turns his head sideways, and takes aim at a spittoon positioned on the floor near the desk. His nostrils exert a quick inhale, and his lips pucker. With a sharp exhale he delivers a forceful spitball. The brown stained saliva sails through the air and lands accurately within the wide copper reservoir. A slight echo reverberates from the hollow core, alerting us to a successful hit. He cracks a prideful smile that he has shot on target. Of course, the splattered surface of the spittoon and surrounding floor mark many failed attempts.

Mother often complains to Father, Wade, and me about our smoking of cigars. She cites the smell as being quite repulsive. I can only imagine her tizzy should we acquire a taste for this disgusting habit. This could also well be the secret to his celebrated bachelorhood.

Sheriff Cleary wipes his mouth and continues speaking, "We have issues with highwaymen along the King's Highway, robbing money, goods, and livestock. Nothing or no one is sacred to these scoundrels. This isn't the first suspicious disappearance either."

"Nathaniel, I hope you collar these no-accounts quickly. The city's economy and reputation are at stake. We can't afford to have people missing or the rich wagon trade threatened," Mister Middleton interjects, appearing miffed.

"I know, Henry. I know. Our posses have been unsuccessful at locating and flushing all of them out. By the time we investigate a complaint, many times the varmints are long gone. Most victims passing through don't want to spend the necessary time here for identification or prosecution. Many of the local citizens don't even report a crime, fearing retribution. We're focusing on an area where there seems to be increasing problems and are expecting arrests within days. Believe me Henry, we're doing our best with the resources I have."

"I know you are, Nathaniel. We're all just very frustrated. Let me know if there's anything I can do. Adam, do you have Wade's sketch?"

"Yes, Mister Middleton, right here. This is a good likeness, Sheriff."

He studies the drawing while savoring his chew. After hearing the sheriff my thoughts turn to Lavinia. I am reminded of her husband's unsavory character friends.

"We have a new printer in town, Samuel Morse. I'll see if he can duplicate this sketch for posting about town."

"Why that's an excellent idea, Nathaniel," Mister Middleton remarks.

"Sheriff, your Postmaster Thomas Bacot also suggested Morse. He even offered to display the sketch."

"It's hard to get one up on Thomas. Morse should be open for business tomorrow. Stop by my office, Adam, and I'll take it over to him. If it can be replicated, I'll give Thomas a copy."

"Thanks, Sheriff. I'll drop it off."

Everyone stands.

"Henry, Adam, I will keep you informed."

We thank the sheriff and walk out to the courthouse lobby, pausing in conversation.

"Adam, Sheriff Cleary is a fine lawman and will investigate Wade's disappearance thoroughly."

"He appears to take his work very seriously."

"Yes, he does. Now let me show you other elements of Charleston. Perhaps we'll garner information on your brother in the process."

"Very well, sir. I see Tamba."

He pulls up along Meeting Street Road across from Saint Michael's, and we cross over toward the carriage.

"Adam, we'll ride through town so you may develop a comfort level with the surroundings. Where else have you been besides the sheriff's office and post office?"

"Only the marketplace and Battery."

"Very well, I'll show you more light-hearted scenery and other mentionable interests. If I comment too much, speak up. Sometimes the politician in me takes over," he tells me grinning.

We board his carriage and trot down Meeting Street Road toward the Battery. Mister Middleton speaks proudly of the Charleston landmarks and families, while Tamba and I listen.

When reaching land's end, Tamba is instructed to turn around onto Church Street heading north. The sunny afternoon temperature is pleasant, and a strong breeze refreshes us. Seagulls navigating the wind currents coast effortlessly high above the waters. Indeed this is a perfect touring day for all.

We travel a few more blocks toward Dock Street, and I notice a throng of people entering and leaving one of the corner buildings. There is also a congregation of carriages.

"What is attracting the crowd?"

"The Planter's Hotel, Adam. The land originally housed the old Dock Street Theatre, but that was long before my time. Now it becomes quite booked with planters from the inland and wealthy local merchants, especially during horse racing season. You will only see the finest dressed ladies patronize this establishment. It has a reputation for fine food and drink. I also hear discrete indulgence of the flesh is an available menu item."

He winks and cracks a smile.

"Can we stop?"

"Oh, you find my last remark appealing?"

His grin turns to chuckles, and I laugh before responding.

"I know Wade. If celebrating with a drink of spirits, his insatiable thirst for women might lead him astray. The ambiance of such a hotel would certainly strike his fancy."

"We should stop so you may inquire within."

"Tamba, halt the horses."

"Yaas, Mass Adam."

I enter the hotel lobby and briefly stand in line at the front desk.

"Good day, sir. Reservations?"

"No, I am inquiring on the stay of a guest."

"The name, sir?"

"Wade Shiloh of Savannah. He would have registered sometime during the past month."

The clerk looks at me puzzled.

"He never returned home from a Charleston visit. Here is a likeness of him."

The clerk seeing the drawing immediately responds, "Yes, sir, I remember this gentleman. He was in the company of his wife, a most attractive, well-dressed, blond-haired woman."

"Wife? There must be some mistake. Look at this sketch more closely."

This time the clerk studies the drawing and points nodding.

"Yes, this *is* the same man. He rented lodging for the evening and paid in advance."

"How long was his stay?"

He leans over the counter, whispering, "Sir, the couple left shortly following registration. Their room door was found open with the key still in the lock. No belongings were inside. Another patron brought it to our attention."

"On what day did this occur?"

"I do not think we should divulge further information. We respect the privacy of our guests and operate a reputable business."

"I have no doubt. Perhaps your business will increase with the presence of Sheriff Cleary," I declare scowling.

"There is no need for that, sir. I believe it was Saturday, a few weeks past. Let me check the registry."

He turns the pages backward, scanning his forefinger down the entries.

"Yes, sir, right here. It was on a Saturday."

His finger stops, underscoring the entry.

"Let me see," I demand, reaching for the journal.

He turns the registry around, and it is simply signed:

Mister Shiloh & Wife

Although not certain, the handwriting appears to be that of Wade.

"Did the gentleman have a limp in his gait?" I inquire further. Wade was permanently injured in a gruesome battle during the War of 1812.

"Why, yes. I believe his left leg was favored."

"The woman, did he call her by name?"

The clerk pauses, pondering the question.

"Sir, I believe it was Marguerite. Yes, I am certain it was Marguerite."

I thank the hotel clerk for his assistance and return to the carriage.

"Adam, how did you fare?"

"Well, Mister Middleton, it seems Wade may have patronized the establishment in the company of a woman named Marguerite."

"Marguerite, you say. Perhaps that's the reason for his extended absence. Do you know who she is?"

"No. The hotel clerk said she was quite attractive with blonde hair. The registry has them as man and wife."

"Wife? He's in more trouble than we thought."

We chuckle.

"Is there a possibility Wade did wed? We have some beautiful women in Charleston."

For a brief second I visualize Lavinia.

"It is possible, but more likely he was married to a lustful stay."

Our chuckles turn to laughter.

"It also appears they left in a hurry, not lodging the evening."

"Adam, perhaps his stay was extended elsewhere. We do have other regarded establishments in town, if you care to stop. Free blacks, Jehu Jones and his wife Abigail, operate the Jones' Hotel on Broad Street. It has an excellent reputation with many Europeans."

"Thank you, but I will call on the boarding houses later this week. Hopefully, sketches will be available to post."

Wade has a reputation for charming all the ladies. His normal course of conduct does not tout casual liaisons, but neither does mine enamor married women. If he did wed, without Mother's knowledge, I can understand why he is being elusive. Her wrath would be like no wife's. However, the event seems to suggest he patronized the hotel, if only briefly.

Mister Middleton resumes our outing and guides Tamba to Bay Street.

"Adam, over there is where we resolve the nation's headaches, while creating our own. I recall being here for President Washington's dinner party. He wouldn't drink a British porter beer import, only a porter brewed in Philadelphia. This was part of his 1789 Buy American policy. George is no teetotaler," Mister Middleton says nodding, as we pass McCrady's Tavern.

Further down we turn onto Longitude Lane, and he points out a row of houses.

"There sets the first tenement buildings in South Carolina, probably the nation. I remember when Vanderhorst Row was built around twenty years ago. Everyone scoffed at the idea of people living in multifamily dwellings, and now everybody wants to invest. Only in our great nation can a mocked idea transform into a profitable enterprise."

In the middle of Longitude Lane, we turn around at Latitude Alley. Both names seem fitting for this sea faring town.

Turning onto Broad Street at the Old Exchange Building, housing the post office, we ride west toward the Ashley. We pass a newer structure on the right, and I look up to the building gable. It is adorned with a prominent gold leaf eagle, and Mister Middleton observes my interest.

"Adam, that is a branch of the Second Bank of the United States, our only institution capable of handling international transactions. The building is only around two years old. Of course the bank is starting to adopt more conservative policies."

"For what reason?"

"Recently some state banks have suspended payment on their notes, even declaring bankruptcy. There seems to also be a decline in imports and exports. These unfortunate events are starting to cause economic panic and could very well thrust the country into a depression. Since prices are definitely spiraling downward, it was timely that Wade contracted early for your crop export."

"I know. Savannah is still experiencing hard times from last year's fever epidemic. Shipping and business trades never revitalized since the quarantine, and most vessels still will not come into port. In addition, our prime cotton industry is in serious decline."

"Well, it is fortunate our Charleston seaport is nearby. Although an added inconvenience and expense for your delivery, at least goods can be bargained for export."

Traveling further, he draws attention to an adjoining double building.

"Governor John Geddes resides there. He is entertaining President Monroe for a goodwill visit next month. Adam, if time and conditions permit please join me for this gala event. Wade is also welcomed pending his finding."

"I would be honored, and hope for Wade's attendance. Thank you."

A few more blocks away, he gestures toward a house.

"There is the Edward Rutledge house. At twenty-six, he was the youngest signer of our Declaration of

Independence. Did you know the original draft presented by Thomas Jefferson included verbiage to ban slavery?"

"I was not aware."

"Well, Rutledge had a conniption fit when it was presented. Of course, the southern slave colonies demanded the stipulation be removed. Ironically, Edward returned to Charleston and freed all his slaves."

"He probably also freed his conscience."

"I know. Society is confronted with a conundrum. We have created a situation that a document of ink will not erase."

A disheartened expression crosses Tamba's face, as many church steeple bells gong slowly three times. Mister Middleton changes the subject.

"Adam, I did not realize the time. You are probably famished."

"No, I am fine."

"Tamba, are you hungry?"

"Yaas, suh, Mis'tuh Middleton."

"Tamba is always hungry."

"I can understand why. He has to eat for four men."

Everybody laughs.

"Well, since we missed lunch, an early supper is in order. Is anything else in town of immediate interest?"

"No, thank you. I have new information regarding Wade and a good appreciation for the town layout. I thank you again for your time. I found everything quite informative."

"Adam, you are so welcome. Anything I can do to assist. Tamba, let's start our journey home."

"Yaas, suh, Mis'tuh Middleton."

"Oh, and Adam."

He pauses.

"Yes, sir?"

"Please call me Henry. It makes me feel younger."

"Very well, sir. I mean, Henry."

We both grin.

Although the age of Father, I find Mister Middleton's company most enjoyable. An air of friendship prevails between us in lieu of authority. His genuine concern and assistance are most appreciated. I can understand why he and Father have been lifelong friends. Both are courageously noble in mind and heart, and share many common convictions.

Henry and I continue chatting, while Tamba routes the carriage back to the river ferry. After crossing the Ashley, Middleton Barony comes into sight as dusk nears.

5

Highwaymen

At Middleton Barony, Tamba stops the carriage near the tower entrance to the big house.

"I will see you in the morning."

"Yaas, Mass Adam."

"Good night, Tamba."

"Good night, Mis'tuh Middleton."

Henry and I walk toward the turret stairway.

"You can tell he is a dedicated and dependable house servant, just like Jessie. I recall your father speaking highly of him and his family."

"Tamba is very much part of Shiloh, and I am going to speak with Father about his release from servitude. He is like another brother."

"I too am close to many of our slaves, and do not know how Middleton could operate without them. I didn't want to talk further on the subject of slavery in Tamba's presence, but their welfare without us is questionable. Many plantation owners, like Thomas Jefferson, also speak of this dilemma. The subject has recently been under intense discussion in Congress."

"How so?"

"Well, many settlers are slave owners within the new territories and want to join the Union. However, many congressmen are unsure about permitting the legal spread of slavery to new states."

"Is a resolution being proposed?"

We pause at the bottom of the tower steps.

"Early last year Missouri petitioned Congress for statehood admission, but heated sentiment floored the bill. The request was resubmitted, and this past month we debated the issue again. Jim Tallmadge, our congressman from New York, proposed an amendment to the bill with several controversial stipulations. These included clauses not allowing additional slaves within the state, and freedom for current slaves' children at the age of twenty-five. Jim's amendment obviously supports a path for eventual emancipation. We passed this bill in the House of Representatives, and it was just sent to the Senate."

"Does it have a chance to pass?"

"I have reservations. I believe this issue will manifest into a constitutional crisis, perplexing even to a founding father. I know the sentiment on this issue differs deeply among the states. I just hope our nation's divide can be mended."

"Henry, any sanction to curtail the spread of slavery is positive. I know our federal laws now prohibit human trafficking."

"I just delivered a speech in Congress, citing that 'thirteen thousand Africans are annually smuggled into the Southern States.' "

We begin climbing the stairs, and I question Henry further.

"Why are we not enforcing the law and arresting offenders?"

"It's a difficult situation, and until now our mandate has been loosely enforced. Congress enacted the ban on American participation within the African slave trade in 1807 at the encouragement of Thomas Jefferson. Great Britain also abolished their Slave Trade Act that same year. Our country and Great Britain plan to sail a small naval squadron to the coast of West Africa, to deter the flesh smugglers and enforce our anti-slavery legislation. Realize Adam, even though some southerners profess support of the abolitionist movement, their agenda is not always honorable. With the slave trade eradicated, the value of their servitude properties and offspring is enhanced."

"A most complicated issue."

"Yes, it's an issue of morals, emotion, and economics confronting us. We can only hope for guidance from the Almighty."

"Henry, I am glad to hear we are searching the soul of our great country. No longer can we look with a blind eye."

Reaching the top of the landing, Henry sounds winded as we enter the big house. The conversation of our short walk brings premonition of a longer path facing our nation. Over a quiet dinner, we enjoy more discussion and then retire early. We are tired from hours of travel.

Lying in bed, I ponder over the many late night conversations with Wade regarding slavery. We shared staunch fundamental differences. He totally valued the slaves as property first and human beings second. I recall him touting to friends how well off the slaves were on our plantation compared to other venues. He possessed a skewed sense of obligation toward them, rationalizing their servitude was rewarded through his provision of food, shelter, and clothing. He told me God's will delivered their fate and position in society.

My convictions differed greatly on the humanity of slavery. I always respected Wade's mindset, but stood strong when mine was to the contrary. Unable to accept the possibility of my beliefs, Wade simply dismissed them to youthful inexperience. In the end our debates would stalemate, going by way of our swirling cigar smoke.

I spend the next day questioning city merchants and posting Wade's sketches. The printer replicated the likeness well, and Sheriff Cleary is displaying it in public buildings, including the post office, courthouse, hospital, and banks. I focus on business storefronts such as hotels, dry good stores, saddler shops, and apothecaries. I also call upon physicians and many tradesmen.

On my return trip to Middleton Barony, I go by route of Meeting Street Road and Six Mile House. After my search efforts, I stop almost nightly to rendezvous with Lavinia. Through conversation we come to know more about each other, building a friendship of amorous disposition.

"Lavinia, you have no family other than your mother and half sister?"

"Papa died when I was young. Mother remarried and had Olivia. She is only ten years old."

"Where do they live?"

"Virginia."

"What nationality is your family?"

"They are of German descent."

"Just as my Mother."

"What is your maiden name?"

"Thurman."

"Mother's is Hickman."

"How long have you been in Charleston?"

"Almost ten years. John and I came here shortly after being wed."

"You are very articulate. Where were you educated?"

"I grew up on a farm. Mama was a schoolmistress."

"So was mine."

"You have never had children?"

"I always wanted a child, but have never conceived. John says I'm barren. I dare not suggest it might be his inadequacy."

"And you Adam, have you ever been married?"

"No."

"Have you been in love?"

"Once during the youth of my college years."

She smiles, looking at me with piercing eyes.

"How did you meet John?"

"He was a laborer for my mother. At the time, I was only sixteen, and charmed by his good looks and brawny build."

"Lavinia, if I may ask, how old are you?"

"How old are you, Adam?"

"I will be twenty-four on the tenth of May."

"Well, I'm only a few years older than you."

"So, you are not going to tell me?"

"Maybe if we kiss, I'll tell."

She cracks a devilish grin that almost makes me forget what I even asked. I lean over and kiss her dimpled cheek.

"Adam, I'm not your mother."

She leans toward me.

Her tender lips meet mine, and our tongues entangle in a web of passion. Never before have I experienced such lingering and intense desire.

"That was nice, Adam."

"Yes, yes it was, quite nice."

"Would you like to do it again?"

I smile and she delivers another kiss that would embarrass the devil himself.

"Now you'll tell me your birthday?"

"The twenty-third of September, Adam."

We resume talking, and each new visit nurtures a deeper relationship. Our affection toward one another becomes increasingly passionate, but falls short of making love. I find myself still conflicted inside, knowing she remains married.

On Thursday morning, February eighteenth, I again prepare for travel to town. But first, I join Henry in the dining room.

"Good morning."

"And Good morning to you, Adam. Did you rest well?"

"Yes, thank you."

"Any more news on Wade?"

"Not yet, but I am canvassing more businesses today."

"I leave this morning for Whitehall, before Mary Helen and the children forget me. I told Jessie to tend to all your needs."

"Thank you, Henry. When will you return?"

"I should be back within a month."

I wish him safe passage, and we express our farewells after eating.

While walking to the stables, I think about my daily quest to find Wade. My mind becomes weary as the compulsive desire increases with every tidbit of information. I am still bewildered by the hotel clerk's account. If Wade had been inebriated, a beautiful woman could have led to a clandestine tryst or worse yet marriage. However, he would have communicated by now. God willing, I will discover his whereabouts regardless of the outcome.

At the stables Tamba has saddled and bridled Gabriel and Nicodemus.

"Good mo'nin', Mass Adam."

"Tamba, good morning. Ready to mount up?"

"Yaas, Mass Adam."

"The horses are well rested. We will race short of the main road."

I nudge my heels hard into Gabriel's side, and he follows suit with Nicodemus as we charge ahead neck to neck. We halt just feet from the roadway. The snorting horses catch their breath, while we each claim victory to a dead heat.

"Tamba, I fail to understand how Nicodemus maintains stride carrying your weight. When I mount him, the result is still a tie."

"Mass Adam, hiz heart iz stronger den hiz legs. Winnin' iz not in'portant, he jes doesn't wanna loose."

I chuckle.

"He does have heart. Well spoken."

We trot down Ashley River Road and cross the ferry into the Charleston countryside. Once in town, I again call on several more King Street merchants. At last, one proprietor recalls Wade after viewing the sketch.

"Yes, I remember him. We did business several weeks ago for a rice harvest. I have a signed agreement of terms."

The exporter finds the contract and presents it to me. I notice the document date is also the same as the purported hotel visit.

"Yes, that is his signature seal and the correct information. By the way, was he in the company of a woman?"

"None I recollect. Do we still have a deal?"

The merchant's brow and palms rise as he questions me.

"Yes, sir, these terms will be honored," I reassure, offering a firm handshake.

There is no doubt Wade arrived in Charleston, and this confirmation raises my spirits greatly. I return to tell Tamba of the findings, and we ride to apprise the sheriff.

At the courthouse, a band of armed men are milling about in the street. Tamba waits outside while I proceed into Sheriff Cleary's office. Several deputies are congregating, and the sheriff is holstering a pistol. The lawmen seem jittery and impatient to leave.

"Sheriff, what is all the commotion?"

"Adam, it's those highwaymen we talked about. I formed a posse to rid that problem area we've been monitoring. Citizens and members of the Charleston Riflemen, Washington Light Infantry, and Northern Volunteers are deputized and ready to go."

"Sheriff, if these highwaymen have anything to do with Wade's disappearance, I want to be there."

"Can you shoot?"

"I fought under General John Floyd in the Georgia First Militia Brigade during the War of 1812."

"Enough said. Let's go. I'll update you along the way."

Everybody hastily leaves his office as Daisy curls up again in the corner chair.

Outside, the sheriff cries out, "Boys, I hereby deputize each of you. Make Charleston and the State of South Carolina proud. Mount up and follow my lead!"

I quickly approach him, pointing to Tamba.

"That is my house servant. He can shoot as well as any man here."

"He's a posse by himself. We're obliged for the help."

I motion for Tamba.

"We are in pursuit of highwaymen possibly having knowledge of Wade. Stay back, keep your head low, and only fire if fired upon."

"Yaas, Mass Adam."

Our band of deputies gallops full stride out of town on Meeting Street Road. I pull away to the forefront position.

"Sheriff, one of the exporters conducted business with Wade a few weeks ago. It was definitely his seal on the contract," I holler, over the clatter of hooves.

"I reckon he made it here," yells the sheriff.

Our shouting continues over the rhythmic racket of tromping horses.

"It also seems he registered at the Planter's Hotel that same day but left unexpectedly. He rendezvoused with a well-dressed attractive blonde, claimed to be his wife."

"Hell, Adam, it sounds like he was doing a bit of celebrating. He's probably still with her. You know how the flesh of a woman can captivate a man."

"I know all too well. I hope it turns out to be that simple."

He smiles through his tobacco-stained teeth. At this fast riding pace, downwind horsemen are unknowingly thankful he has no chew.

"Where are we headed, Sheriff?"

"From the complaints I've been receiving, it appears the trouble spots are in the vicinity of the Five and Six Mile Houses. The property owners gave permission to treat the dilapidated premises as seen fit. The landlords acknowledge some of the inhabitants are of questionable character, and want them evicted anyway. So maybe we can kill two birds with one stone, if any of them are outlaws."

"I lodged at the Six Mile House during last Friday's storm. Although some of the men appeared untrustworthy, no one posed any harm."

"If you had Goliath with you, I understand why."

He chuckles, and we draw rein at the Five Mile House. The halting hoofs kick up a cloud of dust.

Remaining on horseback he shouts, "Hold steady boys."

Almost in unison, many deputy gun hammers cock.

"You in there, this is Sheriff Cleary. Come out peacefully."

No sooner said, a windowpane breaks, and a protruding rifle fires. The posse hurriedly dismounts, seeking cover. The sheriff, Tamba, and I rush to cover behind a chicken coop. A barrage of lawmen bullets blankets the air, showering the piazza with shattered window glass.

More rifles and pistols emerge from the broken windows and a cracked doorway. Undeterred by our sign of force, the suspected highwaymen engage our shelling. We exchange round after round, but they stand strong.

"Boys, hold your fire!" the sheriff orders, after several minutes of gunshots.

Momentarily, all shooting stops as I peek out from behind the outbuilding. My vision is blurred from the lingering cloud of smoke, and I cough from the drifting stench of powder.

"Adam, they appear well armed. This standoff could go awhile, so I'm going to smoke 'em out. I hate to eat a late supper."

He grins.

"You in there! Come out now, or I'll give the order to burn you out!"

Without hesitation more gunfire erupts from the house.

"Let 'em have it boys! Light the torches!"

As an exchange of more lead blitzes the air, several deputies ignite oil-soaked clubs. The torches are flung atop the roof, and the side foundation is doused with the slimy liquid. Hungry flames gradually intensify, feeding on the wooden structure. Eventually the house is swallowed by fire, and the busted windows belch dark smoke.

Before long, the siege ends as incoherent yelling and coughing emanate from inside. The blazing house starts crumbling, and half-a-dozen culprits flee from the rear. They dash toward the woods barely escaping the searing flames.

"Let the no-accounts scatter from town. Good riddance. We have more business a mile down the road," exclaims the sheriff.

Our posse gallops to the Six Mile House, leaving the raging fire to burn. Halting in the front yard, the sheriff instructs the deputies to stay mounted.

"Adam, since you have acquaintance with these people, maybe we can avoid a fight. Let's go to the door, and see if they'll reason."

"Fine, Sheriff."

Not knowing whether Lavinia is inside, avoiding a confrontation is paramount. We step onto the piazza, and he raps on the hewn oak door. Once more, it slowly cracks open. Only this time a vision of disgust appears, namely Hayward.

"What can I do for ya?" he slurs, reeking of alcohol.

"Remember me? I'm Sheriff Cleary. The landlord wants everyone off this property. Hell, you're not supposed to even be in this state. Vacate the premises now, peacefully or by force," he warns scowling.

I did not expect the sheriff to know Hayward, but I am not overly surprised.

"We're not looking for trouble, Sheriff. We'll leave," Hayward mutters, observing the sizable number of lawmen.

"You've got ten minutes to collect your belongings. Make your leave away from town and this state, or you'll be arrested," the sheriff threatens.

"Hayward, is Lavinia inside?" I interject.

"Nope. John's here, but she made a special trip to the market. You're the one looking for his brother, right?"

"Do you know anything?"

"Nothing I'm telling you."

With this response I lunge toward him as Sheriff Cleary restrains me.

"Adam, I have a mind to do the same, but this derelict isn't worth jail time."

Hayward shrugs and snickers, slamming the door closed.

"Sheriff, you know that despicable character?"

"I'm familiar with him, and also did some research on John Fisher, following a few complaints. About two years ago, a previous Governor pardoned Fisher of thirty lashes for theft, on the condition he never return to South Carolina. Hayward was indicted around the same time for assaulting one of Charleston's finest family members."

My intuitive dislike of Hayward is finally validated. Apparently, his course of conduct follows a path of criminal activity.

A few minutes later, Hayward, John Fisher, and several others exit the house. They leave reluctantly, blustering while stepping off the piazza toward the barn. I recognize all of the men with John as the scruffy cardplayers. Part of our entourage follows the presumed robbers to assure their leave is toward the state line.

Fortunately, Lavinia is not in their company, and the discord ends peacefully. The sheriff indicates the landlord wants a citizen posse member to temporarily secure the vacated premise.

"Mister Ross, the band of ruffians is gone. You're free to safeguard the property."

"Thank you, Sheriff Cleary."

The watchman enters the house, and the sheriff turns toward the posse.

"All right, boys, you did your jobs well. South Carolina and the City of Charleston thank you. Hopefully, we're rid of these reprobates once and for all. Now let's head home!"

Everyone disbands, and Lavinia is forefront on my mind. Based upon Hayward's comment, Tamba and I ride hard to the town market.

I soon spot her picking over a bushel of apples. My mind sighs relief as I approach the fruit stand. I notice she is conversing with a tall, bald, and bushy-mustached mulatto. Before reaching her, the unsavory character vanishes into the mass of people.

"Lavinia!" I call out.

"Adam, how did you know I was here?"

"Hayward said you were here. We must talk right away."

"What's wrong?"

"Everybody was evicted."

"Evicted?"

I quickly lead her away by the arm. Her face etches with concern as we scurry along.

"John, Hayward, and the others have been vacated from Six Mile House by the sheriff. Everyone is suspected or known as outlaws, and someone is standing guard for the landlord. You cannot return."

"Adam, John will seek me. Where am I to go?"

"They will look in town if anywhere, so it is not safe here. You will spend this evening with me, until I arrange permanent lodging tomorrow. Trust me, Lavinia."

"I do, Adam."

We share a quick hug.

"Who were you talking with?"

"Merely a friend of John's, not mine."

"He appeared to be a lowlife. Is there a problem?"

"No, but I fear you will not love me because of my past deeds."

"I care not for bygone times, only our future. Are you sure that mulatto poses you no problem?"

"Adam, everything is fine."

"Where is your wagon?"

"On State Street."

I continue to rush her along, and we board her wagon.

"Where are we going?"

"Where you will be safe. Quickly, we must leave!"

We hastily ride toward the Ashley River Bridge and Tamba follows. Although the ferry route is faster, it is more conspicuous.

I do not want to impose upon Henry another personal dilemma. However, I am sure he will understand my precarious position. This evening there is no other choice. I will explain the situation when he returns from his Whitehall retreat.

Soon we cross over to Ashley River Road, finally arriving at Middleton Barony. Tamba boards her wagon in the stables. She stands speechless with her mouth agape.

"Adam, the grounds are magnificent! I never thought I would set foot on Middleton Barony. It is sublime, even more beautiful than people speak."

She spins around wide-eyed and awed.

"Yes, it is truly a paradise on earth," I remark, smiling from her enjoyment.

"Come, Lavinia, let us explore the pastures."

I mount Gabriel, and she rides sidesaddle with me. However, the bumpy wagon journey tired her backside, and she only survives a short distance. After returning to the stables we walk past the south flanker and big house. Along the way, I notify Jessie of an evening dinner guest.

When entering the north flanker, she is overwhelmed with the opulence. We sit in the library to rest and talk.

"Lavinia, if we are to share a future, let it begin now. We know your presence in Charleston is not safe, but I must remain until Wade is found. I will make arrangements with Tamba for your escort to Savannah. You will be safe and well cared for on Shiloh. Plan to leave early morning."

"Thank you, Adam. No one has ever done so much for me in so little time. I am deeply indebted."

"Caring is not bound by time or debt. Your happiness is my reward."

She glows contentment.

"I love you," she says softly, laying her hand atop mine.

"And I love you."

I kiss her tenderly.

"What of my belongings?"

"There is a respectable citizen guarding the property. On the way home, Tamba will detour so you may request your possessions. I will also accompany you there on my way into town. Mister Ross is a gentleman, and has no reason to deny a lady of personal items."

She nods in agreement.

"This land bears so much elegance. Never have I seen such an abundance of flora," she exclaims.

"The beauty of this land is only enhanced by your presence."

She smiles and walks toward the window. I follow her, embracing her waist from behind. As she looks outside, her arms rest atop mine. I bury my face within the fragrance of her long silky hair.

"Lavinia, let us stroll the gardens so you may truly experience the grandeur," I suggest, playfully kissing her neck between words.

Holding hands, I lead her outside, and we casually explore the grounds. Coming upon the wood nymph statue, she gazes intently.

"Adam, the sculpture and gracing flowers are so calming. If only life could be this serene. Her face, what does she meditate?"

"I think the sight of beauty greater than hers."

She smiles again, squeezing my hand along with a quick schoolgirl kiss.

"You are too kind, Adam."

I snip off a long-stemmed rose from a bush and hand it to her.

"Lavinia, these petals opened over time, as the blossom of our love shall grow."

She takes the crimson beauty, and hugs me tightly while smelling its fragrance.

"My favorite flower, Adam."

Completing a long walk, we make way to the big house and enjoy a most stupendous Jessie meal. Afterward we return to the north flanker. Lavinia immediately goes to the piano. Her fingers fly across the keys, playing a most invigorating melody.

"Lavinia, I had no idea you were an accomplished musician."

"Do you play an instrument, Adam?"

"I can only wish, but I do admire those that are gifted."

She continues to play a compilation of tunes.

Eventually, our yawns and tired eyes induce thoughts of retiring.

"Lavinia, you will be most comfortable sleeping in the big house."

"Near your room, Adam?"

"Actually, I lodge in the south flanker gentlemen quarters on the other side of the big house."

"Is anyone else staying the night there?"

"Mister Middleton is out of town, and no other guests are present."

"May I sleep there in one of those bedrooms?"

Pausing from this unexpected request, I must insist she lodge at the big house.

"Lavinia, it is highly unorthodox and ill-mannered for a lady to occupy those premises."

"Perhaps. But Adam, even ladies sometimes compromise their manners," she says sheepishly, taunting me with a flirtatious smile.

"Are you always this assertive?"

"What do you think?"

Unlike my steadfast grip, my stance weakens from her leering demeanor.

"Very well, but not a word to anyone."

"Adam, there is no one to tell, unless it be your mother," she teases.

I grin and grab her hand as we saunter to the south flanker. Two flickering candles guide us upstairs. We pause and stand in the hallway outside of her bedroom.

"I will bid you goodnight in a moment, Adam."

She places two fingers over my lips and slowly starts to close the door. Before shutting it completely, she smells the rose and peeks at me mischievously.

I enter my room, placing my candlelight bedside. Within moments there is a soft knock accompanied by a light shining beneath the doorway. Slowly I open the squeaky hinges.

"Adam, may I come in?"

"Please."

Although I realize our situation is completely inappropriate, I cannot deny my desire for her. If Lucifer has just called, my soul surrenders. She places her burning candle beside mine, and rubs her crossed arms.

"Adam, I have no gown for sleeping. The night air brings a chill."

"My body warmth will blanket you like our embracing candles," I answer spontaneously, nodding toward the flutter of intertwining flames.

I surprise myself with this bold response. She reacts with a naughty smile. Satan has truly possessed me.

We sit on the plump goose feather bed Indian style, and face each other to talk. I am reminded of doing the same with childhood friends, except Lavinia is no little girl. One side of our faces illuminates from the glimmering candles, while the other captures moonbeams from the window. Our long shadows cast upon the wall in the dimly lit room.

As our conversation pauses, I notice all of her hair bunched together, draping down one side of her neck. The long dark strands, covering half of her bosom, glisten from the moonlight. I look up and meet her twinkling eyes, begging for passion. My desire heightens with foregone conclusion.

I gently push her hair away, and she slowly bends her head sideways. I ravage her neck with kisses. My lips warm from her skin. I tenderly caress her full succulent breasts, and her nipples excite, jutting from under her dress. Seconds later our tongues tangle in a web of desire. My forehead beads perspiration and I flush with heat. I feel my heart pound, as rushing blood accentuates every nerve ending.

Excitedly, we undress one another as I blow out the candles. We lie naked in nature's light. Following our lovemaking, I gasp for air, almost breathless. My body tingles with satisfaction, and is consumed with goose bumps. I lay motionless on her, feeling our hearts racing from exhaustion. A cool evening breeze rolls across my clammy back.

"I do love you, Adam," she whispers panting.

"Lavinia, I love you, as I have never loved before. I shall take you away from your dreadful life. Each day you will smell the fragrance of flora gardens and be at peace."

We kiss tenderly and blissfully fall asleep in a warm embrace.

The next morning we awake to more passionate lovemaking. After bathing and a speedy breakfast, I compose a short note.

February 19, 1819

Dear Mother,

I have fallen into love with the beautiful woman now in your company. Please care for her as a daughter until my return.

I have verified Wade's arrival in Charleston, and the search for him continues. I will write of any new findings.

My lodging is at the gracious hospitality of the Middletons. Mary Helen is vacationing at Whitehall with the children, and Henry has been most helpful to me. He sends his respects and best wishes for Father's recovery.

I trust all is well on Shiloh.

Your loving son,
Adam

Tamba arrives at the south flanker with Lavinia's wagon prepared for the Shiloh journey. He also has Gabriel saddled for my travel to town.

"Tamba, give this letter to Mother. It explains all. I will return to Shiloh whenever possible. I am escorting you as far as the Six Mile House, so Lavinia may collect her belongings from the citizen guard. After this detour, proceed to Savannah by our arrival route. Care for her well."

"Yaas, suh, Mass Adam."

We leave Middleton Barony and ride down Ashley River Road, crossing at the ferry. Nearing the bend before Six Mile House, I spot a stranded wagon careened from the roadside. It is setting somewhat lopsided.

"Tamba, halt. Lavinia, I do not know whether we approach friend or foe, so hide in the wagon bed under the hay."

She quickly disappears, and we travel closer. I observe a man with a small boy.

"Pull over."

"Yaas, Mass Adam."

"How goes it waggoner? Do you need a helping hand?"

"Much obliged, I'm having trouble fixin' this wheel. The wagon weight won't let me mount it. My boy is too small to assist."

Tamba and I look at one another and grin, well knowing a wheel dilemma. We jump down from our wagon.

"I am Adam Shiloh of Savannah. This is my house servant, Tamba."

"I'm John Peoples of Savannah, and this is my son, Joshua. It's good to meet another Savannahian. Are you of Shiloh Plantation?" he asks, while shaking hands.

"That I am."

The waggoner and I grab the wheel while Tamba prepares to lift the wagon.

"On three. Ready, One, two, THREE!" I count out.

Tamba lifts with a groan. His face reddens from strain as every massive arm muscle and neck vein bulge. The waggoner and I promptly seat the wheel firmly in place on the axle, while his boy stares in awe.

"Very much obliged, Mister Shiloh. We've been toiling a spell. I think we'll eat a bite, rest, and water the horses before forging on."

"Go back a few hundred yards to the Six Mile House, and you can water the animals. By chance have you seen my brother?"

I hand him the sketch.

"Sorry, Mister Shiloh. He doesn't look familiar."

"Thanks anyway, Mister Peoples. Hope good weather guides you home."

He thanks us and waves goodbye. The boy continues gawking at Tamba in disbelief. Once we round the bend and are out of sight, Lavinia rises with hay-covered hair.

Nearing nine o'clock in the morning, we stop roadside. We observe the Six Mile House from a distance. All appears quiet as the watchman sits on the piazza. Tamba waits in the wagon while Lavinia walks toward the house. I bid both farewell and travel onward to town.

After my vigil of morning inquiries regarding Wade, I stop by Sheriff Cleary's office early afternoon. As usual, the tail-wagger solicits attention, and the sheriff's jaw swells with chew.

During our conversation, the office door slowly opens, and Daisy jumps from the chair. I turn to look, and a man enters. He is holding the hand of a small boy. Why, it is the waggoner we assisted earlier, but he appears frazzled. He recognizes me immediately.

"Mister Shiloh, you helped fix our wagon this mornin'."

"Yes, Mister Peoples. Did it fail you again?"

"Nope. The wagon's fine. It's the ambush we took afterward. They beat me and robbed me of all my money. There were too many of them to fight off. Besides, I was worried about my son."

His voice quavers as he pulls his child close to him.

The sheriff stands and approaches the waggoner.

"I'm Sheriff Cleary. Your name again, sir?"

"I'm John Peoples of Savannah. This is Joshua."

"Pleased to meet you, Mister Peoples."

The sheriff shakes his hand and kneels by the tyke.

"Hello, Joshua, I'm Sheriff Cleary. We're going to arrest those bad people. Don't you worry."

The little guy looks scared, and wraps his arms around his father's leg. He buries his tiny face, peeking at us. Daisy sniffs the boy's feet and wags for affection.

"When and where did this take place, Mister Peoples?"

"This mornin', Sheriff, around eleven o'clock. I stopped at the Six Mile House to water the horses, and a man told my boy to give up our watering bucket. When he refused the man became perturbed. Nine or ten other people came outside carrying clubs, rifles, and pistols.

They gave me a pretty good beatin' and cut me above the eye with a stick."

He pauses, pointing to the slashed skin covered with dried blood.

"Go on, Mister Peoples."

"Well, Sheriff, after the whippin' they swiftly withdrew into the house. I limped to the wagon with my son, and left as fast as I could. We got to where we broke down earlier, and two of the outlaws caught up with us. They robbed me at pistol point of about thirty-five or forty dollars."

"Mister Peoples, did you recognize any of them?"

"I don't know all their names, but two of them went by John and one by Hayward."

"Did you see my servant along the way, Mister Peoples?"

"Nope. I sure didn't, Mister Shiloh."

"All right, Mister Peoples. I will look into this matter right away. Can you stay in town another day?"

"Yes, sir, Sheriff."

"Good, stop by my office tomorrow morning and fill out an affidavit. For now, you better get that gash tended to."

Mister Peoples thanks us for our help before leaving.

"Adam, I thought we rid the town of those highwaymen yesterday. I will organize another posse for tomorrow. The arrests will be for suspicion of highway robbery. That's a swinging offense in our great state. I hope no harm came to David Ross, the property guard."

Now I am somewhat alarmed. Although the waggoner's misfortune happened after I left the area, Tamba and Lavinia were traveling in the vicinity.

The sheriff no sooner expresses concern over the watchman, and his office door swings open. Standing before us is the dazed and bruised citizen guard.

"Mister Ross, we just heard something was wrong. What in damnation happened out there?"

The sheriff leads him to a chair.

"Sheriff, I woke up this morning to an intrusion of gang members beating, biting, and gouging me. First, a woman approached me on the piazza followed by several men. Realizing I was alone, one of them pushed me inside, cursing and collaring me. I was choked and my head boxed through a windowpane, giving me this forehead wound. Then I was shoved outside, but went back to ask for my belongings. One of them drew a pistol on me, yelling, 'You damned, infernal rascal. If you lay your hands on anything, I will blow your brains out.' Suddenly, more of them arrived from the yard, and I found myself surrounded. They took turns beating me outside," he blabbers, between breaths.

His body trembles as he leans over, burying his head in his hands.

"Mister Ross, calm down and take your time. Tell me, did you recognize any of the people present?"

"Kinda, Sheriff, but I was busy trying to fend them off. I know the Fisher couple and the man called Hayward were there."

"How did you get away?"

"Well, Sheriff, two of them struck me with whips, just before I leaped from the piazza. I ran like hell while gunshots whizzed past me. Someone yelled, 'You damned infernal rascal, if I ever catch you, I will give you a hundred lashes.' I finally made it to the woods and onto the main road to here."

He remains visually shaken up, and the sheriff hands him a glass of water.

"Thank you."

"What time did this happen?"

He gulps down the drink and catches his breath.

"About nine o'clock this morning, Sheriff."

"Mister Ross, did you see a colossal man of color along the way? He was with the posse yesterday," I interject.

"I remember, but I sure didn't see him today."

"All right, Mister Ross. I'll take it from here. You better go to a doctor and have that cut bandaged. Stop by in the morning and file a written complaint. I'll arrest these culprits, and you can positively identify them. Seems like they also robbed a waggoner a couple hours after your misfortune. Now we have two solid grievances."

"Thanks, Sheriff. I'll be here bright and early."

He walks out the door holding his head.

"Adam, are you joining the posse tomorrow?"

"Absolutely, but for now I must locate Tamba. He was traveling in the proximity of Six Mile."

"Be careful of that area. I don't need anymore problems," he warns.

We bid farewells and go our separate ways.

There is no way I can leave Tamba unaccounted, no less than Wade. I can only surmise Lavinia is a hostage of sort. I am hesitant to reveal our true relationship, labeling her an adulteress.

I mount Gabriel and hurry out Meeting Street Road toward the Six Mile House in search of Tamba and Lavinia.

6

Fires of Hell

About halfway out of town, I see a distant oncoming wagon. It is Tamba! Thank God for his well-being! When we meet, his face carries an expression of failure and disappointment.

"Mass Adam, I'm sorry! Nothin' could be done!" he expresses frantically.

"Tamba, you did nothing wrong. Is Lavinia all right?"

"I think so, Mass Adam."

"Tell me what happened."

"Miss Lavinia got to dah piazza, and a man came behind her from dah barn. He went een dah house wid Miss Lavinia and dah watchman. Later a man's head came crashin' through dah window. More men came from dah barn, and I hunkered down in dah wagon, Mass Adam. Dey carried rifles, pistols, whips, and clubs. Dey beat dah watchman wid whips, and he ran away."

"Did you see Lavinia, Tamba?"

"No, Mass Adam. She was een dah house."

"What happened next?"

"I rode down dah road a bit and hid dah wagon, and went back on foot to help Miss Lavinia. I waited a long time, but there were too many men, Mass Adam. I went back to dah wagon and headed een to town, lookin' for you."

"You did the right thing, Tamba."

"So you did not see the waggoner we helped earlier?"

"No, Mass Adam. Why?"

"It seems he also had an encounter with the scoundrels later this morning."

I explain tomorrow's plan to arrest the highwaymen, and a troubled look asks, "Mass Adam, what 'bout Miss Lavinia?"

"I do not know, Tamba. Until I talk with her, the situation cannot be fully explained. Although she is being held against her freewill, I believe she is safe from harm. Let us return to Middleton Barony and prepare for morning."

After supper I immediately go to bed, but sleep restlessly. Saturday morning, February twentieth, I awake tired and perplexed, facing yet another dilemma.

Following a fast breakfast, Tamba and I ride horseback to the courthouse by way of the Ashley River Bridge, avoiding the ferry and Six Mile House proximity.

When I enter the sheriff's office, the watchman and waggoner John Peoples are completing their affidavit testimony. The sheriff walks the documents to Judge Charles Jones Colcock's courtroom for issuance of an arrest bench warrant. Meantime, a posse is again forming outside.

Moments later the sheriff returns waving paper overhead.

"I have the warrant! Mister Ross, Mister Peoples, I will contact you when we have them in custody, so you can provide positive identification. Now, I must do my job."

"Ready, Adam?"

"That I am."

"Is Tamba joining us?"

"Yes, he is waiting with the horses."

We walk outside, and everyone looks to the sheriff.

"Let's go boys!"

As our thundering horses again gallop to Six Mile House, I agonize over Lavinia's fate. When we near the property, I see chimney smoke and window silhouettes. A cloud of dust rises from the pounding hoofs halting on the parched ground.

"Circle the house, and wait for my signal!" Sheriff Cleary shouts.

The lawmen scatter, taking refuge behind trees, stumps, and outbuildings. Each man aims his firearm on the house. Tamba and I take shelter behind a water trough with the sheriff, about fifteen yards in front of the hewn oak door. I know the gang members inside must be grossly outnumbered. Since they continued a crime spree after being evicted, it is unlikely this will be settled amicably.

"Walk out peacefully, and no harm will come!" the sheriff commands.

Someone inside smashes a windowpane, showing fight.

I look at the sheriff, and he pulls back his rifle hammer muttering, "Dumb bastards."

Gunshots erupt, and all hell breaks loose. My thoughts are only of Lavinia, hoping for her safety if inside. After several minutes of ricocheting gunfire, there is a silent pause. My arm feels wet. I discover the trough I've been lying behind for protection is leaking like a sprinkling can.

The house is also riddled with holes, and not a pane of glass remains unbroken.

"You're surrounded and outnumbered five to one! Come out, or we'll burn you out!" Sheriff Cleary threatens.

Following a brief hesitation, a white cloth waving atop a musket barrel protrudes from a window.

"Boys, hold your fire! You are all under arrest for assault and suspicion of highway robbery! Drop your guns, and come out with hands in the air!" the sheriff cries out.

Momentarily, the door creeps open, and one by one the occupants come forward. Deputized citizens begin to stand with rifles in hand and approach the outlaws. The first to exit is John Fisher, slowly followed by several of the scruffy cardplayers recognized from my stay. Each are manacled and placed in a prisoner transport wagon. The sides of the boxed jail on wheels are a framework of latticed iron bars.

Just when I thought everyone had exited, Lavinia walks through the doorway. She hesitates and saunters off the piazza steps with a distraught look. Even now her beauty captures the delight of every man present, including Sheriff Cleary. I walk toward her, happy for her safety but abruptly stop. For now, it is prudent to conceal the emotions of our relationship. Two deputies promptly restrain and escort her to the rolling jail. The gang members are arrested and charged.

As the suspects enter the transport wagon, a deputy has each one call out their name.

"John Fisher, James McElroy, Seth Young, Lavinia."

"Lavinia who?"

She looks with no response.

"Lavinia Fisher, my wife," John screams angrily, realizing she is avoiding any association.

The sheriff divides the posse as Tamba walks toward me.

"Boys, half of you ride back with the wagon, and guard the prisoners well. Make sure they are placed in the holding cell at the City Jail. The rest of you search the outside grounds for anyone else."

"Are you all right, Tamba?"

"I'm fine, Mass Adam."

He is seemingly shocked by the turn of events and told to stay with the horses.

"Adam, let's check the house, and make sure no more varmints are hiding inside. I'll also keep an eye out for any reported stolen property."

"I am with you, Sheriff."

We enter and search the premises, finding about ten muskets with fixed bayonets and a keg of powder. Lastly, I walk down the hallway and investigate the wayfarer room of my stay. Thoughts of Lavinia flood my mind. While reminiscing our first encounter, the sheriff enters.

"Adam, anything of interest in here?"

"Nothing I see, Sheriff."

"It's not what I see, it's the smell that bothers me. What the hell is that?"

His nose twitches, sniffing out the source.

"Sheriff, I recall a damp and musty odor, but did not think much about it at the time."

He makes his way near the bed and pushes it aside. Motioning toward the floor with his pistol, a trap door is revealed. I too take aim. Leery of what lurks underneath, he slowly pulls open the squeaky hinges. Cautiously, we peer into a large opening which reveals only darkness.

Then both of us quickly jerk our heads back as a pungent stink emits.

"What is that horrid smell?"

"I don't know, Adam. Daisy smells better on her worst day."

Both of us cover our nostrils with a handkerchief as a deputy enters from the hallway.

"We're searching the outside grounds, Sheriff."

"All right, Horace, but fetch me a lit lantern for now."

"Right away, Sheriff."

The sheriff walks over to the dresser, and grabs a dainty floral pot. He drops the breakable into the black hole.

"Adam, it took awhile to hit bottom. Judging by that echo, the space is fairly large and deep. Any guesses on its purpose?"

"A strange place for access to a cellar without stairs."

We nod at each other in agreement.

The deputy finally brings a lantern. The sheriff lowers the light by hand, but it falls short of deciphering any contents.

"We'll need some rope here."

The deputy promptly returns with a lasso.

"See if the boys found anything outside, Horace."

"Will do, Sheriff," he acknowledges and leaves.

The sheriff knots the rope to the lantern handle, and he eases it deeper into the pit. Finally, we observe a small underground room similiar in size to a root cellar. As the light descends further, a murky rock and dirt floor comes into view, reflecting on a collage of objects.

"Oh my God," Sheriff Cleary exclaims, kneeling aghast at the image.

"Human bones!" I utter shocked.

He continues shining the lantern about the remains.

"There must be a dozen skulls down there in a pit of lye. Adam, you boarded here last week?" he asks rhetorically.

"What satanic deeds took place here?" I think aloud, observing the remnants of heinous crimes.

"Adam, the skeletons appear old, having been here quite some time. It's doubtful any are your brother. However, if word gets out about this discovery we'll have widespread panic in the region. We must remain silent, treating this as a private law enforcement matter. The news writers have a way of sensationalizing and distorting stories. It will needlessly mar our city's image, and further hurt the wagon trade and economy. Besides, these criminals will hang for highway robbery the same as murder."

"Very well, I will not speak of this unless required in a court of law."

"Adam, only the devil himself could bless this place. It must be sent into the fires of hell."

Once outside he thunders, "Boys, remove the keg of gunpowder, and burn this den of inequity to the ground!"

The deputies light torches and set the Six Mile Wayfarer House ablaze from inside. The spreading fire rapidly engulfs the property, and plumes of smoke fill the air. We step backwards from the intense heat as the wind fans leaping flames to greater heights.

While standing with Sheriff Cleary, another deputy approaches and points to an outbuilding.

"Sheriff, I found a fresh cowhide over there."

"That's got to be the property of Stephen LaCoste. He reported the animal stolen several days ago. Take the hide for indentification, and burn all the outbuildings. Be sure to remove any horses and livestock."

Without warning, an explosion sails debris toward us as we duck our heads.

"Adam, the fire must have set off a cache of unfound powder."

I look up and see Deputy Horace jogging toward us, while he waves off hot ash.

"Sheriff, we just found some people buried in two shallow graves behind the house, near the far tree line."

"They could be dead from natural causes. Leave them undisturbed until Coroner Stevens gets out here."

"Yes, sir, Sheriff."

The sheriff and I exchange glances, and he gestures me aside.

"Well, two corpses won't spread as much panic as twelve, but I pray neither gravesite holds your brother."

"Likewise, Sheriff."

I am nervous by the finding of two more unidentified souls. I must speak with Lavinia. She surely has an inkling to the nature of these discoveries. I just pray she is not complicit.

Another fireball erupts, shooting more powdery residue our way. We flinch to dodge the burning fragments.

"Sheriff, I want to be present when the coroner examines the graves. I would like to also interrogate and advise the woman Lavinia. My formal education is in law. She was very cordial during my stay, and I believe her only guilt is through association."

"Her or any other woman certainly doesn't seem capable of such atrocious acts. Of course, the court will decide the fate of all arrested. When we return to town, I'll introduce you to Jervis Stevens our coroner. I will also let our jailer know you are free to speak with her. She definitely needs an advisor and legal counsel."

"Very much appreciated, Sheriff. Where is the City Jail located?"

Before he could answer, the wind shifts, and we are engulfed within a cloud of smoke. We squint our watery eyes and cough while rushing toward fresh air.

"Whoa, that was unexpected. You asked about the City Jail. Well, to get there you'll head west down Dutch Church Alley off King Street, crossing over onto Magazine Street. You can't miss the building because it has a twelve-foot high wall around it. You'll also spot three other structures comprising that city block, the Sailor Hospital, Poor House, and House of Correction. The Poor House operates a manufactory for selling coffins. The House of Correction occupies the previous jail building, and we locals call it the Sugar House."

"I remember my grandfather speaking of this place, indicating it use to be a sugar refinery."

"Adam, your grandpa is absolutely correct. It originally was on the site of the old refinery at Savage and Broad Streets. The name just stuck with the new location."

Within minutes the wild flames die and transform into smoldering embers. Only a charred foundation leaves evidence of the Six Mile House existence. Our remaining posse regroups on the scorched grass and rides to town.

We pass the weathered wayfarer road sign that days earlier signaled refuge. Once more, I take a deep breath, sensing changing texture and fragrance within the air. A new storm is signaled far more tumultuous than Mother Nature's. My deep concern for Wade is compounded by thoughts of Lavinia's predicament. I agonize more than ever.

We return to the sheriff's office and sit a spell, while Tamba waters the horses. A messenger is sent to summon the coroner. I pet Daisy and Sheriff Cleary practices targeting his spitoon. All at once two deputies bolt inside.

"Sheriff, look who we caught selling beef at the market."

"No law against making a living," the outlaw snickers.

"Only if it's an honest one. La Coste's cow no doubt. Get him out of my sight, and jail him with the Six Mile gang."

The lawmen shove Hayward out the door as a tall thin man dressed in a suit and top hat enters.

"Nathaniel, you have work for me?"

"Yes, Jervis, unfortunately. Adam, this is Coroner Jervis Stevens. Jervis, this is Adam Shiloh of Savannah."

I stand and shake his hand, finding his grip weak and unmanly soft. He is soft spoken with beady eyes and skin a ghostly pale. With pronounced high cheek bones and sunken chin, his elongated face displays an eerie smile.

"Jervis, we found two shallow graves behind Six Mile House. Adam is in Charleston looking for his missing brother. I'd like him to accompany you in case any remains can be identified."

"Why, of course. Adam, do you have a weak stomach?"

He cracks a ghastly grin.

"I am fine, sir. I fought in the Creek War campaign under General John Floyd. My gut was sickened to the point of immunity."

"Oh, I am looking for an assistant."

"Sir, I prefer working with the living."

I find his demeanor quite unnerving.

"Jervis, this isn't an employment solicitation. Now when can you exhume the gravesites?" Sheriff Cleary interrupts, obviously irritated.

"Say tomorrow morning, around ten o'clock. The odors are better before the heat of day. Do you find the time suitable, Adam?"

"The hour is fine. I will meet you there."

"Oh, by the way gentlemen, the Charleston Theatre is presenting "Lock and Key" with the afterpiece being, "Forty Thieves" for tonight's showing. The town is quite eager to profit from your labors. Good afternoon."

With this departing comment and grim smile, he tips his hat and leaves.

"Adam, old Jervis is a morbid sort, but he does a good job. Although I must admit, he does give me the jitters."

"Understandably, he is eccentric, not working with any lively clients."

The sheriff chuckles.

"Well, Daisy and I will stop by the jail before heading home. I'll be sure to clear your visits with Lavinia. Just ask for Rufus. He's the head jailer."

"Thank you, Sheriff."

He stands and pats his leg. The sleepyheaded mutt springs from the chair, and a wagging tail follows us out the door.

Tamba and I return to Middleton Barony before nightfall, and I anguish over all that has happened. The day has left me mentally exhausted. My stomach's resistance to the grotesque suddenly knots from mere emotion. I substitute Jessie's traditionally superb dinner with an elixir of Seidlitz Powders dissolved in water. Then I lie down and desparately try to fall asleep.

Morning follows a night of tossing and turning. Still feeling tired and queasy, I partake only in a light meal. After Tamba arrives at the south flanker with Gabriel and Nicodemus, we ride to the Ashley River ferry, and travel our initial arrival route to Six Mile House.

Although this journey is unimpeded by storms, I feel pelted by drops of looming unknowns. Is one of the shallow graves Wade? What explanation can prove Lavinia's innocence? I anxiously await fate's answers.

By ten o'clock, we arrive at the sooty ruins of the Six Mile House. About two hundred yards behind the charred foundation, the silhouette of a man is shoveling. Drawing closer, we see that it is Jervis.

"Good morning, Coroner."

He is so peculiar, I dare not engage serious conversation. Pausing between loads of dirt, he wipes his brow.

"Why, good morning, Adam."

While excavating the first grave a tapping sound from the shovel indicates solid matter. Kneeling graveside, he removes loose earth and debris by hand. Finally, a skeletal remain comes into view settled between two layers of dense brush. I am filled with anxiety, praying neither grave holds Wade.

"Oh, this is just a young girl. I believe her to be a Negro," he offers, following a brief examination.

I breathe a sigh of relief although Tamba seems disturbed.

"One down, one to go, Adam."

The creepy coroner starts the second exhumation.

With each scoop of dirt he hums what mimics a funeral dirge. Tamba and I look at each other, and I roll my eyes. How can anyone take pleasure from such morbid work? Again the shovel alerts contact with a foreign object, and signals a large mass. Once more, he kneels on the ground and pushes away a mixture of loose soil, leaves, and twigs. A coffin top built of rough wooden slabs is revealed.

"Adam, over there, my wedge please."

I hand over the tool located a few steps away.

He lodges it under one of the top slabs, while circling and prying it loose. Then he jams his shovel into the jimmied opening and removes the wooden slat. He repeats this exercise for the rest of the planks. We look inside and a decayed body with discolored hair lies at rest.

The coroner studies the remains, finally concluding, "This one is a white man. He's been passed at least two years, just like the Negro."

Again, I breathe a sigh of relief.

"Thank you, Coroner. We will be on our way now."

"My pleasure, Adam. Anytime."

He cracks another bone-chilling smile.

Tamba and I, anxious for different surroundings, ride to town seeking Sheriff Cleary. At the courthouse, Tamba waits with the horses as usual. Upon opening the sheriff's door, Daisy scrambles from the chair for affection. No doubt, the pet knows me by now.

"Adam, did you meet with the coroner?"

"Yes, thank God neither grave held Wade."

"Well, it still leaves him missing, but hopefully alive. By the way, we did arrest several more Six Mile gang members. There's only three others on the loose, and we'll hopefully round them up shortly."

"Good, Sheriff. I am heading to the City Jail to question Lavinia and will let you know her story."

"You'll have to wait until the identifications are completed. I'll be there shortly with Mister Peoples and Mister Ross, so they can point out the attackers. There will be a couple dozen citizens present to validate the session. With the affadavits and the outlaws identified, I can let Mister Peoples go home to Savannah. There's no need to hold him in a witness cell, especially since he is caring for his son. Mister Ross will be available to testify whenever there is a court hearing. You might want to join us. I can introduce you to the jailer afterward."

"Fine, Sheriff. I will see you there."

"When arriving, just pull around to the eastside jailyard. Everyone will congregate inside the vestibule behind the large double doors."

"Thanks, Sheriff."

I resume my leave toward his office door.

"Oh, Adam, one more thing. You might want to read these stories of yesterday's events."

He hands over two news publications.

"Thanks, again."

I read the article accounts outside. The Charleston Courier reported the Six Mile House was set afire intentionally, while the Gazette printed the blaze was accidental. I understand the sheriff's concern regarding reporters. A misstated or sensationized article could stir undue public panic. Indeed, this could further taint the city's image and jeopardize an already fragile economy.

I mount Gabriel, and Tamba climbs atop Nicodemus.

"Tamba, now we are heading to the City Jail."

"Yaas, Mass Adam."

While trotting along, my thoughts focus on Lavinia and her troubling arrest and incarceration. If only the detour for her belongings was minutes earlier she would be en route to Savannah. Now she travels an unknown path steered by judge and jury. Accused and arrested for assault and suspicion of highway robbery is no minor offense. The robbery charge bears punishment by the hangman's noose.

7

City Bastille

Before long the prison comes into sight, along with the three neighboring buildings mentioned by the sheriff. Tamba and I pause to observe all four structures, occupying the block bordering Magazine, Mazyck, Back, and Queen Streets.

We sit high atop our horses, and a shoeless slave steps toward us. His apparent master is escorting him. The Negro is an emaciated figure, clad in loose, ragtag garments. His eyes walk the ground, navigated by a drooping head. Ankle chains swish with each stride he takes. Both of his wrists are bound facing forward, forcing folded hands as in prayer. While passing us, he glances up. My eyes behold a familiar dispirited image, while his silence speaks years of neglect and torment. The sound of his restrained walk ends, when the property of flesh reaches the infamous Sugar House of Correction.

"Mass Adam, what 'bout dah slave?"

Tamba's voice expresses helpless empathy, knowing the prospects are troublesome.

Grandfather told of this Sugar House disciplinary facility. As we trot toward the City Jail, I begin to impart the story to Tamba, and a disheartened look transforms his face.

"This correction house is used to punish slaves for bad behavior. It also serves as a jail for minor crimes, such as curfew violation. The major offenders are imprisoned next door at the City Jail. If a slave is not claimed within sixty days, he is sold to compensate the cost of room and board. During my grandfather's time, the cost for punishment was one shilling for thirty lashes. Old-fashioned flogging used to be the most common form of discipline. The warden of the facility could also use other methods of inflicting pain, while whips of black overseers maintained order."

"Colluh's whippin' Colluh's?"

He shakes his head in disgust.

"I know, Tamba. There are good and bad people of all races."

"What else would dey do, Mass Adam?"

"Grandfather mentioned another cruel punishment was a treadmill mechanism. Slaves walked this device in relays, providing power to grind grain. Their hands were bound overhead while their bodies were severely beaten with a cat o' nine tails. Salt would be rubbed into the bleeding welts."

Tamba cringes as I tell the story. It is as though he feels the inflicted pain. I hesitate with a reluctant expression.

"You can tell me, Mass Adam."

"Are you sure you want to know?"

He nods.

"Well, another barbaric practice consisted of a hoisted pulley system, housing two ropes. The feet of the slaves were chained to the floor and nooses bound each wrist. Opposite ends of the ropes were pulled tightly through the pulleys, and their body stretched from the floor in excruciating pain. I understand all of these disciplinary methods are still in practice today."

His eyes tear, and he looks at me hopelessly. Even though he has never been subjected to physical abuse, the persecution of fellow slaves hurts him deeply.

"Why, Mass Adam, why?"

"I am sorry, Tamba. Their actions will be reckoned with on judgment day. Why Masters resort to such unconscionable behavior escapes me. But not the Almighty!"

Then muffled screams emerge from the whipping house. Grandfather told me the original structure was built using double walls, with sand filling the separating barrier. This was to dampen the sounds of the agonizing cries. He was vehemently opposed and deeply troubled by such inhumane treatment.

Not wanting to expound further on this horrific place, I direct Tamba's attention toward the Poor House. The main building is three stories high, crowned with a large cupola. The courtyard appears stacked with salable coffins from their manufactory.

Finally, we reach the eastside prison yard and face the cold, uninviting City Jail. Grandfather said its forebidding appearance reminded him of a French bastille. He also mentioned the building was constructed upon an old eighteenth century graveyard. This seems sacrilegious to me.

As we dismount, a chained group of slaves is guided past us. Grandfather said the prison also held undocumented and unclaimed slaves, which were publicly auctioned for the city coffer.

These grounds seem to imprison the spirits of all, living and dead. Its aura is rooted with torment and doom.

No souls can rest in peace. However unpleasant, Tamba still prefers any distance from the Sugar House.

The opened jail double doors alluded to by the sheriff easily facilitate entry of the prisoner transport wagon. The entranceway leads to a ground-level vestibule where twenty to thirty citizens are milling about. Sitting idle nearby is the jail on wheels that delivered Lavinia and the others only hours earlier.

Sheriff Cleary has yet to arrive, so I decide to walk the imposing grounds. Tamba seems somewhat uneasy and prefers to remain with our horses.

Other than a few live oaks, the surrounding complex is desolate. At the rear of the building stands an unorthodox man-made hanging tree, towering as a statue in a garden of evil. I move closer to study the contraption architecture.

"It's not your normal gallows, but the result is the same," a passing guard volunteers.

He stops to talk.

"I see there is no trapdoor."

"No, sir. The body is lifted from the scaffold instead of fallin' below. The hangman's noose travels from the victim's neck over that pulley," he describes pointing.

"How is the body hoisted?"

"The other end of the rope attaches to that heavy iron cylinder. Beneath this counterbalance sets a ten foot deep hole. When that pulley lever is yanked, the cylinder plunges into the earth. Some souls are lifted into heaven swiftly, others dance their way. It seems cruel, but no more than that French guillotine. Of course, people of small stature have been beheaded from the tremendous jerkin' force. After the hangin' they're eventually cut down.

Sometimes, we let 'em dangle awhile for the prisoners. It seems to better their manners."

"Thank you for the information."

"Wanna know what happens to the bodies?"

Before I can respond, he proceeds to elaborate.

"If the bodies aren't diseased we wait a day or two for claimin'. If they're unsound, or no one shows up, we'll take 'em to the lumber mill. They'll burn with the excess sawdust. On a real nice day we'll dump 'em a few blocks west in the Ashley River marsh grass. They'll be a meal for the gators, or river dogs as we call 'em."

"Thank you, again. I must be on my way."

The sentinel, although informative, provided more knowledge than I either anticipated or desired.

I do believe in punishment by death for killing except in defense of life, country, or property. Even though other crimes are inexcusable, such as highway robbery, the death penalty seems excessive. It is unfortunate the state's judicial system does not afford life imprisonment for hardened criminals of lesser offensives.

Walking around the three-story brick exterior, I see every opening patterned with bars. Having no sashes or shutters, the entire building is openly exposed to the elements. Several iron gates provide access, and the roof is of slate.

As I return to the eastside yard, the sheriff arrives with Mister Peoples and the boy. Feeling raindrops, I motion Tamba to join me.

After everyone assembles in the vestibule, Sheriff Cleary instructs the citizen witnesses.

"Gentlemen, this is Mister Peoples, the waggoner who was assaulted and robbed. And this is Mister Ross, the assaulted property guard. Each person arrested for suspicion of these crimes will be escorted here, one by one. These victims are prepared to identify the people who they remember being present. I want everyone here to simply witness this affirmation."

The sheriff orders the guard to bring down a member of the Six Mile Gang. Momentarily, he returns and presents one of the male suspects in manacles and ankle chains.

Sheriff Cleary addresses the accused and orders, "State your name and age aloud for all to hear."

"John Fisher, twenty-eight years old."

The sheriff looks to Mister Peoples and Mister Ross, receiving positive nods.

"Let the record show this man is identified as a perpetrator," the sheriff shouts.

Now, Lavinia is escorted, also restrained in chains. Not looking at the band of citizens, her head hangs shamefully. She appears disarrayed and scared, but her natural beauty still commands a presence.

Again the sheriff repeats the request.

"Lavinia, twenty-seven years of age."

"Please state your *last* name."

She pauses, reluctantly replying, "Fisher."

Mister Peoples and Mister Ross both shake their head affirmatively, and I look at Tamba with an expression of concern.

"Let the record show this woman is also identified," the sheriff hollers.

Chatter blankets the citizenry. The thought of a woman being accused of a hanging offense is appalling to all. The identification process continues for the remaining suspects.

All are recognized. The identified culprits are returned to an upper-level holding cell, and the bystanders disperse.

"Well, Adam, she was recognized."

"I'll know more when I speak with her, Sheriff."

"Let me know what she says."

"I will."

"I'll show you where the prisoners are incarcerated, and introduce you to the jailer."

"Most appreciated, Sheriff. Tamba, do you prefer to remain here?"

"Yaas, Mass Adam."

I follow the sheriff up a stairway, passing through an iron door to the second level. Prison cells of various sizes line each side of the corridor.

"Adam, this level houses the lesser criminals and an overflow of minor offenders from the ground floor. These patrons also have limited recreational usage of the prison yard."

Climbing upward, we walk through another barred entrance and up a winding corridor. At the top of this stairwell we enter the uppermost story. He unlocks a final security gate.

"This is where the worst of the worst are imprisoned. All of them are hardened criminals."

The top level is divided into small and larger confinement areas. Each side of the hallway has grated cell doors with large iron locks. I notice the inner ceiling of this level, unlike the others, is constructed of pine planks.

As I go by the large cells, a fireplace is observed in each corner. These detention areas are crammed with prisoners. There are also iron rings bolted to the floor that shackle the most violent inmates. This highest story especially reeks of odors, even with open-air barred windows.

Each floor consists of east and west wings separated by a nine-foot corridor. The interior walls and floorboards are constructed of strong oak timbers. Filth is everywhere, surely harboring a variety of disease and vermin. Mosquitoes fly freely, plaguing prisoners and guards alike. I continually swat the bloodsuckers from my neck.

Throughout the facility inmates yell profanity and some profess innocence. Others shout in unknown tongues because of a busy Charleston seaport that harbors foreign criminals. The jail living conditions are abhorrent. Undoubtedly, the majority of occupants are most deserving.

Not seeing the jailer on the upper stories, we return to the ground level. Tamba stands facing the open double doors, watching the rain.

"Tamba, you seem bored. Join us."

"Yaas, Mass Adam."

We trail the sheriff down another narrow passageway leading away from the vestibule.

"Adam, we're flanked to the east by the jailer's flat. The west wing houses the kitchen and cells for debtors, court witneses, and persons of social rank."

The sheriff knocks on the jailer's residence, and I hear heavy footsteps pace toward us. A short stout man appears, chewing and wearing a towel atop his shirt. The makeshift bib is stained with missed bites, although the food escaping his mouth is far less than entering his belly.

"Rufus, didn't mean to interrupt your meal."

"Not a problem, Sheriff, just finishing up. How did everything go with the identifications?"

"Looks like you'll have new boarders. Rufus this is Adam Shiloh, the person we discussed with clearance to see Lavinia Fisher. Adam, this is our jailer, Rufus Crutcher."

"Oh yeah, I remember. Good to meet you, Adam."

"Likewise, Rufus."

After I shake his stubby small hand, mine feels slightly greasy.

"This is Tamba, his house servant and part-time deputy," the sheriff jests.

"Tamba," the jailer greets and nods.

"Hello, Mis'tuh Rufus."

"Rufus, I should have more Six Mile Gang members in custody shortly. They'll all go before a judge within a couple of weeks."

"We always make room for more guests," he replies, chuckling.

"Rufus, is there a place I can chat with Lavinia privately?"

"Adam, we'll be moving her from the upstairs holding cell to permanent quarters. Meantime, I'll bring her to a confinement meeting room down here. Of course, we'll have to lock the door on both of you. Give me about ten minutes."

"Thank you."

"We'll let you finish eating. Tell the wife, 'hello.' "

"Will do, Sheriff. I'll talk to you later."

We walk away, and the sheriff excuses himself, citing other business. The rain stops, and the sun struggles to peek through the overcast sky. Tamba returns to the horses, and I wait for Lavinia.

A cooking smell lures me to the nearby kitchen. Unlike the other building flooring, the kitchen is paved, probably as a fire precaution. Food is being prepared for the inmates. It is served on prison china of forged tin. Their staple seems to be bread, soup, plus meat of a questionable nature.

"Adam!"

I turn, looking down the hallway.

"She is down here," Rufus hollers, waving his hand.

I walk swiftly toward him.

"Just call for the guard when you want out."

He unbolts the solid oak door, which features a barred window. After refastening the lock, he peers through the iron bars before leaving. Lavinia stands with her back to the doorway.

"Whoever you are, be gone!"

"I think not."

Without hesitation she turns around.

"Adam, I never thought you would see me again!"

She rushes to my open arms.

"Lavinia, Tamba told me what happened. Are you all right?"

"I cannot believe I am imprisoned! This is a horrible place! I would rather be dead!"

Her voice quivers, and her pretty eyes swell with tears.

"Have you ever been arrested before?"

"Never, Adam."

"I must understand what brought you here. Why were you involved with assaulting the property guard and waggoner? What explanation do you have for the Six Mile House cellar skeletons and outback graves?"

"I know nothing of any skeletons or graves. When I arrived for my belongings, John and the others were hiding in the barn. He thought I was merely returning home. I stepped onto the piazza, and John forced Mister Ross and me into the house. I told John I heard about the sheriff's eviction visit and slept in my wagon that evening. Later, he discovered the wagon missing, and I said it must have been stolen. I am thankful Tamba left unseen, or they would have killed him. John was leery of the story, making me strike the watchman and waggoner to prove truthfulness and allegiance to him. I was afraid, Adam. Otherwise, he threatened me with bodily harm."

She sniffles, hugging me tightly.

"What about the robbery of the waggoner?"

"I took no part in any such crime."

"And the dead people?" I reiterate.

"I have no knowledge of anything so vile. Several patrons have left before I woke in the morning, and John merely said they had an early departure. I discovered he prepared a beverage from oleander leaves. This was used in their drinks to paralyze their senses so he could rob them. Remember, when you first arrived he offered tea, and I said there were no more tea leaves?"

"Yes, I recall."

"I know of some livestock theft, and at the time was unknowingly party to card cheatings. He would direct the attention of unsuspecting travelers toward me, then swindle them by sleight of hand. I was not involved with any other crimes, especially murder. I told you, John made me do regretful deeds. What is to become of me now?"

Distraught, she bursts into tears.

"Just be patient until an attorney is appointed. I will be at your side."

"Oh, thank you, Adam. I am truly sorry for these burdens. I love you so."

"I love you too, and together we must concentrate on your release. Meanwhile, I will speak with the sheriff and try to have your stay here less harsh. I must be on my way now."

Before leaving, I blot her tears with a handkerchief, and we kiss in a close embrace.

"Guard! Guard!" I cry out.

The door is unbolted, only to be relatched. She grasps the cold window bars, watching me leave. I turn, and we wave goodbye.

"Tamba, let us question more town merchants. Afterward, we will proceed to Sheriff Cleary's office."

"Yaas, Mass Adam."

The storekeeper inquries and posting of sketches are now a daily routine, but no new information regarding Wade has come to light. Late afternoon we enter the sheriff's office.

"Well, Adam. How was your talk with Lavinia?"

"Needless to say, she is quite upset. She confessed to striking Mister Peoples and Mister Ross, but only from fear of retribution by her husband. As far as the bones and graves, she claims no knowledge. Neither did she participate in robbery of the waggoner. She admitted being used to distract cardplayers for the purpose of cheating, and was aware of livestock theft. I believe her."

"Well, I'm inclined to also, but the fact remains she acknowledges committing an assault. Of course, that falls far short of highway robbery or murder."

"Sheriff, what lawyer is prominent in the state?"

"One of the better attorneys is Robert Y. Hayne. Unfortunately, he is the State Attorney General and Solicitor in the Eastern District. This includes Charleston, meaning he'll be doing the prosecuting. If you have an overpowering Philadelphia lawyer, it might have the appearance of guilt. If she is only guilty of assault, a sound counselor like John Davis Heath is certainly qualified for her defense."

"Adam, can I ask a question in confidence?"

I nod, anticipating the nature.

"Do you have a personal interest in Lavinia?"

I hesitate briefly before admitting, "If you must know, we have fallen in love. I intend for her to return to Savannah with me. Please bury this with the trapdoor skeletons."

"It's already forgotten. I'll help by any means possible."

"There is one small request. Could she be jailed where there is a window for sunlight and fresh air?"

"I will speak with Rufus tomorrow."

"Thank you."

"Just be careful. To love a woman as beautiful as Lavinia can blind a man. Remember, she was in the company of some unsavory characters."

"How can I love her, yet not believe her?"

"I understand. I'm inclined to think she is also innocent of any heinous crimes. Just a word of caution."

"I appreciate the concern."

"So you want me to have Attorney Heath review the case?"

"That will do well. You will represent me as a professional advisor to Lavinia?"

"Absolutely. The counselor conducts courthouse business frequently. Are you available to meet here?"

"Certainly, any day is fine. Just let me know. Thanks for your help and discretion, Sheriff."

A long, firm grip seeds a budding personal friendship.

Over the next several days, we resume our search for Wade, which is followed by a daily visit with Lavinia. On Thursday afternoon we pull into the prison yard, and I notice the sheriff's horse.

"Tamba, wait here. I will return shortly."

"Yaas, Mass Adam."

I enter through the weather-beaten double doors, and a guard approaches me.

"I am looking for Rufus."

He directs me upstairs, and I climb the steps one level.

While walking down the corridor, I see the sheriff and Rufus placing two men into a holding cell. A third man is manacled and escorted past me. I recognize him to be Joseph Roberts with the cropped ear. As I near the holding cell, the scruffy cardplayers James Sterritt and John Smith are also identified as the other captives.

"Hello, Sheriff, Rufus."

"We have the remaining Six Mile gang members," the sheriff touts.

"Roberts is returning for more lodging. He was here two years ago but escaped. The conniving cutthroat pretended to be with a party of visitors. This time he goes to more secure confinement on the top level," Rufus interjects, but leaves momentarily when summoned.

"Adam, I cited Lavinia's case to Rufus and the fact she is a lady. He assigned her to a west wing cell on this level. She will have a window and prison yard privileges."

"Thanks, hopefully she will be more comfortable."

"Oh, Attorney Heath is stopping by my office this afternoon regarding another matter. Are you available to meet around four o'clock?"

"Yes, I will be there."

Rufus returns.

"Are you here to see Lavinia?"

"Yes, Rufus, for a short visit."

"I will have a guard accompany her to the same ground level confinement room."

"Thank you."

I excuse myself, and head downstairs where Lavinia arrives shortly thereafter. We enter the confinement room behind locked door, and she waits for the watchman to leave.

"Adam," she says, while embracing me, "they moved me to the debtor wing today. The cell room is small but has a window."

"Now you can feel the sun, and breathe fresh air."

I smile and kiss her.

"How long must I remain here?"

"I hope for only a short time. Attorney John Heath will represent you. My meeting is scheduled with him this afternoon. He will confer with you later. Admit to the witnessed assaults, and cite your fear of retribution from John. Emphatically proclaim your highway robbery innocence. Remember to always conceal our personal relationship. My role must be perceived purely as an advisor, so not to damage your character further."

"I understand. When will there be a court hearing?"

"After talking with Attorney Heath more will be known. This is troubling I know, but everything possible is being done."

"Thank you, Adam. I do love you."

She kisses me, hugging me tight.

"I love you also, and look forward to the day we are together. Now, I must bid farewell."

"When shall you return?"

"Soon, my love."

"Guard! Guard!"

I feel somewhat relieved. Lavinia now occupies better quarters, although all are horrid. Tamba and I proceed to the harbor and distribute more sketches on the wharves. Afterward, we ride to the sheriff's office to meet Attorney Heath, but arrive later than expected. When reaching for the knob, the door abruptly opens from within.

"Adam, in the knick of time. This is John Heath. John meet Adam Shiloh. I just informed him of your consulting capacity to Lavinia."

"Sheriff, Mister Heath, I apologize for the tardiness."

Each shake my hand.

"So Adam, the sheriff indicates Lavinia was witnessed commiting two assaults."

"She admits to those crimes, citing coercion. Her husband threatened bodily harm if she did not participate in the ruckus."

"This will be difficult to prove, but we'll try to garner sympathy for the helplessness of the weaker sex. We must present her as being victimized by an overbearing spouse. What about the robbery of Mister Peoples?"

"Counselor, Mister Peoples cited two men as the robbery perpetrators, not a woman," the sheriff interjects.

"Well, that's definitely to her advantage. The two graves behind the property, Adam?"

"She disavows any knowledge of buried corpses."

"Has she a criminal record?"

"None, she claims."

"Again to her favor. I will stop by the jail and speak with her directly."

"Very good, Counselor. I told her to expect your visit. How long before the initial hearing?"

"Probably within a few weeks. I'll keep you informed. The sheriff also spoke of your brother being missing."

"Yes, we are trying to locate him."

"Best of luck. Now, if you'll excuse me, I have another meeting to attend. Good day, gentlemen."

We bid him goodbye.

"Adam, I'll let you know if I hear anything about Wade. At this point, let's hope someone comes forward. Regarding Lavinia, she's in the hands of the judge."

"Thanks for your help, Sheriff."

I also begin to walk out.

"Oh, I almost forgot. Postmaster Bacot said this just arrived."

He pulls a letter from his desk drawer, handing it to me.

"Thanks again."

I resume my leave to the wagon.

"Tamba, head back to Middleton Barony."

"Yaas, Mass Adam."

He signals Gabriel and Nicodemus onward with a whistle and yank on the reins. I open the letter, as the paper jostles from the uneven street pavers.

My Dear Son,

I am glad to hear of your safe arrival, and hope more information arises on Wade. Everyone is doing well, and your father's condition remains unchanged.

Jeremy and Sanie have been unusually well behaved. I believe Colossus even senses gentler treatment.

President Monroe is scheduled to arrive in Savannah early May. I was in the company of Julia and William Scarbrough and understand the President is lodging at their abode. They are also entertaining him on the steamboat Savannah. At their invitation, I am attending this gala event.

Fatu sends Tamba her affection, and baby Gumbu, otherwise healthy, has a touch of colic.

I pray you find your brother soon. I agonize daily over his welfare. Please keep me informed, and care for yourself.

Your loving parent,
Mother

"Tamba, Fatu sends her love. Everybody is doing well, but Gumbu has a touch of colic."

"Mass Adam, someone's not sleepin'."

We chuckle as the wagon wheels bump along the cobblestone, but it bothers me knowing Mother is so distraught. My thoughts turn to Wade.

8

Coming of Age

When we reach the woodland bridle trail along the Ashley River, the terrain reminds me of our military days. It was six years ago when Wade and I trudged through thicket in the untamed Georgia and Alabama frontiers. Memories of the war flood my mind. The visions, sounds, and emotions of another time become vivid. I think about our fighting endeavors that preserved our way of life. The past becomes present, and the presence of my brother is surreal.

Although four years my senior, Wade and I have been close since childhood. Even during our college years, periodic visits and letters kept each of us informed of our life doings. Wade is always quick to serve as my protector and advocate, much as a surrogate parent. I always admire his tenacity and sound business judgement, indoctrinated most notably through Father. However, as we grow older the degree separating our knowledge and experiences lessen.

Wade always postures himself as the wiser, seasoned sibling. He refers to me as "*Little* Brother", but we share mutual respect. As for being the protector, Wade learns to appreciate my coming of age. Manhood and brotherhood quickly rise to task, as does defense of our nation's freedom.

* * *

It is Jeremy's first birthday, Thursday, June eighteenth, 1812, when our United States of America declares war on Great Britain. It was after supper, the following Saturday, when we received word of the war.

Father, Wade, and I convene from our evening meal to the upstairs portico. We enjoy stimulating conversation in the shade of dusk, imbibing in sherry and Cuban tobacco. I celebrated a seventeenth birthday last month, and Father acknowledges my adulthood. Next year I enroll in Franklin College, and Wade graduates.

Partaking in alcohol, tobacco, and debate are Father's manly pleasures besides hunting. However, Mother refers to alcohol and tobacco as masculine vices. She only partakes in wine during special celebratory occasions. Given my age, she solely condones the activity of debate. Mother has a history of chastising me for indulging in these perceived taboos, and I for rebutting her remarks. Father notes the lashing of a woman's tongue teaches patience for the most punishing deliberation.

Out of nowhere, Mother frantically scurries down the hallway toward the portico. I hurriedly hide my spirits and cigar from her sight.

"We just received news. War has been declared on Great Britain," Mother announces.

She pauses to catch her breath.

"I feared this day would repeat itself," Father remarks.

"What is our reason for war? Britain has not fired on us," Mother declares.

A puzzled look crosses her face.

"Not with the trigger finger, but through their hand of diplomacy. They are undermining our shipping trade and scheming covertly with menancing Indians to stifle our expansion westward. Since the Revolution, Brits continue to condescend us. So it is no surprise that our patriotic war drums again march to the beat for independence. I personally find the Crown's prima donna behavior reprehensible," Father responds.

"The Redcoats forget we won our freedom years ago and treat us as unruly children," Wade interjects.

"Men are stubborn and too quick to draw blood. We need womanly compassion and diplomacy in this world. Sit and ponder another creation of man," Mother vents.

She walks away shaking her head.

Father whispers, "Sons can you imagine our government controlled by women? Maybe they could defeat the enemy by gorging them to death with pies."

Everyone chuckles.

"Our Revolutionary War Whigs could have been War Bustles," Wade comments.

We roar in laughter. After our frivolity subsides, the conversation turns more serious.

"Father, how do we prepare for this threat?"

He hears my question but remains quiet, nervously puffing away on a cigar. Soon his head is engulfed in a gray cloud of smoke. He waves a hand back and forth to dissipate the static air. Gradually, his face emerges, revealing squinting and watering eyes. Father wipes his tears and coughs as the swirling tower of suffocation slowly evaporates. His facial expression is etched with concern, while he deliberates before answering.

"Sons, our preparedness for such a foe is less than satisfactory. I have deep concern. Our Federal troops are grossly outnumbered, supported only by undisciplined state militias and patriot volunteers."

He further expounds, following a sip of sherry and long inhale of his cigar.

"We are fortunate indeed, that a substantial number of British soldiers and ships are preoccupied warring with France. This affords us time to mobilize our defense. However, the Crown will not take our act of war lightly. Sons, in either case, we just confronted the most formidable military power in the world."

Realizing the graveness of Father's tone, Wade and I know when to stifle ourselves and pay attention. He befriends many prominent political and military families, here and abroad. We know the information spoken is well founded and presented scenarios highly probable. Likewise, he is methodical when posturing convictions, never rushing to judgement.

He again hesitates in thought, finishing his glass of spirits and enjoying several more puffs of smoke. We follow suit and heed, listening intently.

"Boys, what bothers me greatly are the Upper Creek Indians of central Alabama territory. You both know the close proximity to Savannah, this plantation, and our summer home. Although the Lower Creeks will ally with us, damn well fearing our retribution, the Upper Creeks will support Britian. Not that I trust any of the red devils mind you, ally or otherwise. The Upper Creek savages are known as Red Sticks because of the red war clubs they carry into battle. I understand they can be quite belligerent, and will war relentlessly to stifle the westward encroachment of our settlers."

He pours himself more sherry, while grimacing and shaking his head.

"My particular concern for Georgia is our miles of coastline and extensive frontier. We are quite vulnerable from both the Redcoats and Redskins. Indeed we are an inevitable venue for conflict. May God be with us."

We spend several more hours discussing the war ramifications. The patriarch finally bids good night, after satisfying his thirst and snuffing out the cigar stub. Wade and I are also tired, but our patriotism is awakened.

"Wade, we must take up arms to defend our country."

"Yes, Little Brother. I agree. We need to protect our land and family. Our nation will need all able-bodied men."

"We shall inform Father and Mother tomorrow."

"Very well, Little Brother. I will tell Father and you tell Mother."

"I think not. We will approach them together."

"Direct and forceful. You are truly growing up, Little Brother."

He chuckles.

Everyone knows Mother's emotional sensitivity regarding matters of personal welfare. She is also likely to vent great displeasure on the disruption of our education.

Yawning and tired, we head to bed.

"Good night, Wade."

"Sleep well, Little Brother."

Even though Wade's room is a distance away, I know when he is fast asleep. Only the dead rest well, not hearing his infernal snoring. At least my childhood sleepwalking amused the family. Mother said her conversations with me during my catatonic state devulged many mischievous brotherly doings.

Come morning, we proceed to inform Father and Mother of our intent to enlist. He is working in the study as we stand outside his hallway door.

"Wade, he always says not to interrupt him unless it is a matter of importance."

"We're getting ready to fight a war for God's sake."

Wade knocks lightly.

"Jeremy, if that's you, your bottom is going to feel my hand."

"No, Father. It's Wade and Adam," Wade responds.

I hear footsteps approach and the latch unlock.

"Sons, come in, come in."

We walk into the room and stand in front of his desk, where he resumes sitting. There is a long silence while Father completes a writing thought. I notice a slight tremor in his pen hand. Finally he looks up, removes his spectacles, and rubs his eyes.

"Sons, rest yourselves. I trust you have an important problem for discussion?"

"Yes, Father. I mean no, Father. There is no problem. We want to enlist for the war," Wade answers.

We sit at attention in the mahogany high-backed chairs.

"Boys, boys, what about your education?"

His forehead wrinkles and arms fold as he leans back in his chair.

"Sir, I promise to complete my studies after service to our country."

"I will do the same as Wade, Father."

"Wade, you must first complete this final year of college. And Adam, your last year of preparatory schooling. You may start university studies later. At such time both of you shall have my permission," he advises.

His stern look and raised brow let us know his decision is final.

"Father, the war may end before then," I protest perplexed.

"Sons, it will be a blessing if it does, but I think not. There will be plenty of time remaining to defend our freedom."

Looking at us, he pauses, and a grin transforms his face. Father stands and we do likewise. He walks over and embraces each of us with several heavy pats on our backs.

"You both speak the words of true patriots. If only I could join you."

I do not recall a time Father appeared so proud, other than the birth of Jeremy. Although he never served in the militia, Father is an ardent patriot. He was a child during the revolution, and the onset of his unknown aliment precludes service in this war.

"Sons, have you spoken with Mother?"

"No, Father, not yet," Wade replies.

"Good, it is prudent not to mention your enlistment now, or she will needlessly anguish over your plans. Do we have an understanding?"

His brow again raises.

"Yes, Father," we acknowledge.

Although disheartened by Father's ruling, we respect his wishes and foresight.

* * *

A year quickly passes. Wade graduates from college, and I complete my preparatory studies. As Father predicted, the war is nowhere close to ending. Following dinner Saturday evening, the third of July, Wade and I decide to inform Mother that we plan to enlist.

We thought it fitting to join for duty on tomorrow's Sabbath, asking for the Almighty's blessing. At the same time, we can celebrate our Declaration of Independence from Great Britain. Unable to locate her in the house, we pass Fatu watering floral pots on the downstairs portico.

"Do you know Mother's whereabouts?"

"Yaas, Mass Wade. She iz een dah secret garden."

We follow the cobblestone footpath, leading to Mother's place of solitude. There she is kneeling in front of the holy crucifixion statue. We stand quietly behind her, knowing she senses our presence. After completing her reverent whispers, she stands silently and faces us. Her expression is distraught, and a reservoir of tears erupts.

Wade and I glance at one another, and ask, "Mother, what is wrong?"

She approaches and hugs us all together.

"Sons, I love you so much. I know without freedom there is no light of dawn, but sense your intentions and fear for you. May the Lord be with you both."

She squeezes our hands, and whimpers while walking away.

We look at each other surprised and confused. How can she know? Turning our sight to Mother's statue, perhaps there is divine intuition. We are aware Mother is fretful of maiming and death handed through conflict, but now realize she understands our undertaking for liberty. I am also shocked, but grateful, she did not raise any discussion on my postponement of college.

The next day Wade and I arrive at militia headquarters in Savannah, standing in line with other volunteers. Receiving assignment within the same infantry platoon squad, we sign our names to the roster.

First Brigade Georgia Militia
July 04, 1813 Year of Our Lord

Wade Shiloh, 22, Savannah, Georgia, Infantry
Adam Shiloh, 18, Savannah, Georgia, Infantry

We promised Mother to remain as close as possible during battle. If either is to die, it will be in the presence of family. Knowing this will help console her in the event of our demise.

Our deployment is not yet scheduled, pending more volunteers and supply provisions. We return home and await our campaign assignment. By nightfall, Father and Tamba have prepared for an Independence Day firework display. This annual tradition is conducted near the riverbed for everyone on Shiloh to enjoy. Jeremy, Sanie, and all the children are especially awed by the noisemaker orange flashes and white sparks.

During the next few weeks, Wade and I help Father wherever possible, knowing we will soon be absent from plantation chores. Mother still has her moments, but seems more accepting of our departure each passing day.

Father's concern of likely Indian insurrection readily proves real. The last day of August we receive word of a Red Stick Indian uprising in Alabama territory just north of Mobile, close to home indeed. Hundreds of well armed

Red Sticks, with rifles and ammunition supplied by the British, attack and annihilate Fort Mims. The massacre results in hundreds of men, women, and children killed. We hear several hundred scalps are taken, and about fifteen people escaped.

The decimation of Fort Mims spurs widespread panic. All Georgia patriots rally to avenge this bloodbath and defend families, homes, and country. Two days later Wade and I report for duty, as Tamba takes us to Savannah in the wagon. On the way, I tell him of the Fort Mims slaughter.

"The Redskins enslaved most of the Negroes, certainly worsening their servitude conditions."

"Mass Adam, sufferin' iz dah road to heaven, like dah Mas'tuh Jesus."

Tamba always perceives the benefit from hardship. He often expresses profound thoughts similar to the most learned. Even though Tamba is mentored in many disciplines, he is rooted with an intellectual inner being. Since childhood I always regarded his words as thought provoking and sincere, even delivering unintentional humor.

At army headquarters, I see a crowd of patriots milling about. Like Wade and I, everyone is anxious to finally defend our homeland.

"Farewell, Tamba."

"Goodbye, Mass Wade."

"Watch over everyone, Tamba."

"I will. Be careful, Mass Adam. You too, Mass Wade."

"We will, Tamba," I assure.

Tamba shakes our hands and leaves.

We are proud to serve and eager to avenge the Fort Mims carnage. Before long, our troop detachment, under the gallant leadership of General John Floyd, marches deeper into Indian territory.

From time to time that month, we engage several scrimmages with the Red Stick warriors, but no fight is more gruesome than on the twenty-ninth day of November. Just before daybreak, at approximately seven o'clock, we inflict a surprise attack on the Indian Village of Autosse stronghold.

The evening before arriving at the battlesite, we quietly advance through longleaf and marshy woodland. A slow saturating rain plagues our tedious march. Finally our infantry platoons arrive at the end of a tree line, fronting a large open meadow. The village lies across the grassland several hundred yards away, and everyone hides quietly behind the bordering foliage and thicket.

Twilight breaks the horizon, and an eerie silence blankets the ranks. Dense morning fog hovers atop the field, making visibility extremely poor. The grueling march left our feet cold and damp inside water soaked boots. Wade and I crouch behind a cluster of pine trees, and smack our necks to ward off biting mosquitoes. These flying pests are unduly active, given the unusually crisp winter temperature.

The annoying insects will soon gorge themselves unharmed on a fortuitous feast of bloodshed. In a matter of minutes, the serenity of sunrise will be shattered by smoke and violence. I prepare mentally for the looming onslaught. As bird chirps announce the first morning light, I feel a chilling wind stir.

The artillery division rolls powerful cannons past the tree line onto the meadow grassland, and we affix our bayonets.

"May God be with you, Little Brother."

He grips my shoulder.

"May He be with us both," I solemnly respond, laying my hand atop his.

Cannon fuses ignite one by one, and the sparkling lights inch toward the powder. Seconds later, the sounds of shooting cannonballs erupt in succession, signaling our charge. We start advancing across the foggy field, careful not to overrun our line of sight. The field grass is tall and overgrown, further limiting the pace to a slow trot. My boots squish into the soggy ground with each stride, as cannonballs whistle overhead.

The relentless discharge from artillery subdues many of the red devils, and the cavalry charges from the opposite direction. Although fog obscures the view of distant Autosse, hundreds of oncoming war cries converge closer. Finally, Red Stick silhouettes appear directly ahead. Our infantry line pauses, aims, and fires. The red heathens return the gunfire and blanket the sky with countless deadly arrows.

The screaming of tribal women and children, warrior cries, and tumultuous noise of battle is a mutation of sounds from hell. The smoke filled air reeks of gunpowder. Minutes later the battlefield is strewn with uniformed and painted warrior casualties. Trampled tufts of green grass are stained crimson.

Many of the charging Red Sticks escape our infantry fire, and the crazed savages quickly engage our advance. We are positioned on the front line, with Wade standing about ten feet to my left. As we clash with the screaming Redskins grisly hand-to-hand warfare ensues.

I hear Wade yell, and turn to see an arrow penetrating his left shoulder. He staggers back in pain. Another yelping Indian quickly approaches him, but there is no time to reload my rifle.

"Wade, hold on!" I shout, running to his aid.

All at once, the deranged red devil is staring in my face, with hatred exuding from his eyes. He starts furiously swinging a tomahawk. I lift my rifle barrel to block the blows, feeling the vibration ripple down my arms. The forceful strikes are diverted, except for one which grazes my temple. The blow stuns me and hurts like hell.

"Damn you!" I cry out, feeling warm blood oozing down my cheek.

The savage quickly resumes attacking, screaming a tongue of gibberish. I retaliate in a rage, and thrust my bayonet forcefully into his abdomen. He stands momentarily wide-eyed and staring bewilderedly. I pull the bloodstained blade from his stomach, and he plummets to the ground. His war cries quiet to a muffled gurgle, as blood hemorrhages from his mouth and nose.

I pivot on the mushy ground, looking for Wade. Morning fog blended with gunsmoke continues to cloud my vision.

"Wade! Where are you?" I repeat. My yells are drowned out by the deafening sounds of mayhem.

Hearing no response, I move in the direction of his last position. Then I spot him. The feathered arrow still portrudes from the shoulder of his blood-soaked coat. He fires his pistol to fend off another attacker, but the chamber is empty. The uncivilized human is yelping insanely and flailing a red war club as Wade flinches. Before he can fully draw his saber, the savage swings the club and lands a crushing blow to Wade's right leg. He drops to his knees, barely visible above the tall meadow grass. Wade is too injured to combat this ferocious attack, and I again dash to confront another assailant.

The painted warrior looms over him grinning and slowly unsheaths a hunting knife. The barbarian appears to be pleasuring himself as if on the brink of killing prey. I am seconds away when the mad savage pounces on Wade, knocking him backwards out of my sight. Suddenly, the redskin's knife-clutching hand rises above the tall grass, and my heart plummets as the blade thrusts downward.

"Wade, noooooo!" I scream, finally reaching him.

Now standing above them, Wade uses both hands to barely restrain the Indian's plunging arm. The tip of the blade breaks the skin on Wade's chest, and draws a trickle of blood. I quickly swing my rifle butt, bashing the savage's head. He rolls off Wade limp and bleeding profusely. At that moment, more war yelps lead the red devils to abruptly retreat. They scatter like scared rabbits, many escaping into the woodland. We raise our weapons, shouting victorious battle cries, and I immediately tend to Wade.

"I'm suppose to care for you. Thanks, Little Brother. I mean Brother. You just graduated," Wade mumbles in pain.

"Time to care for my elders, Wade."

Panting, his half-laughter response turns to moans, and perspiration drips from his mud splattered face.

"That was real close, Brother. Are you all right?"

"I'm fine, Wade. Just a grazed head. Almost thought you ..."

"I know, Brother, a few more seconds and Grandfather would be calling."

"Wade, the arrow?"

"Just take the damn thing out Adam," he pleads, cringing in pain.

I am apprehensive about the task at hand, but realize Wade cannot bear the arrow any longer. The battlefield remains in turmoil, and many wounded require medical dresssing.

"Wade, lie down with your left arm against your side."

I place my left heel on the ground, and cross my foot over his left bicep and chest area. My right foot is planted firmly into the soggy earth for balance and leverage. I snap off a piece of the arrow just below the colorful feathers, placing it between his teeth.

"Bite down hard!"

After closer inspection, the stone head almost penetrated his shoulder. I feel its tip formation beneath the skin on Wade's back. I grasp the wooden shaft with both hands, and hope the head will not disengage when I push. The Indians intentionally attach the jagged head loosely, making easy removal difficult if not impossible.

"On three, Wade."

He nods emphatically, squinting his eyes closed and gritting his teeth.

"One, two, THREE!"

I push the arrow through his outer flesh as he screams from excruciating pain.

The deeply embedded triangular head is at last removed, and I pull the remaining shaft through his gaping sinew. Wade grabs the arrow and slings it to the ground, cursing its very existence. Unbeknownst to him, I recover and save the painful memory. Afterward I rip out a section of his torn shirt and compress the cloth into his wound. The material saturates with blood. He stands up, but can barely walk. I raise his pant leg to examine the other injury. His right knee is purple and swollen like a ripe melon. I help him hobble to the wayside, where he sits and leans against a tree.

"Wade, I will find a doctor and assist others where possible."

He responds with a shivering halfhearted wave, as his face wrinkles in pain.

I jog back onto the somber battlefield.

The once tranquil meadow is now planted with harsh realities of war. More tufts of blood-soiled grass nest the recklessly strewn bodies of soldiers and savages. The morning breeze reeks with the odor of gunpowder. The smell nauseates me, and I gag with every breath. My distant vision remains obscured by dense fog and smoke, but I can see scurrying silhouettes staggering and collapsing from injury. I hear voices cry out for help, and moans resonate from the severely wounded. Hundreds lie silent, but clutched weapons of lifeless limbs speak their valor. As a cutting wind stirs my hair, I feel the coldness of death intensify the winter chill.

I proceed to lend assistance to our wounded, and observe a doctor speaking with General Floyd. Our leader is on horseback, yelling commands to the troops. The physician insists he accept medical dressing, but he orders the surgeon to assist all other soldiers first. Hearing this, I direct the doctor to Wade's location. When I return, I find Wade bandaged but still distressed in pain. I attempt to lift his spirits with a serious face.

"Wade, remember Mother wants our portrait in full military dress."

He barely smiles and starts to chuckle.

"Adam, do not make me laugh, it hurts," he grumbles groaning.

Our second-hand uniforms are tattered, soiled with blood and mud. Wallowing with the pigs would have made us more sightly. We know Mother would faint seeing this day's portrait.

The Red Sticks prove to be fierce warriors. After tending to our wounded, we bury our dead. A few of the graves belong to men within the platoon squad, and one patriot in particular had developed a close friendship with me. James was a family man of sound principle and stature. I recall our last conversation before reaching Autosse.

"Adam, I don't have a good feelin' 'bout these marching orders."

"Why, James?"

"I don't know. I just don't. If I should die in battle, tell Abigail how much I love her, Sarah, and little Jimmy. And give her this."

He handed me a locket from his pocket.

"Go ahead, open it."

Inside is a lock of hair.

"It's Sarah's from when she was a baby. There's always something special 'bout your firstborn."

"James, this is one request I hope to never honor."

"Thank you for being a good friend, Adam."

We exchanged firm grips, and he slid his keepsake back into his pocket.

One can only imagine the burden of sorrow to be shouldered by his wife and children. I know in my heart this good compatriot continued marching onto the cloud meadows of heaven. Not since Grandfather have I lamented over a death.

Our detachment returns to Fort Mitchell exhausted and famished. All of the human hardships of this campaign seed my mind and soul with new thought and emotion.

Within the safety of the fort, Wade remains in the infirmary pending partial healing of his wounds. The shattering of his knee proves critical, forcing a permanent gimp in his gait. The left shoulder slowly heals, and he gradually regains mobility in his arm. To Wade's dismay, the severity of his injuries precludes further military service. Knowing his return home is imminent, I bore a hole into the infamous arrowhead and thread it onto a leather neck strap. Before Wade departs, I hand him the souvenir.

"Wade, this is your strength during bad times."

He grins when recognizing the memento, and places it around his neck.

"Thanks, Adam. I will wear it to remember my brush with death, and a little brother that is bigger than me."

From that time forward, he always wore the cherished keepsake. He is discharged honorably from service, returning home in time for Christmas.

Our next major campaign is not yet devised, so plenty of time exists for soul searching. Soon it is Christmas Eve and yuletide songs and liquid spirits abound in the barracks. However, my inner spirit feels a loneliness as I lay on my cot, yearning for the company of family. I would even welcome Wade's aggravating snoring.

This war affirms the fragility of life, and I come to grips with my own mortality. Never again will any day pass nonchalantly, but with substance and purpose. I also reflect upon country and family, never before realizing how fleeting each can be. The war challenges not only our nation's defense of freedom, but our total being and fortitude as a people. God willing, we will prevail to preserve our cornerstone of liberties and beliefs.

I remember Mother's reluctance to our military enlistment, yet her reserved understanding. My mind echoes her secret garden words, 'Without freedom there is no light of dawn.' Mother's comment concisely justifies our human sacrifice for this war. Our lives are unimaginable without freedom. However, when I ponder her statement further, Tamba and the slaves come to mind. The interpretation in the context of slavery is even more profound.

Although I am thankful that Grandfather despised physical abuse of slaves, I remain troubled by minds born into shackled torment. These properties of servitude live in a mental prison, chained with agony, locked with hopelessness, and crumbling from despair. The many different faces of bondage mirror the same hidden image. Each reflect the hardship and immoral disfranchisement of a people.

For the first time, I begin to envision the quiet desperation and psychological scars bore through slavery. How can we, as God-fearing people, validate such unconscionable practices? As innocent souls forfeit to servitude, are we not complicit with Lucifer himself? I recall the writings of philosopher Rousseau.

Man is born free, but everywhere he is in chains.

Although a freeborn aristocrat, the chain of hypocrisy weighs on me. My conscience anguishes over society's condoned bondage. Knowing the enslavement and freedom of races has been cyclic throughout history, I wonder when all Negroes will realize true liberty. At such inevitable time, I also ponder how our plantation ways will endure.

"Mail call!" a soldier thunders.

All of us clamor around the mailbag, as names are hollored out. I anxiously hope for word from home.

"Shiloh!"

I grab the letter and sprint back to my bunk. My fingers cannot open the seal fast enough. It is a precious holiday gift, and my spirit lifts in anticipation of this Christmas Eve greeting.

December 10, 1813

My Dear Son,

We wish you a joyous holiday with good health, and are so proud of your defense of Wade. Had you not foiled the attackers, your brother's marker would be certain. Wade frustrates from the limp, but I thank God he survived the brutal attacks. Father now tutors him in the ways of plantation business.

Jeremy is growing like my trellis of roses, latching onto everything within reach. I show him your hallway portrait each day, and he now says your name.

Father still shows signs of failing health, some days being more fruitful than others. Thus far, the doctors do not prescribe any ailment cures, and my concern heightens. However, he is in good spirits this season.

We have Christmas gifts upon your return. Tamba and Fatu inquire to your well-being often, wishing you good health.

Everybody prays for a speedy end to this war and your safe arrival home. Please do not unduly place your person in harms way, and care for yourself cautiously.

Your devoted loving parent,
Mother

After reading her letter, my loneliness greatly subsides. Her words paint a portrait of family love and caring, comforting to the soul. I awake Christmas Day blessed with strength from God's paper present.

Shortly thereafter, General Floyd is reassigned to a new command in Savannah. He is to protect our beloved city from British aggression. My enlistment expiration, along with other Georgians, coincides with the General's assigned departure. Several of us have the distinct privilege of accompanying him homeward.

Arriving in Savannah, the General personally thanks each of us for our service and sacrifice. Thoughtfully, he arranges a military supply wagon to see everyone home. I am first on the route and tense with anxiety, not having seen Shiloh or family for the past year. Stopping at the foot of our entrance road, I jump off the wagon with my knapsack. Fellow soldiers bid me farewell, and the mile-long walk begins under the strong sentries standing guard. While passing beneath Father's revered oak, a bond with nature inexplicably fills me. I view all of God's creations with renewed respect and admiration as each step brings me closer to family.

Mother eventually comes into sight, sitting on the downstairs portico. She is sipping tea and fanning herself, while Fatu holds a fidgety Jeremy. I approach crouching along the side of the railing. Fatu spots me with surprised eyes and her mouth agape. With a forefinger across my lips, I alert her to hush.

"Mother!"

She startles, quickly standing and turning around.

"Adam! Oh my God, it is you!" she screams, starting to cry.

I vault the portico railing, and she embraces me tightly. Pulling me down, she kisses my forehead repeatedly, overjoyed with my presence. I find no feeling more sublime than coming home to a loved one.

"Welcum home, Mass Adam."

"Thank you, Fatu. It is so good to be here."

I outreach my arms for Jeremy as he squirms within Fatu's grip.

"Ad-dam," he recites, pointing to me.

Mother again bursts into tears and darts into the house. She alerts everyone to my presence.

Seconds later, Father, Wade, and Tamba are on the portico, shaking my hand and giving me welcoming hugs. When the excitement subsides, Mother and Fatu begin preparing a special wild turkey supper. Mother voices concern about my weight loss, vowing to stuff me like a pig. After dinner the family retires to the sitting room, where Father, Wade, and I imbibe brandy. Mother actually partakes in a glass of wine.

They present me with belated Christmas gifts, including a box of Cuban cigars and a tantilizing small wooden box. I slide the lid open, and inside is a small pistol. The small but lethal weapon fits easily within the palm of my hand. This novelty gift is quite unique, yet practical. Father had it forged and crafted as one of a kind by a Philadelphia gunsmith.

"A special thanks to everyone for your thoughtfulness."

"Adam, even the strongest man is equalized by the smoke from such a small object," Father remarks.

"Sir, do you mean the cigars or pistol?" Wade interjects.

Everyone chuckles.

I hoist my glass upward with one hand and the pistol in the other.

"I shall dub it, Equalizer!"

Father lifts his crystal in a toast, "To the safe return of Adam and Wade. May God bless Georgia and the other parts of our country."

Laughing, all raise their drinks to the clinking of glass. As everybody knows, Father is a strong state rights man and loves Georgia with a passion.

Father, Wade, and I eventually convene to the upstairs portico, discussing the war and plantation business until the wee hours. After we retire, I remain awake awhile from Wade's irritating but welcomed snoring.

The next day I attempt to resume my normal life, but the memories of battle haunt me. I pull out the locket belonging to my close friend, James. Reluctantly, I ride

Gabriel to his family's countryside Savannah home. As I approach the house, his wife walks onto the front porch. She is carrying one small child while the other grabs hold of her dress.

I remove my hat.

"Ma'am, I am Adam Shiloh."

"James wrote of you. Do you have his holiday letter? Is he all right?"

I briefly bow my head.

"I am so sorry, ma'am."

Her face cringes in agony.

"Oh my God, no. Noooo!"

She sits on the porch step, distraught and wailing uncontrollably. The baby and little girl also start crying at the sight of their mother. Lord knows they are much too young to understand.

"Ma'am, James wanted me to tell you how much he loves you, Sarah, and little Jimmy. And he wanted me to give you this."

I hand her the locket, and a smile crosses her face amid streaming tears.

"Thank you, Adam."

"Do you have other family, ma'am?"

"No, only our children."

"Take this, ma'am."

I hand her an envelope, and she opens it.

"What is this?"

"James had pay coming, ma'am."

"But there are hundreds of dollars here."

"Never mind ma'am, it's for you and the children."

"Oh, thank you, Adam. May God bless you."

"Take care, ma'am."

I return to Shiloh, feeling so sad for his wife and children. The price for our freedom is not without a lifetime of pain to those held so dear. With the advent of more invading British troops, my concern deepens for the welfare of my own loved ones.

The following month we heard of British soldiers invading and capturing Washington. The Redcoats set the President's Mansion, Capitol, and other buildings ablaze.

Hearing about the fall of our national government angers and disheartens me. Wade and I discuss the gravity of the situation, and I feel compelled to reenlist. Mother, acquiescing to my initial enlistment, is not so passive this time. She pleads with me to reconsider, citing every reason imaginable to bolster her position. When I stand firm, she has nothing short of a temper tantrum.

"Adam, I will not hear such talk. You already served our country. I could have lost both you and Wade," she vents, quavering with teary eyes.

"Mother, I must do what is necessary to protect our lives and land," I insist calmly.

"And I must do what is necessary to protect my sons. Give me a rifle and point to the enemy. I can shoot as straight as any man!"

Her face reddens with anger.

"Now, Mother, settle down," Wade interjects, trying to pacify her.

By now Father is alerted to Mother's seldom heard boisterous voice and enters the room.

"Caroline, what may I ask has you so riled?"

He rests his hand atop her shoulder.

"Adam has thoughts of reenlistment. I will not hear of it!"

She stamps her foot against the floor with fists on her hips. Father and Wade attempt to squelch her fears, but to no avail.

Finally, Father walks past me frustrated, imploring under his breath, "Say something. We must all live here."

I look at him and nod with a raised brow.

"Mother, I promise to serve for the defense of Savannah and Shiloh under General Floyd, should reenlistment be necessary."

Hearing this, she pulls me down and kisses my forehead. After this usual gesture of affection, she leaves the room without further comment. My appeasing vow seems to unruffle her feathers.

Anxiously awaiting any new war word whatsoever, we hear chatter about another major British offensive. With Washington in shambles, the Redcoats marched onward toward Baltimore. Only Fort McHenry separated the enemy from the city and its harbor.

War waged for twenty-five long hours, but the incessant British bombardment of the fort failed. Our flag of fifteen stripes and fifteen stars boldly endured, touting our victory.

Our family is elated to hear of the great triumph, and Father breaks out his best spirits and Cuban cigars. We men celebrate into early morning. Mother is pleased to hear of our major battle redemption, but foregoes the late night frivolity. She retires much earlier with Jeremy.

The successful defense of Baltimore rejuvenates our nation's patriotism. It marks a turning point in the war and signals our tenacious resolve to the British.

Three months later the Treaty of Ghent signing ends the war stalemate. Ironically, we discover that two days before Congress declared war, Britain stated it would repeal the legislation deemed our pretense for fighting.

Shortly after the war, the Red Sticks amassed a final offensive, and General Andrew Jackson defeated the entire Creek Nation at New Orleans. This solidified our expansion westward.

I hope to never witness war again in our great nation. This is the second time our country fought to preserve freedom. However, our will for independence is unequivocable, and all states stood steadfast in unity. Our nation defended freedom as on the grassy meadow at Autosse, a brotherhood bonded with our very blood.

I learned many life lessons from the conflict, and the meaning of freedom is truly understood. However, I have an emptiness inside for taking human lives. I am torn between the commandment of God and Country. I feel my love and bonding with the Almighty rise to deeper fulfillment, but I can only pray for His forgiveness.

For the first time, my eyes are open to the reality of death and the fragility of life. I treasure the love and caring of family as never before. The core of my soul is opened, acknowledging the wrongness of slavery. During battle, I discovered unselfish love deep within my inner being. This most profound love emerges without reservation, willingly self-sacrificing life for another.

From tribulations of war, I learned the unteachable and discovered the face of my true being. Through the quest for freedom, I experienced the reality of Father's strongest conviction, 'Strength of character evolves through adversity.'

*   *   *

After I reminisce about Wade and the war, I feel our strong brotherly bond. Although comforting, the sentiment is tainted with anxiety about his disappearance.

9

Presidential Ball

Several more weeks pass, and Henry returns from his Whitehall home. It is late evening when I notice his carriage arrive. I assume he is weary from the trip. Morning will be more appropriate for conversation.

Unable to drift asleep, my restless mind runs amok. I anguish over the inability to find Wade. Thus far, my pursuit of information has introduced more questions than answers. No matter how glum the outlook, I try to remain resilient like Father's oak.

Tomorrow, Tuesday the twenty-third of March, is Lavinia's initial court hearing. Hopefully, the session will rule favorably and bail can be posted. Attorney Heath did visit her to discuss the case and seems confident in the truthfulness of her statements. Client credibility typically stirs counsel to a vigorous defense. This affords a more convincing court performance.

I last wrote Mother a month ago, and know she is surely curious to any progress. Since I am wide-awake, I decide to compose a letter.

March 22, 1819

Dear Mother,

*Please excuse my tardiness from writing, but I
have been quite busy. An export merchant has
attested to Wade's arrival in Charleston, and I
verified his contract signature seal. He also
appears to have had a brief hotel stay. I am
seeking further clues daily.*

*During my visit, I have also met a beautiful
young lady whose company I enjoy immensely.
Although she is not of aristocrat background, she
is educated and a lady of affectionate
disposition.*

*I trust everyone at home is in good health and
mind. I shall write soon.*

*Your loving son,
Adam*

I choose not to mention Lavinia's predicament,
realizing Mother would needlessly fret over another issue.
After returning to bed, belabored thoughts tire me asleep.

A rising sun soon spurs the sights and sounds of
Middleton Barony. As I walk to the big house, the
plantation comes alive with animals and souls of servitude.
Although Henry, like Father, is a kind and compassionate
plantation owner, indentured negro feet are no less than
working oxen hooves.

I see sheep and cattle leisurely grazing in grassy
meadows, while black bodies toil muddy marshland fields.
I hear obstinate mules protest and kick like thuds of slave
hammers submitting to chores. Overhead, I observe
singing songbird flying freely, as chanting slaves obey

overseers below. The dawn gives birth to another day of human oppression and their lingering hope for freedom. I empathize more each day for these deprived lives and possess a sense of obligation for solutions.

I walk into the dining room, and Henry is reading news articles.

"Welcome home, Henry!"

"Thank you, Adam. I was just updating myself on past events."

"Yes, much has happened. How was your stay? I trust everyone is doing well."

"Just fine. Of course the children were so preoccupied, my presence became readily forgotten," he tells me grinning.

"Any progress on Wade?"

"I did verify he contracted the rice harvest with an export merchant. This was the same day of the Planter's Hotel registry."

"Interesting. Has Sheriff Cleary uncovered anything?"

"He has been extremely supportive, but nothing yet."

"Somebody has to know something more."

"I agree."

"I read where Six Mile Gang members have been arrested."

"Yes, I was with the posse."

I explain the sequence of events leading to Lavinia's arrest.

"I apologize if her evening stay here was intrusive. I did not know what else to do. Only Jessie and Tamba were aware of her presence."

"If you feel that strongly about Lavinia, you took the right action. Your personal relationship with her remains unspoken, by Jessie and myself. I only hope the hearing goes well this morning. By the way, who is presiding?"

"Judge Eliau Hall Bay."

"The old geezer is at least sixty-five years old and should be retired. He can barely hear, stutters badly, and is real crotchety. Although I've heard that he's partial toward women, especially attractive ones. This can be to her favor."

"I hope so."

"Oh, Adam, remember, President Monroe is arriving next month. Can you still join me for the gala?"

"Absolutely, I am honored, sir."

*   *   *

After breakfast, Tamba and I ride the wagon to the courthouse. He waits with the horses, and I walk upstairs to the Court of General Sessions. Attorney Heath is standing outside the courtroom, fumbling through paperwork.

"Good morning, Counselor."

"Adam, good morning. Sheriff Cleary is bringing Lavinia, her spouse John, Hayward, and Roberts, on the writ of habeas corpus."

"Counselor, I understand Judge Bay can be somewhat cantankerous."

"He can be difficult. I assure you, I'll do my best."

We enter the massive doors to the hall of justice. The courtroom is as impressive as the lobby. A huge crystal chandelier hangs overhead, and paintings adorn the walls. Every railing, baluster, and piece of wood shines from polish. I sit and await the opening swing of the gavel.

Other individuals, including citizens, lawmen, and news writers gradually fill the audience.

Moments later the door opens to chatter, as Sheriff Cleary and deputies escort the four accused to their seats. A court clerk announces Judge Bay's entry and everyone stands. The judge appears older than his actual years and seems frail, but strikes a solid gavel.

"T-t-his c-o-ourt is n-n-now i-i-n ses-s-sion."

Being severely hard of hearing, his boisterous stutter resounds throughout the room. Everyone is seated, and the clerk calls the first docket case, citing a hair-pulling incident. After hearing the facts, Judge Bay wastes no time passing a sentence.

"I o-o-order you j-j-ailed in the s-s-same cell, so you may p-p-ull one a-a-another's h-hair as much as y-y-you please. T-t-ten days, plus a-a-another t-ten for w-w-wasting the c-c-court's time. T-t-take them a-a-away."

"N-n-next case," his earsplitting voice resonates, after clearing his throat.

Upon reading the John Peoples and David Ross affidavits he stammers, "W-w-what is to b-b-be said in d-d-defense of these t-t-testimo-o-onies?"

Attorney Heath, now standing, pleads the case for Lavinia, as the judge implores him to speak louder several times. The frustrated counselor literally shouts the arguments, falling on deaf ears.

"Your Honor, she did not engage in robbery and possesses no criminal record. Furthermore, her association with these criminal actions was prompted under duress."

"D-u-u-u-r-ess?"

"Yes, Your Honor. She was intimidated by her controlling spouse," he affirms, pointing to her husband.

However, Judge Bay recalls John Fisher receiving a governor's pardon several years prior, on the condition of never returning to South Carolina. This violation, along with the testimony and two suspicious grave findings, convinces him to hold John and Lavinia.

The judge further cites that the alleged assaults occurred on premises under their control. He remands them to jail until an indictment hearing on the tenth of May.

Much to my surprise, Hayward and Roberts, who are accused of complicity in the assault, are granted bail. The sheriff reluctantly unshackles the snickering Hayward and cropped ear Roberts.

Teary-eyed Lavinia and stoical John are led to the transport wagon. The wheels of justice return them to jail. I am dismayed by the verdict, and Sheriff Cleary is livid over the prisoner release. Everyone knows Hayward and Roberts have long criminal records, and pose a great threat to the public. Perhaps Henry is right concerning Judge Bay's need for retirement, finding sound judgment going by way of his hearing.

Needless to say, Lavinia is quite upset knowing jail will be her home for at least six more weeks. Ironically, the court proceeding falls on my twenty-fourth birthday. All I wish for this year is Wade's safe return and Lavinia's finding of innocence.

Over the next four weeks, I continue my search for Wade and visit Lavinia daily. Her anxieties build, and rarely do her sparkling eyes or dimpled smiles appear. I try to brighten her spirits through fresh conversation, but discussion always reverts to her release.

*   *   *

President Monroe and his entourage arrive in Charleston, Monday, April twenty-sixth. The town is well prepared for his visit, and a celebratory mood thrives. Decorations, music, and fireworks abound, and not a single boarding room is vacant. The city swells as constituents from the region all hope for a glimpse of our country's leader. Sheriff Cleary, cognizant of crime breeding from swarms of people, increases the presence of lawmen. An event of this magnitude is a haven for pickpockets.

The evening of the gala, Tamba rides Henry and me to St. Andrew's Hall on Broad Street. The landmark is well known for hosting private balls, banquets, and meetings. President Monroe is also residing here during the celebration, organized and hosted by Governor Geddes. While Henry and I stand in line for entry, I notice Judge Bay near the front.

"Perhaps I should approach Judge Bay and lobby for Lavinia."

"I don't think that is wise, Adam. It would be perceived as undue pressure. He won't do anything to recuse himself from future proceedings. Besides, between his hearing loss and boisterous voice, the conversation would be overheard by all."

I nod in agreement.

"Welcome, Mister Middleton," greets a doorman, looking at me curiously.

"My lamppost for the evening, in case I over imbibe," Henry jests.

Everyone laughs as we show our invitations.

"Adam, an arm's-length discussion with the Governor might be a better approach. He and the judge are close friends."

"That does sound like a good alternative."

"I can introduce you, although we don't share a warm relationship. He and I differ on many political issues."

"I would appreciate meeting him, Henry."

Inside the opulent grand ballroom, a passing servant offers a selection of spirits. Henry and I each select a flute of champagne.

"Henry!"

I too turn around, instinctively assuming a stance of attention and salute.

"At ease, son. Henry, good to see you."

"You too, John!"

They engage a long vigorous grip, chuckling from good-natured banter.

"Adam, I'm sorry. John, this is Adam Shiloh. Adam, you recognize this old warrior out of uniform?"

"Yes, sir. I served under General Floyd in the First Brigade Georgia Militia."

"What campaign did you fight, son?"

The general outreaches his hand.

"The Creek War, Battle of Autosse, sir."

I reciprocate his firm greeting.

"Oh yes, we gave the red devils a taste of defeat that day. You Georgia troops were among the finest I ever commanded."

"I also accompanied you on your reassignment to Savannah, sir."

"Why of course, Adam, now I remember you."

"Tell me it is not a small world," Henry interjects.

"So, Adam, what's a Georgia boy doing in Charleston?"

"Sir, I am searching for my missing brother who was also under your command."

"To the well-being and return of your brother," he toasts, hoisting his glass and clinking mine.

"May he be found safe and healthy," Henry adds, sounding another ting of glass.

"Thank you kindly, sirs."

"Gentlemen, if you'll excuse me for now. I hear someone calling," the general jests, and bids us goodbye.

We watch as he beelines toward an inviting spread of food.

While tilting my head to drink, I catch a glimpse of Sheriff Cleary walking toward us.

"Adam, Henry, this is quite a reception."

"Yes, quite impressive, Nathaniel," Henry concurs.

I nod enthusiastically.

"Adam, a piece of mail arrived at the post office. I thought I'd save you a trip."

He hands me a sealed letter.

"Thank you, Sheriff."

I slide it within my side jacket pocket.

Following more conversation, the sheriff excuses himself.

"Henry, is Governor Geddes present?"

"I do not see him," he replies, after glancing around the ballroom, "but President Jefferson and President Madison just arrived. Come, I'll introduce you."

We walk toward the entrance.

"Thomas, James, it's so good to see you."

Henry extends an enthusiastic handshake.

President Jefferson looks my way asking, "Who might this young man be?"

"Oh, Mister Presidents, please allow me to present Adam Shiloh of Savannah."

Although Presidents Jefferson and Madison are aged, their grips are extremely firm. Jefferson is slightly taller than me and freckled. Madison is of short stature. I can hardly believe I am standing in the company of such prestigious patriots.

"So Thomas, how is retirement at Monticello?"

"Henry, you know the word is without meaning to me."

"I would be disappointed if you replied otherwise."

"Our nation will be forever indebted to your service, Mister President," I remark.

"My only regret is not contributing more," Jefferson answers, being the humble man he is.

"President Jefferson, if I may ask, sir, how do you feel our great nation will reconcile the issue of slavery?"

"Son, you believe in jumping right in the hornet's nest," Madison interjects grinning.

"Adam, we have a wolf by the ears and can neither hold him, nor safely let him go. My hope is for the institution to wither and die. I know President Monroe is a strong advocate of the American Society for Colonizing the Free People of Color in the United States. You may want to pose your question to him."

"Thank you. I will, sir."

"James how is your retirement at Montpelier?" Henry inquires.

"Unlike Thomas, I am enjoying privacy and solitude," Madison assures.

"Like Thomas, you too have earned the right to relax."

"Henry, if only my wife Dolly would agree."

Everyone joins in a hearty laugh.

"President Monroe just entered with Governor Geddes," Henry notes.

President Monroe notices the presence of Jefferson and Madison and nods our way. His attire is plain and reminiscent of bygone times. Eventually, he walks our direction, being greeted by many guests along the way. The Governor follows but stops to converse with Sheriff Cleary. The President, tall and striking in appearance, finally reaches us.

"Thomas, James, Henry, greetings to all."

Handshakes and pleasantries ensue, reminding me of an election campaign.

"Mister President, allow me to introduce Adam Shiloh of Savannah," Henry says, placing his hand aside my shoulder.

"Mister President," I respond, engaging a solid handshake from our nation's leader.

"Adam, my pleasure," he replies and smiles.

"So how do you like our beloved Charleston?" Henry asks President Monroe.

"I am duly impressed. The city is pleasantly cosmopolitan, and the town folk are quite hospitable. I'm savoring every moment."

"Mister President, my mother will be aboard the Scarbrough steamboat Savannah for the launching gala next month."

"Adam, I look forward to her acquaintance. William Scarbrough and his wife Julia have been most gracious, welcoming my upcoming Savannah stay."

Having President Monroe's attention, I follow with questions regarding our nation's resolve to end slavery.

"Mister President, I ..."

"Excuse me, Adam."

He turns to select a flute of champagne from a passing tray.

"I'm sorry, you were saying?"

"Mister President, I understand you are an advocate for the American Society for Colonizing the Free People of Color in the United States. Do you think it will be a solution to end slavery?"

President Monroe takes a drink and pauses in thought.

"Henry, he is persistent," Madison again remarks chuckling.

"Adam, slavery is a most complicated subject indeed. I do support this society to assist the emigration of freeborn and emancipated Negroes to their homeland of Africa. It could very well prompt a graduated means to end slavery. The society also looks at this effort as charitable work and a means of spreading Christianity."

"Who originated this Society, Mister President?"

"The Society was formed by the Reverend Robert Finley. The reverend feels Negroes will never fully integrate into our American society, and will better serve themselves in their African homeland. He perceives them as detrimental to our country's well-being and quality of life. He also cites the Negroes as being unfavorable to our industry and morals, leading to problems of interracial marriage and whites supporting poor blacks. Although I don't agree with all of the reverend's convictions, he does espouse the popular mindset of our nation today."

President Monroe sips his champagne and suggests, "Gentlemen, the food looks enticing. Shall we?"

"Absolutely, Mister President," Henry concurs.

Our entourage strolls across the reception hall.

I walk beside President Monroe, following with more questions. Everyone listens intently to his responses.

"Mister President, how is this Society funded?"

"Congress has appropriated one-hundred thousand dollars for the cause, and we are helping to secure African soil for the colonization. Even with federal aid and support, the venture is falling short of funds, so the Society is selling lifetime certificates to raise capital. They plan to actually implement the colonization process next year."

"This emigration could be viewed by many as deportation, Mister President."

"Whenever a process reaches Washington, Adam, it automatically becomes politicized. Reverend Finley's strongest support is from the slave states, but not without a hidden agenda. Please bear in mind, I am not saying you or anyone here have dishonorable intentions, but most slave owners have no desire to free blacks or end slavery. They simply desire to deport free Negroes, securing a black population of slaves only, thus bolstering white superiority. This led to protesting against colonization two years ago in Philadelphia. Over three-thousand Negroes demonstrated to fight against slavery and remain in America as citizens."

When reaching the appetizing cuisine, President Monroe turns around. He shifts his eyes across all of us, professing, "The divide in our nation increasingly widens over this subject matter. We must look to the Almighty for guidance and pray for a peaceful Christian resolution."

"James, I could not have summed it up better," Jefferson concurs.

"Amen," Madison adds.

"Now to discuss these delectable dishes," Henry jokes.

Everybody partakes in a sampling. I am still awed by the presence of Presidents Jefferson, Madison, and Monroe, standing before me.

"Adam, Governor Geddes appears to be free now."

We excuse ourselves and approach him.

"Governor, how are you?"

"Henry."

"I would like to introduce Adam Shiloh of Savannah."

"Governor Geddes, sir."

"Adam."

We exchange handshakes.

"Count your fingers, Adam. The governor is a true politician."

"You never miss a chance, Henry. Adam, we try to work together, but Henry is good at giving you the sleeves from his vest."

Everyone chuckles.

"Gentlemen, if you'll excuse me, there's room for more dessert."

Henry leaves.

"Governor, I am advising an individual currently jailed in Charleston. Perhaps you could offer some direction."

"I am a politician, Adam, not a practicing attorney."

"I understand, sir, but the experience of your diplomacy is equally valuable."

"You appear experienced yourself, in the art of flattery. What is the situation?"

"A woman by the name of Lavinia Fisher is jailed on serious but erroneous charges."

"I am aware of this case, and most familiar with the past criminal activities of her husband."

"Yes, but she has no arrest record of ill-doings."

"Adam, you seem to be an intelligent young man. She may very well be innocent, but my advice is not to forgo caution to the wind. Let the evidence speak for itself."

"Thank you, sir."

"If you'll excuse me."

I nod, and moments later find Henry still standing around the dessert table.

"Well, Adam, how was your chat?"

"I think he just gave me the sleeves from his vest."

"That's the governor!"

As the evening progresses, Henry introduces me to several other prominent legislators and Charlestonians. The food, drink, and music are superb. Charleston can hold its head high for delivering the hospitality and fanfare that befits our nation's leaders and honored guests.

I am absolutely awed by the figures in attendance. Undoubtedly, history will speak well of these gallant patriots' leadership and contributions.

While leaving the gala, I wave to Tamba who is speaking to a mulatto on the front walkway. He notices Henry and me, and immediately brings the carriage around for departure.

"Mass Adam, that iz President Madison's servant, Paul Jennings. He was born and raised on Montpelier."

"He appears quite young to be the President's servant."

"Yaas, Mass Adam, he's just twenty years old."

"Is Washington calling you?"

"No, Mass Adam. Shiloh's my home," he tells me grinning.

After arriving at Middelton Barony, Tamba leaves us at the big house and proceeds to the stables. I remark to Henry on a most enjoyable evening.

"Have you ever tasted such delicious dishes?"

"Shush, I learned to tone down compliments about any food not cooked by Jessie. If I don't, my morning flapjacks may well be burnt. But the food was scrumptious," he whispers.

"Thanks again, Henry, for a most memorable time."

"My pleasure, Adam. Sleep well."

"Good night."

I walk to my south flanker quarters tired but ecstatic over such an extraordinary event. While removing my jacket, the forgotten letter falls to the floor. I pick it up and begin reading by candlelight.

April 18, 1819

My Dear Son,

I am thrilled to hear of Wade's known arrival. Please inform me immediately of any new developments.

Everyone on Shiloh is doing well, and it is comforting to know your stay is with the Middletons.

Jeremy constantly inquires to your whereabouts. He has an illusion that you are again fighting a war. His overactive imagination has gotten the best of him.

Father plans to return home in August to manage the rice harvest. I do hope Wade, you, and Tamba are here to assist, so chores do not overwhelm him. Afterward, he will depart to London for additional medical treatment.

You mentioned a lady acquaintance of affectionate disposition. Is there difficulty in pronouncing her name?

Your birthday is less than a month away, and I hope the day is pleasurable and relaxing wherever you are. We shall celebrate it on Shiloh as always.

Please care for yourself, and send warmest regards to Henry and Mary Helen. Know my prayers are with you.

Your loving parent,
Mother

It is comforting to know all is well on Shiloh, and I am glad to hear of Father's upcoming return home. This unforgettable night and Mother's letter well serve to relieve my tensions, if only temporarily. I fall asleep quickly, not waking until seven o' clock.

I arrive in the dining room later than normal, and Henry has already eaten. The table is cleared, and he is reading the newspaper.

"Good morning, Adam."

He motions for Jessie, gesturing his cup.

"Henry, good morning."

"Breakfast for Adam, and tea for both of us please."

"Yaas, suh."

"Henry, I am sorry to be late."

"Nonsense, I overslept myself."

"Last night was tremendous."

"I'm glad you enjoyed yourself, Adam. You needed the relaxation."

"Yes, it was extremely pleasurable. Thank you again. Yesterday's letter from Mother indicated Father is coming home in August."

"Did the treatment cure his ailment?"

"Not yet. He is returning to London after our fall rice harvest."

"Please let him know he is in our prayers."

"Thank you. I will, Henry."

"Mother also sends her warmest regards to you and Mary Helen."

"Tell your mother she also is in our thoughts and prayers. Between your father and Wade, I know these must be difficult times for her."

"I know she is most grateful for your help and concern."

"Helping one another is the food for friendship, Adam. Speaking of which, here comes Jessie."

She enters with another servant, carrying a plate of eggs, ham, a mountain of grits, and hot baked cinnamon bread. Of course, I could not escape the piping hot tea.

*   *   *

Over the next two weeks, preceding the indictment hearing, I repeat my inquiries on Wade and visit Lavinia. My thoughts are again consumed with looming uncertainties, as the euphoria from the gala dissipates.

I continue to communicate with Sheriff Cleary frequently. He is supportive of all my efforts, and our friendship deepens daily. On Saturday afternoon, the eighth of May, Tamba and I stop by his office. He appears anxious to see me.

"Adam, I have word on Wade. A dock man swears he saw him."

"Where, Sheriff?" I exclaim.

"Barbados."

"Barbados? What? Wade would never leave the country unannounced."

"I know. It does sound farfetched, but he swears it was him, if not a twin."

"Who was this person?"

"Just a drifter en route up east. He saw the sketch posted on our wharves."

"Sheriff, mistaken identity no doubt."

I become aggravated with the preposterous notion.

"Don't let his claim bother you. We'll just keep on searching, something will surface."

"I hope so."

We bid farewell, and Tamba and I return to Middleton Barony.

10

Voyage of Faith

Wade could feel his back and legs shimmy up and down against the hard wagon floorboards. Peeking out the bottom of his blindfold he saw only darkness beneath the tarp. He was extremely hot and thirsty, perspiring profusely. Wade squirmed to free himself, but tight rope bound his wrists and ankles. His mumbled calls for help only returned the warmth of his breath. The bandana gag was pulled snug.

He heard occasional conversation, but the trotting horses drowned out the words. Wade knew he was in a real predicament, and solving it would be a dilemma in itself. He found himself alone and scared.

Finally the thumping hooves halted, but his head continued pounding. Before long, approaching voices whisked the canvas from his body. A strong breeze instantly started to evaporate his sweaty skin. Two sets of hands yanked him up and cut the binding from his legs. The menacing men directed him ahead, prompted by several kicks to the pants. Wade hobbled along. He heard rough waves sloshing on either side of the wooden planks, and knew he was on a pier.

"You're late, mate!" yelled an oncoming person.

"We waited for nightfall."

A club slammed against Wade's legs from behind. He groaned and quickly collapsed on his knees.

"I see he's a cripple."

"No, just a slight gimp in his gait."

"I'm changin' the terms of our agreement."

"What do you mean?"

"I'll give you half."

"Half?"

"Take it, or leave it!"

There was a pause.

"On your feet!" shouted one of Wade's captors.

He felt the slap of a hand against the back of his head.

"All yours, Captain."

Wade was dragged away, but aware of clinking coins being counted. Soon he was swaying, trying to balance himself, as he limped aboard a large sailing vessel.

"Throw 'em in the bowels with the others," the captain ordered.

Wrist and ankle shackles substituted for rope constraints, and he was shoved down a flight of steps. Wooden splinters gouged his skin as he tumbled hard onto a damp floor. Moaning and exhausted, he struggled to remove his gag.

"I'm Wade Shiloh. What do you want?" he managed to shout.

"Excuse me, your majesty," replied a voice from above.

"I need water."

"Of course, Sire."

A stream came rushing down from a pail. The liquid drenched his head and splashed to the floor.

"Water, Your Highness!"

One of the hoodlums bowed, and the others busted out laughing. The hatch door slammed closed.

Wade laid in a murky puddle, and pushed himself into a sitting position. He dripped with the stench of urine from the privy bucket. He removed his blindfold only to again be in darkness. As the belly of the ship rocked side to side, he vomited.

His dilated pupils saw silhouettes of bodies, as coughing and rattling chains accompanied their movements. Feeling lightheaded and shaken to the core, he wobbled to stand. Nausea overcame him once more. He leaned back against a support beam and slid down to the floor. He overheard muffled talking, but the language was unknown. He so wished this was a horrible nightmare from which he would awake.

"Who's here?"

There was silence.

"Someone talk to me. I know you're there."

He felt a hand grasp his shoulder, and he jerked away.

"Take this," a voice uttered.

Wade gulped down a tin mug of fresh water. He looked at the Good Samaritan, but barely saw the whites of eyes.

"Where am I?"

"You don't know?"

"It smells like Satan's den."

"You'll soon get used to the odors."

"What do they want with me?"

"They are pirates and slave traders. Down here you are among slaves."

"Slaves? No, you don't understand. I am a slave owner."

"But now you are a property of flesh, like one of us."

"No, this can't be. Who are you?"

"I am Zazu. Your name is Mis'tuh Wade?"

"Yes, how did you know?"

"You hollered it out."

"Oh, yeah. I forgot. You ..."

His conundrum was far worse than he ever imagined. He hesitated, shaking his head to clear the cobwebs.

"You speak good English."

"I was brought here as a child and sold into slavery, Mis'tuh Wade. My master was a Charleston businessman. I became his house servant."

"So, why are you here?"

"He passed away. I was unable to bear children for new lives of servitude, so his heirs sold me."

"Who are these people?" he asked, observing shadowy profiles.

"They boarded this ship at foreign ports. None of them speak English. They will probably be rebartered at profit along with you and me, Mis'tuh Wade."

Pausing in a catatonic state, he stared in disbelief.

As he focused more clearly, he looked upon a young black face. He could tell she had an attractive physique, and that her head was shaved.

Suddenly, out of nowhere came a scamper of feet, and a figure leaping through the air. A horrible screech liken to a baby's cry reverberated throughout the dark chamber.

"My God, what was that?"

"Lucy. She pounced upon another rat, Mis'tuh Wade."

He never thought he would see the day he welcomed a feline. Wade was bitten by one as a child and forever leery of the species. Of course the thought of a rodent bite was dreaded more.

"Has anyone escaped from this hellhole?"

"Several have tried, Mis'tuh Wade, but met their death."

"What is done to pass time?"

"Some slaves have tasks. Others simply sit and await their fate. Any belligerent ones are beaten. I have the duty of cooking."

The overhead door creaked open.

"Zazu, come. We're hungry!"

"Mis'tuh Wade, I must leave now."

"Meals at this time of night?"

She slowly stood, and her head drooped.

"Their appetite is not for food."

As Zazu stepped into humiliation, Wade fell into an agonizing sleep of helplessness.

He awoke to sounds of more jostling chains. Daylight started to penetrate the crevices and portholes of the dingy area. Although he felt somewhat rested, his head was still throbbing. He brushed his hand across the top of his scalp.

"Ouch!"

A protruding hickey was very swollen and tender.

The trap door again opened as he squinted from the sun's rays. Two loaves of bread were slung to the floor below. Black bodies clamored to rip off a piece of the nourishment.

Wade observed about a dozen men plus one older woman and a toddler. Their leg irons were tethered to the ship with chains about four feet long. Only Zazu and the child were free of all restraints.

Even though famished, he again felt the urge to regurgitate. He gagged, smelling an intense odor of more urine along with feces.

"Mis'tuh Wade, you must eat."

Zazu reached out with a clump of bread and a cup of water.

"Thank you."

He started cramming his mouth.

"What else do you eat?" he mumbled between bites.

"This is our staple, Mis'tuh Wade. When at sea we might receive raw or half-cooked fish."

He spit out the food.

"I can't bear this any longer!"

Angry and mortified, he placed his hands on the floor to boost himself up. His palms squashed into a moist substance. Further observance proved it to be vermin droppings. This infuriated him even more.

Once standing he screamed, "You up there!" over and over while warding off flies.

The other slaves looked at him confused, and muttered among one another. Surely they never saw a white man enslaved.

Eventually the hatchway opened.

"I want to speak with the ship captain, now!"

"Oh, it's the king of the slaves. The captain awaits you, Your Grace," said a smirking sailor.

He motioned Wade to come atop. His links of bondage swished with each ascending step.

Once on deck, he shielded his eyes from the blaring sunlight, but did notice the trapdoor key hanging on an adjacent post. Without warning, flying fists pummeled his stomach. He doubled over trying to catch his breath. Two of the hooligans continued roughing him up as he was jostled back and forth. Wade dropped to the ground, beaten and bloody.

"Enough, mates!"

"But Captain Clarke, we're just softenin' up the lad. He seems to have a bad attitude."

"We need 'em able-bodied to barter a good price. Any tribal king will pay handsome for a white man. Bind him to the hull below with the Negroes."

"Aye, Captain."

Wade again toppled down the splintered stairs.

One of the henchmen descended below, and manacled Wade's leg iron to the vessel. After kicking him in the groin, the thug climbed back atop.

"Mis'tuh Wade, just do as they say if you want to live!" warned Zazu.

"I'm not sure I want to," he groaned.

She helped scoot him against a hewn timber upright. He sat while she dabbed a wet cloth over his cuts and bruises.

"Ow!"

He flinched.

"Hold still, Mis'tuh Wade."

"Sorry, Zazu."

"I have to remove the splinters now. This will sting."

"Ouch!"

Wade grimaced and squeezed his eyes closed. Moments later she finished nursing his wounds.

"Thank you."

"You're welcome, Mis'tuh Wade."

"Consider me a friend. You don't have to address me by mister."

She nodded and smiled.

"Why aren't you bound?"

"I've been here for quite some time, and honor their every demand. They don't fear me."

"What they did to you last night was immoral. Are you all right?"

Her eyes drifted toward the floor.

"I am, Mis'tuh Wade. I mean, Wade. You said you own slaves."

"Yes."

"Don't you ravage the young ones?"

"No. No, I don't. Our slaves are treated humanely."

She looked up at him with uncertainty.

"We must escape, Zazu."

"And go where? We are at sea now. Besides, your limbs are bound."

"When they go into port, there must be a time of opportunity. Tell me their ways."

"Most of the lowlifes go into town at night. They stumble back the next morning, reeking of spirits. Many sleep well into the afternoon. But there are always guards."

"How many?"

"At least four, sometimes more."

"Do you know where we dock next?"

"I overheard the Captain order a charting to Barbados, but how can we get away? We're always watched, and everyone is chained."

"Not you, Zazu. Trust me. I have a plan."

He imparted his thoughts, and concern etched her face.

"If it doesn't work, Wade, we'll be killed."

"We may as well be dead. This is no life, merely tortured existence. At least we'll go down fighting for our freedom. Together we can do this."

"But for now, you mustn't provoke them."

"I know. I won't, Zazu."

He continued to endure maltreatment from the rogue privateers. They levied just enough to enforce an upper hand, but not enough to damage their human goods. His days passed slowly, abused and locked to the belly of the ship. Wade frequently thought of his family and life at Shiloh. He soon realized how much he had taken for granted, and began to see the world in a different light. Although he knew Adam would surely try to find him, he was aware the task was next to impossible. His only option was to escape.

After several weeks of Wade being obedient, the captain put him to work in the galley with Zazu. Here the oppressed couple schemed daily to further perfect their planned getaway.

Throughout the evening hours Zazu was summoned to satisfy the desires of the kidnapping rapists. Wade sat with the Negroes, and listened to the night-hour chatter of rats. Occasionally, he would see their beady eyes scurry along the rafters. Of course they were no match for the prowess and agility of Lucy. After the demise of each rodent, Wade would reward her.

"Lucy, Lucy, come here girl," he repeated, holding out breadcrumbs.

Green eyes eventually emerged. She was a large Calico marbled in black, tan, and white. He would continue to coax her until she finally nibbled on the food in his hand.

"Meow," the feline would softly utter.

Beneath her distinction as a vermin killer, arose a hidden tenderness.

After time, she would let Wade pet her, as she arched her back and purred. Although a mere cat, Lucy reminded him he was still human, and not the primal animal he feared he had become. She kept alive his sense of compassion and affection. He soon shared all of his meager meals with her, and she slept by his side. He took a deep shining to this predator ally. If it weren't for the friendship of Zazu and the companionship of Lucy, his sanity would surely have been at risk.

Despite the fact spoken words were not understood, the Negroes accepted this white man as one of their own. Wade felt this newfound human bond to be unlike any other. For the first time, he too was rooted with the essence of their desperate despair. The mental and physical consciousness of slavery beset him week after week. Not until now had he experienced or understood the impetus for suicide.

Then one sultry day in July, the port of Barbados came into view. Wade could sense excitement from the motley crew. They had been at sea over a month. The prospect of setting foot on dry land and carousing the taverns was foremost on their minds.

"The time has come, Zazu. They will be intoxicated for sure this first night in port. Are you ready?"

"I think so, but I'm scared."

"I am too, but we must try."

"I know."

"Be brave, Zazu."

Wade squeezed her hand and she nodded.

That evening most of the plundering swashbucklers left for town. At the sound of eleven bells the sentries standing watch could be heard storytelling and laughing. Their drunken state was visible from their slurred speech.

"Zazuuu, we're hungryyy. Come!"

Wade patted her shoulder, and gave her a mixed look of empathy and encouragement. A halfhearted smile crossed her face. She again climbed upward into degradation. Wade sat shackled among the Negroes who were mostly sleeping. He bowed his head and whispered a prayer.

Heavenly Father, please be with me and these souls of servitude. Guide us safely to freedom. I'm sorry for all I have taken as granted and for any transgressions against my fellowman. I repent for my past ways of error. More than ever, I ask for your mercy and forgiveness. Should I die tonight, please grant me the honor of a presence in heaven. Amen.

Wade waited nervously. About an hour later the hatch door barely opened and quickly closed. A thud had sounded on one of the upper steps. Wade extended himself as far as possible from the ship hull, stretching the chain taut. The fallen object was mere inches from his reach. After several attempts, he slumped over exasperated. Then he felt a tap on his shoulder from a tiny finger. A father was holding his small son, and gestured a motion. Wade grinned and took the child. He reached out again, lifting the toddler toward the steps. The father encouraged the boy in his foreign tongue. Moments later an iron key was retrieved that Zazu had seduced from the unsuspecting guards.

Wade unlocked his manacles. He passed the key to the father who aroused the others. Commotion filled the quarters.

"Hush, Hush," Wade told the slaves, placing his finger over his lips.

He couldn't help but chuckle as the Negroes mimicked him.

Silence prevailed except for more clicking of unlocking iron. Wade motioned to four young strapping men to follow him as he climbed up the rickety steps. He tilted his head inches from the overhead door and listened.

"Zazuuu, you're toooo pretty to beee black," hiccupped a voice.

"Both of you come with me. I'll show you the beauty of a black tongue wrapped around your white skin."

Roaring in merriment, the guards approached her closer. They reveled in anticipation.

"But first, count the number of hours I can please you before dawn."

Six stomps vibrated the trapdoor. Soon their boisterous hilarity faded with their footsteps. Wade cautiously cracked open the squeaky hinges and peered about the deck. Fog had set in, but the dismal area appeared clear of any patrols. Although visibility was poor, he was guided by the shenanigan sounds of Zazu's suitors. The whereabouts of the other four guards was unknown.

Wade crouched on the deck, motioning his trailing squad of peers to do the same. Hidden by nature's veil, they snuck toward Zazu. He peeked around a mast, and observed both of her wooers standing and fondling her breasts.

Knowing these watchmen were well distracted, Wade and his following swiftly stormed them. After a brief scuffle the inebriated no-accounts were knocked out, but not before a gunshot echoed.

"Zazu, lead the other slaves ashore as planned. We will join you soon."

"Be careful, Wade."

She squeezed his hand and darted away.

Now alerted to trouble, the remaining guards were charging toward Wade and his band of slaves. The four buccaneers had their sabers drawn and pistols in hand. Wade and the Negroes grabbed what weapons were handy from the two unconscious bodies, and collided with the pirates. Fighting ensued as blades of steel sliced through the fog and pistols fired. White and black flesh colored the deck crimson with blood.

A moment later an eerie calm settled amid the hovering haze. Moaning silhouettes slowly staggered out of the mist.

11

Day of Reckoning

After Sabbath services, the day before the indictment hearing, Tamba and I break from our search endeavors. He spends leisure time with the house servants, and entertains them with conversation, music, and song. Henry and I enjoy an afternoon river cruise on his pleasure barge. After dinner, we lounge in the north flanker until late evening.

"Thank you for a most relaxing day."

"You're welcome, Adam. I always find the water ripples soothing to the mind. Of course, these Cuban cigars and spirits do settle the nerves."

"A good marriage, Henry."

We chuckle.

"Adam, I hope the arraignment outcome tomorrow is favorable."

"Thank you, so do I."

After our fill of relaxants, we bid goodnight.

The following morning I awake to clear skies and bright sunlight, but my vision is clouded with anxiety. After joining Henry in the dining room, I walk to the stables where Tamba is saddling Gabriel.

"Good mo'nin', Mass Adam."

"Good morning, Tamba."

"What day is it, Mass Adam?"

"Another court date filled with tension."

"I hope Miss Lavinia's all right."

"Thank you, Tamba. I will return in time for supper."

I mount Gabriel.

"Mass Adam, I talked to Jessie last night, and she iz preparin' something special for dinner."

"Oh, what is the occasion?"

"Happy birthday, Mass Adam."

He smiles, handing over the reins.

"I truly forgot. Thank you, Tamba. Please express my appreciation to Jessie. I will personally thank her this evening."

"Yaas, Mass Adam."

While riding to town, I recall past presents and celebrations. Although the gifts throughout the years were appreciated, none were quite as special as on my twenty-first birthday. It was only three years ago when Father and Mother surprised me with Gabriel. I remember him as a young colt, wobbling to stand. Now he is a powerful steed, and can journey long and hard. Although well behaved, he is still spirited, and enjoys romping in a wide-open pasture.

Mother says the love of an animal molds our sense of caring and compassion. She believes everyone should experience this unique bond. Gabriel and I have certainly shared the reality of her conviction. After dismounting him at the courthouse, I pat his long muscular neck and slip him a lump of sugar. He looks at me and whinnies, surely a sign of gratitude.

Inside the crowded courtroom, I sit in one of few remaining seats. Attorney Heath is standing and rifling through paper across from the judge's bench.

Moments later the hall doors open to heightened chatter, as Sheriff Cleary and deputies escort the estranged couple inside. The judge enters from chambers, and the Court of General Sessions is called to order. Everyone is seated.

While the fifteen jurors enter the jury box, the court clerk recognizes them by name, "William Hart, Luke Bowes, William Wheelen, David Murray, J.S. Packer, William Owens, I. Gespeale, William Mathews, James Fogartie, Joseph Tyler, William Brisbaine, Caleb Walker, Peter Gaillard, John Davis, John Wilson."

This assembly of citizens, both Charlestonians and others from the adjacent countryside, will pass judgment. A local resident comments that each one is an upstanding pillar of society.

The judge curtails belabored opening remarks from Attorney Heath, reminding the court this indictment hearing is not a trial. Subsequently he orders the assault testimony of the Charlestonian property guard David Ross to be presented.

Sworn to tell the truth, Mister Ross delivers testimony identical to his affidavit. Attorney Heath attempts to negate the assault assertion on Lavinia's behalf. He claims undue spousal duress forced her actions. Each juror listens intently, but many appear skeptical of Attorney Heath's nullification claim.

After all testimony and arguments are presented, the eminent fifteen vacate to weigh the evidence. They return after a brief deliberation, and the judge solicits their verdict.

"Mister Foreman, what say you of the crimes?"

Juror William Hart stands.

"Your Honor, we find the accused to be indicted for assault and assault with intent to murder."

Mumbling ripples through the courtroom as the jurymen nod affirmatively at one another.

"Order! Order in this courtroom!" the judge yells, pounding his gavel. "The accused will be remanded to the City Jail, pending a trial date of May twenty seventh."

Sheriff Cleary escorts Lavinia and John to the prisoner transport wagon.

The next court date is two weeks away. Evidence supporting Lavinia's assault participation does not illustrate the extenuating circumstances. The jury obviously was not satisfied with Attorney Heath's coercion reasoning. However, he will be allowed more latitude at trial. He believes the charges against her will be dismissed, or she will simply be fined.

Hayward and Roberts, scheduled to appear at this same hearing, are noticeably missing. They have skipped bail.

With the verdict date seventeen days away, my tension mounts. Attorney Heath continues to be confident of a favorable outcome, although her destiny will be in the hands of judge and jury. I attempt to mitigate Lavinia's worries during frequent visits, while my vigilant search for Wade continues.

The day before the trial, Wednesday, the twenty-sixth of May, Tamba and I again journey to town.

The bumpy cobblestones of Bay Street slow our wagon while nearing McCrady's Pub. Gabriel and Nicodemus suddenly become agitated, rearing and snorting as if sensing a storm. They abruptly halt in front of the establishment, neighing and shaking their heads for no apparent reason.

"Tamba, what is wrong with the horses?"

"I don't know, Mass Adam."

He whistles and snaps the reins, encouraging them onward, but they stand steadfast.

"They are acting like stubborn mules."

"I know, Mass Adam."

The horses tied in front of the tavern become spooked from the unsettling antics. One in particular tries to break loose, causing a fracas.

"Tamba, wait!"

I jump from the wagon, and rush toward the frantic animal.

"Whoa, boy! Whoa!" I yell, calming him.

There is cause for excitement as he bobs his head and whinnies at me.

"Mass Adam, Mass Wade's horse!"

"Yes, Tamba! Yes! Gabriel and Nicodemus knew it was Isaiah!"

The commotion attracts patrons inside the tavern to investigate. A huge brawny man with large biceps confronts me.

"Hey, that's my horse!"

"Who might you be, sir?"

"I am Benjamin Brown, the blacksmith. What are you doin'?"

"This animal belongs to my brother. Where did you get it?"

"I bought this horse fair and square!"

"Who sold it to you?"

"A man named George Clark."

"That is not my brother. You have been hoodwinked."

"Mister, I don't know who you are or what you're up to, but you're going to get coldcocked."

He draws back his immense fisted arm, but hastily squirms to his knees, grimacing. Behind him stands Tamba, twisting the threatening limb.

"All right! All right!" the man pleads.

"Tamba let him go!"

"Yaas, Mass Adam."

"I'll have you flogged," the stranger threatens, holding his hurt arm.

"You won't have anyone lashed, Benjamin," hollers Sheriff Cleary, appearing out of nowhere. "Besides, it looks like the only one gettin' whipped is you."

The bystanders laugh, but abruptly stop when the fuming blacksmith turns toward them snarling.

"Now what in the hell is going on here?" the sheriff thunders.

"Sheriff, this man's tryin' to steal my horse, and the black savage attacked me," the blacksmith blurts sneering.

"Tamba was only stopping him from assaulting me, Sheriff. This is Wade's horse."

"Benjamin, these two men are deputized posse members. No one's tryin' to steal your horse, and I'm sure these forthright citizens here will tell me who threw the first punch."

"Well, I did buy this animal, Sheriff."

"Adam, how can you be sure this is the right horse?"

"On the saddle underside there is an inscription reading Isaiah the Prophet."

"Benjamin, unsaddle the horse."

"I can't, Sheriff. My arm," he whines.

The sheriff unstraps the saddle and turns it upside down on the ground.

"Well, Benjamin, look for yourself. It seems you bought stolen property. This negates the sale and your ownership. Who bartered this horse, and when did this occur?"

"I swear, I didn't know, Sheriff. A man named George Clark sold it to me about a month ago, right here at McCrady's. I haven't seen him since."

"If you see him, report it to me right away. Don't take matters into your own hands. You see what can happen. Do you understand me?" Sheriff Cleary scolds him like a child.

"Yes, sir, Sheriff."

He walks away begrudgingly, nursing his arm and grumbling.

"Adam, I'm sorry about Benjamin. The big man is a hotheaded town bully. I've never seen him manhandled before, but it's about time he was put in place. Good job, Tamba."

"Yaas, suh, Mis'tuh Sheriff Cleary," he answers grinning.

"Deputies, Sheriff?"

"Well, theoretically you two are still deputized."

"Thanks, Sheriff."

"You know it's never a good sign finding a horse without its rider."

"I know. But until Wade is found one way or another, I have to keep looking."

"I'm right there with you."

"Thanks again, Sheriff."

I shake the hand of a true friend.

Tamba leads Isaiah to the rear of the wagon and ties him down. While passing Gabriel and Nicodemus, the three horses snort with heads shaking and flapping tails.

We curtail our day in town, and take Isaiah back to the stables at Middleton Barony.

*   *   *

Morning brings the day of reckoning, as I find myself again sitting in the Court of General Sessions crammed with spectators. Most in attendance are mere curiosity seekers and largely indifferent to the judicial process.

The young and flamboyant State Attorney General Robert Y. Hayne is prosecuting the case. He projects an air of confidence that could be construed as arrogance. The popular prosecutor is best known for his recent conviction of a Charleston murderer who is scheduled to hang tomorrow.

The judge enters and calls the session to order. The complaint affidavits are presented alleging assault, assault with intent to murder, and robbery by Six Mile Gang members.

Defense Attorney Heath enters a not guilty plea for all charges against Lavinia. Husband John also enters a plea of not guilty, portraying a feeble attempt toward innocence.

Victimized property guard, David Ross, and citizens observing identifications by him and John Peoples present firsthand prosecution testimony. The witnesses undergo a barrage of questions, as a bristly exchange erupts between lawyers.

Attorney Heath cross-examines David Ross with empathetic references to Lavinia. Her lovely face is streaming with tears. She appears to be capturing sympathy from the all-male jury.

"Mister Ross, did the defendant, Lavinia Fisher, due you bodily harm?"

"Yes, Mister Heath."

"Please explain to the Court exactly what transpired."

Attorney Heath slowly paces in front of the seated jurors, grasping his chin between a thumb and forefinger.

"Well, she choked me while boxing my head through a window pane. It gave me a gash on my forehead."

"I see. So she did this by herself?"

"Well, she and her husband were in the house at the time. The others were outside and beat me later."

"How do you know in all the upheaval, it was her hands wrapped around your throat from behind? They must have been extremely strong hands to choke your large manly neck. Do you agree?"

"Yeah, I could hardly breathe."

"Your Honor, and members of the jury, please permit me to enter the hands of the defendant as evidence."

The courtroom stirs with noise, joined by a banging gavel.

"Order! Order!" cries the judge, as calm promptly prevails.

"Your Honor and respected jurymen, please allow yourselves to feel the hands of the accused."

Attorney Heath leads Lavinia to the bench and jury box, while each man caresses her soft womanly hands. Her dimples take shape as she flashes her captivating smile. The men appear flattered.

"Gentlemen, these soft delicate hands harmed the burly neck of Mister Ross? He certainly must be at the mercy of his wife."

The courtroom bursts into laughter.

"Order! Order! Order!" shouts the judge again, hammering blows of the gavel.

"Mister Ross, concerning the gash. You entered the pane head first?"

"Why, yes."

"Could you see behind you at that moment?"

"Well, no."

"So either one could have boxed you through the window."

"No, I know it was her!"

"Just like you know her soft delicate hands were strangling your throat. Your Honor, I have no more questions for this witness."

The courtroom again fills with conversation as the slamming gavel restores order. Now prosecutor Hayne approaches the state's witness.

"Mister Ross, when is the last time you struck a woman?"

"Why never, Mister Hayne."

"As no gentleman would. So in the scuffle your instincts prevented you from retaliation against the accused."

"I would never hurt a lady."

"The defense claims her hands were too feminine to choke your neck. Honorable Judge and Jurymen, I want the accused to place her hands around this witness's throat in a choking position."

The courtroom breaks into pandemonium as a pounding gavel once more echoes for silence.

"This is preposterous!" Attorney Heath complains.

"Counselor, you entered her hands as evidence, and the prosecution is entitled to rebuttal. Mistress Fisher, please approach the witness box," the judge orders.

Lavinia, appearing reluctant, is escorted to Prosecutor Hayne.

"Please stand down here, Mister Ross," the prosecutor requests.

He steps over to the jury box.

"Mister Ross, be so kind to turn around and face the jury, as if the window at Six Mile House. Sir, I am now going to blindfold you."

The prosecutor ties a scarf around the witness's forehead, covering his eyes. The jurymen look at one another confused.

"Madam, please lay your hands on this witness from behind in a choking fashion."

The packed courtroom is completely still as she slowly places her hands around his neck, but quickly withdraws them.

"No, Madam. Let them remain there," the prosecutor requests.

Again she assumes a strangling position without flinching a finger.

"You may remove your hold now. Please repeat the exercise for the court one more time," he instructs, but stops her mid-motion, "however, give me the pleasure of first examining your hands."

"Your Honor! Must we humor this charade?" Attorney Heath objects, while standing up.

"I will allow it. Be seated, Mister Heath."

The prosecutor encloses each of her hands within his own, pausing briefly. She appears perturbed, but complies.

Her hands again wrap around Mister Ross' throat.

"Thank you, madam. Please be seated."

The prosecutor removes the blindfold.

"Mister Ross, you may now resume sitting, and remember you are still under oath. Did you recognize the hands of your simulated assailant?"

"Well, yes and no."

"Please clarify, sir."

"The first time they felt like her hands but not the second."

The courtroom again erupts into chatter as the rapping gavel calls for quiet.

"Mister Ross, as everyone here witnessed, it was her hands each time."

"What kind of nonsense is this?" objects Attorney Heath.

"The kind proving guilt, Counselor!" Prosecutor Hayne shouts.

"This is rubbish, Your Honor!" Attorney Heath protests screaming.

"Order! Or I'll find you both in contempt! Bring closure to your argument Mister Hayne!" the judge thunders, striking his gavel.

"Yes, Your Honor."

The prosecutor takes a moment to regain his composure.

"Mister Ross, please tell the court why you identified the hands of the first choke hold, but not the identical hands of the second."

"I can tell they were different."

The courtroom buzzes with ridicule and chuckles.

"Order!" the judge demands, nodding at the prosecutor to continue.

"How can you expect this court to believe a difference existed through use of the same hands?"

"The first hands I identified wore a ring, Mister Hayne."

The prosecutor walks toward Lavinia while flashing her emerald stone in the air for all to see.

"Madam, I am returning the ring removed from your finger prior to the second strangle hold!"

The hall of justice explodes into total chaos.

"Order! Order! Order!" The gavel strikes repeatedly, eventually establishing decorum.

"Will the accused, Mister Fisher, please raise his hands for the court to observe?" Prosecutor Hayne presses on.

John Fisher sits, seemingly ignoring the request.

"The accused will comply," orders the judge.

John lifts his hands in the air, noticeably absent of any rings.

"Please note Mister Fisher wears no ring. Only his wife does, thus proving her guilt of assault."

Another outburst is subdued from a slamming gavel.

Although Attorney Heath stands his own ground, Prosecutor Hayne is thorough and innovative. The defense alleges her actions were coerced through intimidation by the threatening hand of her spouse. However, the prosecutor poses questions requiring direct answers, which allow little room for speculation. The result is damaging testimony, marring the defense. The jurymen's facial expressions affirm the prosecutor's every summation.

After closing arguments the jury retires to deliberate and returns shortly thereafter. The assembly of men is seated. Expressionless, they patiently await the judge's entrance from chambers. However, the lingering decision unnerves the restless audience, plagued with whispers and squirming seats. Finally the robed man reenters.

"Mister Foreman, how say you on the evidence presented?"

Dead silence hangs on the response.

The stoic juryman stands, declaring, "Guilty of highway robbery!"

The courtroom erupts into mayhem and Lavinia into tears, as reporters rush to publicize the outcome.

"Order! Order in this court! The prisoners are hereby remanded to the City Jail pending a sentencing date," the judge cries out, followed by a final swing of his gavel.

Everyone knows the punishment for highway robbery is death by hanging. I stand stunned by the verdict, and approach Attorney Heath amid the turmoil.

The affidavit of John Peoples, the Savannahian waggoner, did attest to highway robbery. However, the proven testimony shows Lavinia's only wrongdoing was assault. There is no evidence implicating other guilt, but the jury has tried all Six Mile Gang members as one. Lavinia is considered complicit to a crime which she had no involvement. Even husband John was not proven a participant within the theft. Ironically, two of the purported guilty gang members, Hayward and Roberts, were granted bail and remain at large. Indeed, this is a travesty of justice.

Once more, Sheriff Cleary escorts Lavinia and John to the prisoner transport wagon for their return trip to jail.

"Counselor, what the hell went wrong?" I vent.

"Adam, I am presenting a motion for a new trial."

"No proof was presented of highway robbery by Lavinia, only assault. She has no prior record," I stress exasperated.

"I know, Adam. Robbery complicity and the intent to murder charges are less than circumstantial. They are grossly unfounded. The jury didn't identify with Lavinia's brow beating husband predicament either. I'll keep you apprised."

As the courtroom clears, I sit numb in disbelief.

12

Fall Harvest

Several days later Attorney Heath informs me the sentencing date is June second. At such time, he is submitting a petition for an appeal. When visiting Lavinia, I express optimism for the new trial motion. Dismayed and disillusioned, she is inconsolable.

Less than one week passes and another judgment day arrives. The courtroom again overflows with spectators and reporters. Everyone waits to be the first voice publicizing the results. Sheriff Cleary brings Lavinia and John into court, and the judge enters from chambers.

"The Court of General Sessions is now in session. The Honorable Judge Charles Jones Colcock presiding," the clerk announces.

"Everyone be seated," orders the judge, following a bang of his gavel.

Attorney Heath approaches the bench declaring, "Your Honor, I am motioning for the Constitutional Court to grant a new trial."

He hands over a document.

Judge Colcock reaches for his spectacles, methodically perusing the argument. The sound of turning pages breaks the hush of the courtroom. Being quite the opposite of flamboyant Judge Bay, his mannerisms are almost blasé.

Finally, he lays the request down, and contemplates his decision.

After rubbing his forehead, he looks up and responds, "Motion granted."

The courtroom again buzzes as the saga continues. The Constitutional Court will review the appeal next January, providing Lavinia a reprieve from the inevitable sentence of hanging. This affords eight more months of life and jail. She is elated, and a smile of hope reshapes her face. I too feel relieved, if only temporarily. Perhaps Judge Colcock allowed the motion suspecting lack of evidence. The request could easily have been denied.

Today also marks a month since I received Mother's last letter. Her curiosity about the unnamed lady, combined with the recent events, compels me to write a frustrating response.

June 02, 1819

Dear Mother,

I have knowledge regarding Wade, which presents more unanswered questions. A transient dock man claims to have seen a person in Barbados, resembling him closely. The Sheriff and I dismissed this sighting as mistaken identity.

We also discovered Wade's horse in the hands of a local citizen who purchased the animal from an unknown third party. Since the transaction was not proven legitimate, I have recovered Isaiah.

The lady of affectionate disposition is named Lavinia. She currently has legal difficulty of which I am advising. Today she was granted an appeal for her case to be heard next January. It is my wish for you to meet her someday. I will explain more when in person.

I am glad to hear of Father's return home in August to manage the rice harvest. Rest assured that Tamba and I will be there to assist. I can only pray for Wade's presence.

We continue our diligent search efforts daily. I will write of any new findings.

Your loving son,
Adam

*   *   *

Over the next two months, my determined pursuit of Wade continues. I also continue lobbying for Lavinia's defense and release.

On the heels of Judge Colcock's appeal ruling, a fire devastates sections of Meeting and Market Streets on the sixth of July. This disaster sets Charleston in a tizzy, and the vibrant marketplace economy is temporarily jeopardized.

The sheriff also regains custody of Hayward and Roberts following their disappearance. After they jumped bail in March, they were arrested upstate and extradited to Charleston.

*   *   *

August necessitates the Shiloh rice harvest, suspending efforts to locate Wade. Tamba and I set out for Savannah, and bring Isaiah home. Along the way, I stop to visit Lavinia at the foreboding City Jail.

"I am glad the case is successfully appealed, but dread being imprisoned until January."

"I know, Lavinia. At least you remain alive, and everything possible will be done to comfort your stay."

"Please don't forget me."

She squeezes me tightly.

"Forgetting you would be no less than forgetting my name."

I hold her, kissing her forehead.

"Oh, Adam, I do love you."

"As I love you, but now I must return to Shiloh."

"Please don't leave me."

Her head droops sniffling.

"I will never *leave* you, but must assist with the rice harvest. I promise to return whenever possible."

She looks at me teary-eyed while nodding. I tenderly kiss her, and release my close embrace. I look into her eyes, and feel my heart throbbing. In a burst of passion, I press my lips hard against hers. We kiss madly, and cannot hug close enough. She moans with every caress of my hand. I love her so much. Then I reluctantly slide my fingers down her arm, lastly squeezing her hand while walking away. She reaches toward me smiling as a lone tear streams down her cheek.

Tamba and I continue to our Savannah destination, and by mid August ride beneath the strong sentries standing guard. As we approach the big house, Father is sitting on the downstairs portico with Mother.

"Father!" I yell.

He stands as I jog toward him from the wagon. I firmly grip his tremulous hand, followed by a loving hug. He appears frail with diminished color but proves strong in spirit.

"Mother."

I lean over while she kisses my forehead.

"How are you feeling, sir?"

"Fine son, just fine."

Knowing Father prides himself on his strength and leadership, he is reluctant to accept the terms of his illness.

"Mother informs me monthly of Wade's status. Has there been any confirmed development other than the exporter and hotel visits, or finding Isaiah?"

"No, sir, I am sorry to say."

Not desiring to upset Mother, I look at Father and motion my head toward Isaiah.

"We'll be right back, Caroline."

"William, where are you going?"

"To see Wade's horse, Mother," I respond.

While walking over to Isaiah, I tell Father the hotel visit details. When reaching the steed, Father strokes its muscular neck.

"Adam, these events are not a good sign."

"I know, sir."

"If you could only talk, Isaiah," Father says, and hands him a lump of sugar.

We walk back to the portico, continuing our discussion.

"What do you conclude from the purported Barbados sighting?"

"An unreliable reporting. The Sheriff and I considered the drifter's claim simply as mistaken identity."

"I understand you have Wade's sketches posted about town?"

"Yes."

"Likewise, you are soliciting the townspeople and businesses in person?"

"Yes, Father. Unfortunately, no one has come forward with new information. It is a tedious task. The Charleston population is about twenty thousand."

"Be strong, Adam. Persevere and you shall succeed."

"Yes, I will, sir."

Reaching the portico, Father changes the subject. He realizes better than anyone how emotional Mother can become.

"How are Henry and his family?"

"They are doing well. Henry sends his deepest regards for your good health"

"You tell that political war horse I'll call upon him soon."

"That I will, Father."

"Mother, how was the Presidential Gala?"

"Glorious! President Monroe is a man with vision, and I declare such a gentleman. We sailed the steamboat round trip from town to Tybee Island."

"Caroline, steamboats sail only if they lack in power," Father volunteers.

"Oh, pshaw," counters Mother, dismissing him with a wave.

"Your last letter spoke of Lavinia. Are you becoming her beau?"

"In a manner of speaking, Mother."

"Son, when will we meet her?" Father interjects.

"Sir, she currently has a private legal matter of which I am advising. Her appeal hearing for a new trial is scheduled for January. I hope you can make her acquaintance in the near future."

"What type of legal issue?" Mother inquires.

"Caroline, he said it was private," Father exclaims, shaking his head.

"I know, William. I know," Mother concedes, knowing the question was intrusive.

"Jeremy and Sanie are anxiously awaiting your arrival. If I didn't know better, I'd think it was Christmas. They have been exceptionally well-behaved," Mother remarks, quickly changing the conversation.

"Where is the little general?"

"As always, they're trampling around my secret garden."

I follow the cobblestone footpath toward their playful chatter, and a feeling of déjà vu overcomes me. They are still in a rip-roaring wooden gun battle with Colossus chasing.

"Boys! Boys!" I yell, and each comes running.

"Adam!" Jeremy cries out, hugging my side.

"Mass, Adam," Sanie yells, while grabbing the other side of me.

"You brought our sweets?" Jeremy blurts, smiling with his new set of front teeth. Again Sanie grins ear to ear.

"Have both of you behaved?"

"Yes!" they shout simultaneously.

"Very well then."

I reach into my pocket and hand over a large bag of hard-candy. Both boys excitedly jump and scream, then run away with barking Colossus.

During our absence, the day-to-day plantation operations have been handled well by our freed negro overseers. The rice crop fields are plentiful, and the golden grain has matured for reaping. I observe field slaves cutting down the stalks and bundling them together. They pull the bundles, weighing between one and two hundred pounds, from the muddy fields. After drying out, the stalks will be processed. The rice is stored in wooden barrels, made by our coopers, and loaded onto barges.

The harvest caravan will depart for Charleston by route of the inland waterways. Our head overseer is Tamba's uncle, who is also captaining the voyage. He will be accompanied with experienced waterway slave navigators. Upon delivery, the barrels will be unloaded under the guidance of the export merchant. Ultimately, the grain will be resold and transferred onto sailing vessels bound for foreign ports.

Over the next three weeks, I assist Father in managing the harvesting tasks. In September, Tamba and I prepare to revisit Charleston, and resume our efforts on behalf of Wade and Lavinia.

"Father, the barges will be ready to voyage in three days. Tamba and I are heading back to Charleston tomorrow. We want to arrive in advance of their docking."

"Very well, Adam. I will be with you in spirit."

"I know. Take care of yourself, Father."

"I will, son. I will."

I reciprocate his weakened handshake and fatherly embrace.

Our wagon leaves early morning, after we stock up with supplies and bid farewell to our families.

*   *   *

We arrive in Charleston a week later, again lodging at Middleton Barony. Henry informs me of several town citizens afflicted with the fever. His family already departed to his Whitehall retreat as he prepares to join them.

"The disease spreads rapidly, and you should seek a safe haven. Come with me to Greenville."

"Thanks for your concern, Henry, but I really should return home."

"Don't wait too long. The illness can be lethal."

"Once our rice barges arrive for market, I will depart."

The epidemic will certainly last several months, plaguing the living and claiming loved ones. I cannot afford to fall ill and reluctantly plan an immediate return home. Tamba, although demonstrating immunity during past outbreaks, is also apprehensive of the sickness.

The following day, Tuesday, the fourteenth of September, our Shiloh rice barges arrive. Given the circumstances, I am pleased delivery is earlier than expected, and readily complete the export transaction.

I instruct Tamba's uncle to dock two of the barges with oarsmen and experienced vessel captains at Middleton Barony. This will accommodate our imminent leave homeward. I stop by the sheriff's office to discuss any new developments.

"Adam, there was a jail break last night, John Fisher and Roberts."

"Lavinia?"

"Not part of it, although she surely knew."

"She probably was threatened to remain quiet. How did they escape?"

"They dug a hole under the window and used a rope made out of blankets. I understand the material snapped on the last descent, and one of them may be hurt."

"If on foot, Sheriff, they cannot travel far."

"Let's hope not. I don't want to lose them now. My deputies and the city guards are alerting citizens, and Governor Geddes is offering a five-hundred dollar reward for Fisher's capture."

"More missing people."

"Adam, you never know what the day is going to bring."

"Anything on Wade or the man, George Clark, who sold Wade's horse to the blacksmith?"

"I'm sorry, Adam. There hasn't been anymore information."

"Is the fever still progressing?"

"Unfortunately, we're losing people every day. The epidemic is beginning to ravage the town. The City Jail is quarantined until the deadly disease passes. City leaders feel this is in the best interest of the prisoners and public alike. The doctors have their hands full, but there's little they can do. The only benefactors are the Poor House coffin manufactory, the undertaker, and Jervis the coroner. Of course, most of the bodies are being burned."

"I am returning to Savannah until the sickness ends. Can you see that Lavinia receives my letters?"

"Of course, send them to me. Rest assured all will remain discrete."

"Should she fall ill, or if news develops on Wade, please send word."

"I will write of any critical issues."

"Thanks, Sheriff. Stay well yourself."

"Likewise, Adam."

We exchange reassuring grips.

Returning to Middleton Barony, I inform Henry of my morning leave coincident with his.

"I am unsure of my return date."

"Whenever is fine, Adam. The south flanker always has room."

"Thank you for your gracious hospitality."

"You're quite welcome. I just hope the fever passes quickly so we may all come back safely."

"Henry, as you well know, Savannah was struck with an outbreak last year quarantining the whole city."

"I recall, and hope it doesn't resolve to a calamity of that magnitude. Join me for breakfast tomorrow. Neither of us should travel on an empty stomach."

"Certainly, Henry. Thank you."

I inform Tamba of our departure and to prepare for our morning journey home. He packs supplies provided by Jessie, including fresh baked bread, fruits, nuts, and cured meat. The wagon sleeping quarters are also prepared using plenty of fodder for Gabriel and Nicodemus. I write a short note for Lavinia.

September 14, 1819

My Dearest Lavinia,

I am not permitted to see you, for fear of transmitting the fever. The city is in epidemic proportion, and the disease will be prevalent for several more months.

*I must travel to Shiloh for the time being and will
return when able. Know that I will be thinking of
you on the twenty-third of this month. I look
forward to when you can celebrate your birthday
with me on Shiloh.*

*I shall write of my intentions, which will be
discreetly delivered to you. If you are able to
correspond, forward to Sheriff Cleary for
mailing. Care for yourself.*

My sincere love,
Adam

Come morning, I join Henry in a departing meal.

"Thank you again for everything."

"Adam, don't mention it. Give your family my sincere regards, and tell your father he's in my prayers."

"I will. Good health to you and your family."

My hand engages his vigorous grip.

Tamba leads the horses and wagon to the Ashley at the foot of the big house. After loading Gabriel and Nicodemus aboard one of the barges, Tamba effortlessly pushes our wagon onto the other. The barges row toward Savannah, first stopping in town, so I may deliver Lavinia's note. Having eight oarsmen per barge and favorable tide, the current is swift and the breeze refreshing. After docking within walking distance, I jump ashore and make way to the sheriff's office.

"I thought you were headed home."

"Sheriff, I want to first leave this letter for Lavinia."

I hand over a sealed paper.

"I'll personally see she receives it. By the way, we just caught Fisher and Roberts."

"Where?"

"On the wharf. Our grocer, William Bull, spotted two suspicious characters coming ashore in a canoe. One entered his store about eleven o'clock last night and left after purchasing a few food items. Mister Bull followed him, observing both men slipping under an overturned boat at Williams' Wharf. He notified a city guard, and sure enough it was the varmints. They're both back in jail under tight security."

"They are lucky to have been caught by you instead of the fever."

We chuckle.

"Sheriff, I look forward to seeing you before long. Take care of yourself."

"You too, Adam."

I wave while walking out the door.

*   *   *

Tamba and I arrive home the following Sabbath. Mother, Father, Fatu, and the children are surprised and happy for our unexpected visit. Father is preparing for his return trip to London, remaining optimistic for a cure. I hand him the monies from our harvest sale, which is secured in his ironclad strongbox. He soon departs on his voyage, and Mother reverts to her doldrums.

The Charleston epidemic plagues the city through the onset of winter. I write to Lavinia in October and November, and the last reply reveals her innermost feelings.

November 19, 1819

Adam My Love,

I hear the fever epidemic is subsiding. The hand of the scourge took one inmate, cheating the executioner. Several others were not so fortunate when passing from this world.

My days are long and filled with boredom. Fortunately, Sheriff Cleary and Rufus provide me books to pass the time. I am appreciative of the window in my cell, although the stenches still loom throughout the building. The food remains less than appetizing but fills my empty stomach.

I hope for the granting of a retrial that will prove my innocence of highway robbery. The gallows behind the jail greeted a prisoner only last week. He was a despicable character who murdered his wife. Although the sentence delivered justice, his lingering death on the rope was unbearable to behold.

The thought of my demise from such agonizing torture haunts my dreams. I awake choking and breathless while my heart races from fear.

Knowing you truly love and honor me is my only salvation. I pray this nightmare will end so our hearts may join together for all time.

Please return to Charleston as soon as possible. I long to linger in the comfort of your arms.

Your loving Lavinia

With Christmas only a few weeks away, I mail the sheriff a gift package of Savannah tobacco chew. Also enclosed is an envelope for Lavinia. It contains my holiday greeting with a necklace of conjoining hearts.

December 10, 1819

My Dearest Lavinia,

Know I am with you in spirit this Christmas season. Try to relieve your mind of anguished thoughts, and remember that I love you dearly.

Please accept the enclosed gift as a token of our love.

I will return to Charleston next month in time for your appeal before the Constitutional Court. Our arms will then rejoice in the love we cherish.

My loving affection,
Adam

We celebrate Christmas Day on Shiloh disheartened by the absence of both Father and Wade. Jeremy, although a tender age, is becoming more inquisitive. Mother satisfies his curiosity in such a manner not to frighten him. I am additionally troubled with the unbearable uncertainty surrounding Lavinia. During this difficult holiday season the gift of love and empathy is exchanged between Tamba's family and mine.

As the calendar turns to 1820, I reflect on the past year. Although discouraged from the unresolved dilemmas, I am thankful for family, freedom, and our beloved Shiloh.

13

New Year Politics

The week following the New Year, Tamba and I prepare for another Charleston journey. As we pass underneath the strong sentries standing guard, I pay homage to Father's gigantic oak.

Gabriel and Nicodemus forge the King's Highway with seeming comfort as if knowing the destination. Poor weather delayed our arrival to the evening of the sixteenth, just in time for tomorrow's Constitutional Court session. Tired and late, we proceed directly to Middleton Barony. Henry is thrilled to see us but immediately voices alarm.

"Adam, we just read of a downtown Savannah fire."

"Fire? When did this occur?"

"January eleventh. You were probably en route. When did you leave?"

"On the ninth. How severe was it?"

"Reports told of the fire destroying most of the downtown area, fanned by strong winds. The flames roared and smoldered for twelve hours, starting at two o'clock in the morning. It spread to Ellis Square and ignited an illegal cache of gunpowder that fueled the beast throughout the city. We heard over four hundred structures perished. You are fortunate Shiloh is a good distance from town."

"Yes, I am sure everyone is safe, but cannot believe our beloved city is in shambles. Ellis Square you say, well the city market is no more. Father will be especially disturbed with this knowledge."

"The article also indicated area planters are distributing food to the homeless and needy. I know your mother is probably spearheading the effort. I have two barges of grain leaving today to assist with the relief. My slave captain will stop by Shiloh to verify everyone's well-being."

"That is most thoughtful and compassionate, Henry. Savannah and I thank you deeply."

I obviously feel concern from this terrible news, but remain confident all is well on the home front.

"On a lighter side, Mary Helen and the children are home. Come with me, so you can meet them."

Henry's wife and children are most hospitable, and the big house bustles like a small town. I lost count of all the boys and girls scampering about. After introducing everybody, Henry excuses us to the study and inquires about Wade and Lavinia. I know his concern is genuine, but sense he welcomes this discussion as relief from the household madness. He also informs me that President Monroe is appointing him Minister to Russia in April. Since this ambassador position will entail long absences from the states, he is selling his beloved Whitehall retreat.

The next morning I join his family at breakfast. No longer does the table dwarf any place settings. If anything, the mahogany top is barely visible from many plates and overflowing containers. Jessie is truly an accomplished cook to prepare food for this platoon.

After eating, I leave on horseback to the familiar courtroom. Nearly all the seats are full. I meander to the rear and secure one of the few spots available. Before long it is standing room only.

The capacity crowd, comprising all walks of life, anxiously awaits the guests of honor. Finally the doors open with Lavinia appearing distraught and malnourished. Her haggard image is reminiscent of the slave I saw entering the Sugar House with wrist and ankle manacles. I notice her necklace chain and smile. The conjoining hearts signify the freedom of our love and spirit that no one can imprison. As Sheriff Cleary escorts her and John, I can see Lavinia's natural beauty shimmer through her gaunt appearance.

A clerk announces the court in session with the entry of presiding Judge Colcock.

"Everyone be seated," directs the stern looking robed man. He follows with one blow of his gavel.

The crotchety and deaf Judge Bay is also present.

Attorney Heath stands and approaches the bench.

"Your Honor, I am presenting the court with an appeal for a new trial."

"On what grounds, Counselor?"

"Insufficient and circumstantial evidence, Your Honor. In addition, the Court was insensitive to the spousal coercion induced upon my client Lavinia Fisher."

"Counselor, I along with Judge Bay find the known crimes evidenced by testimony reprehensible. The Six Mile Gang infested our city, and waged crime against our citizenry and travelers alike. We believe the accused to be complicit with liability and the rendered verdict equitable. We cannot in good conscience overturn the conclusions of our honorable jurymen. Let these consequences of wrongdoing be an example to anyone entertaining illegal activity against the City of Charleston."

"But, Your Honor," Attorney Heath pleads.

"Motion denied!" Judge Colcock declares, slamming his gavel.

The courtroom bursts into an uproar, and I stand shaken from the ruling.

The gavel raps several more times as Judge Colcock cries out, "Order! Order! Order in this court!"

The onlookers eventually quiet and listen for the foretold sentencing. All well know the punishment for highway robbery, only needing confirmation of an execution date. During this silent moment, Lavinia's sobs echo throughout the packed room. Before rendering the official ruling, both judges admonish the weeping Lavinia and stoical John.

Lastly, Judge Colcock decrees, "For crimes against the State, each are condemned to hang by the neck until dead. The execution shall be performed in public view on Friday, the fourth of February. Until such time, you are remanded to jail. This session is now adjourned."

The gavel falls a final time. I sit dumbfounded, almost unable to move. Reporters dash from the courtroom. Spectators express mixed emotion as several clergy voice concern.

"The execution date is only sixteen days away. That doesn't allow adequate time for repentance!"

Rumbling from many citizens supports the sentiment. Sheriff Cleary leads Lavinia and John from the courtroom upheaval one last time.

Everyone was optimistic a new trial would be granted. I am most certain John's recidivism and jail escape tainted the possibility. The court has tried the Six Mile Gang collectively as one, and now only Governor Geddes can commute her sentence.

Attorney Heath passes me in the courthouse lobby.

"Adam, I am truly sorry. I did all possible. This is a miscarriage of justice for Lavinia."

I speak no words, nodding with a look of despair. I leave for the City Jail to be greeted by Sheriff Cleary and another man in the vestibule.

"Adam, you were at the hearing?"

"I was."

"I'm sorry, old friend. Unless the governor commutes the sentence, we'll have to carry out the court order. Although I hear the clergy and a few citizens are petitioning him for more repentance time."

"Sheriff, there is not much time to react regardless."

"I know. This is a more than difficult situation. Well, even under adverse circumstances, it's still good to see you. Adam, let me introduce Francis Deliesseline. He'll be assuming the sheriff's position starting next month."

I exchange greetings with the new lawman.

"Sheriff Cleary, are you retiring?"

"Oh no, Adam, just passing on the torch. I'll still be around, only as a deputy. I've informed Francis of the events surrounding Wade."

"Adam, I will help you in any way possible."

"Thank you, Sheriff Deliesseline. It is greatly appreciated."

"I was just on my way out. If you'll excuse me gentlemen."

The new sheriff leaves.

"Adam, when did you get in?"

"Tamba and I arrived last night. We're staying at Henry's."

"I just heard about the extensive Savannah fire. Everything all right on Shiloh?"

"As far as I know. We are located a fair distance from town."

"Some Charlestonians are organizing to help out."

"I know. Henry is delivering barges of rice. Savannah appreciates the neighborly assistance. Any word on Wade, or the horse thief George Clark?"

"I'm sorry. I wish there was information or more could be done. You know some of his sketches have been posted a year next month."

"I realize his fate is not favorable, but he must be found to bring closure. I cannot give up."

"I admire your tenacity. Wade is fortunate to have you as his brother. Let me know if there's anything more I can do. You can also trust Francis. He's a good lawman."

"Thank you, Sheriff."

"Oh, and thanks for the holiday chew."

"My pleasure. I appreciate the letter forwarding between Lavinia and myself. How has she been faring?"

"As well as can be expected, until today. You probably noticed a weight loss. Rufus and I tried to comfort her as much as permitted."

"She wrote of the reading material, thank you."

"Right after Christmas I did notice her wearing a necklace," he remarks smiling.

"I only wish I could have given her the gift of freedom. Is Rufus manning the Bastille?"

"He still has the keys to the kingdom. He was just upstairs on the top level."

"I will find him."

I hurriedly climb the stairwell.

"Rufus, how are you?"

I take a second to catch my breath.

He turns toward me while locking a cell door.

"Why hello, Adam. You sound winded."

"There are more steps than remembered."

"It's been awhile, good to see you. I suppose you heard about the sentencing?"

"Yes, Lavinia is what brings me."

"She was quite upset when placed in her cell. I'll have her taken to the usual confinement room."

"Thank you, Rufus."

I head back to the ground level, and shortly thereafter Lavinia is escorted downstairs. Seeing me, she smiles and becomes teary-eyed. When locked in privacy she throws herself into my arms.

"Adam, I missed you so. Now I'm going to die!"

She sobs uncontrollably between words.

"The governor is being petitioned for a stay of execution. The clergy and citizens alike feel more repentance time is needed. This will give additional leeway to convince him of a sentence commute. So all is not lost."

The crying gradually subsides as I blot her eyes with my handkerchief and try to console her.

"Do you think he will commute my sentence?"

She whimpers, and her glazed eyes widen, reflecting a glimmer of hope.

"By no means do I know the man well, but hopefully he has compassion and common sense. The evidence does not support this condemnation."

"All I want is to be with you!"

"And I with you, Lavinia."

We share a passionate lingering kiss.

"Make love to me Adam, if only one more time."

"Here?"

"I know, but I want you terribly so."

"No more than I desire you."

Again our lips embrace as my hands fondle her.

"The guard," I caution, hesitating.

"I will keep watch."

Her hand slides down atop my trousers while our tongues wrap madly together. I playfully squeeze her supple breasts and feel her nipples harden. She turns around facing the door, peering out the barred window. I move her long silky hair aside and tenderly kiss the nape of her neck. Seconds later, I slide into a warm yearning body as she moans quietly with each standing thrust. Afterward, we kiss with faces flushed in warmth. Her sparkling eyes speak her love as we quietly cherish the closeness of a long embrace.

"Adam, the guard approaches."

"I will return soon."

Our lips bid farewell.

"Guard! Guard!"

I mount Gabriel and leave for Middleton Barony, retiring early.

Early morning Tamba and I ride the wagon into town. The execution is street-corner conversation. We stop by the sheriff's office, and Tamba waits outside. As soon as I open the door, Daisy leaps for affection. She headbutts my hand, fanning the air with her tail. I rub the playful mutt's snout.

"Good morning, Sheriff."

"Hello, Adam. Did you hear about the execution delay?"

"No, not at all!"

"The clergy and citizen's plea for more repentance time has been granted. Governor Geddes approved a two-week respite, until Friday, February eighteenth."

"That is great news! He reacted swiftly. This affords more time to focus on commuting her sentence. Maybe the Governor is sympathetic."

"Political, yes. Sympathetic, maybe. Full of himself, definitely. The original execution date falls during our most revered race week sporting and social event. I think he gave the petitioners nothing more than patronage. I also hear that our fashionable and straight-laced women are organizing to solicit him for an execution pardon."

"Why would these prim and proper socialites come to Lavinia's aid?"

"I hear the ladies feel execution of a white woman would stigmatize womankind."

"How do you think he will respond?"

"Not sure, but I do know the governor resents being cornered. He can also be very elusive. Let's just hope his decision is a favorable one. By the way, there has been no new knowledge regarding Wade."

"I still think someone besides the export merchant and hotel clerk had to see him."

"Adam, we blanketed town thoroughly. I can only suggest combing the countryside and neighboring boroughs. These people don't come into the city often, if at all."

"At this point, I will call upon anyone. Thanks again."

I leave and board the wagon where Tamba patiently waits. In short time, we arrive at the City Jail. Again I meet with Lavinia in the confinement room to inform her of the recent information.

"Lavinia, the governor has granted an additional two week respite period!"

"Does this mean my sentence will be commuted?"

"I do not know his full intentions. However, this does provide more time to press for a pardon."

"Oh, Adam, my mind is weak from worry and my body exhausted."

"I know this ordeal is trying, but this latest development is promising. For now, go rest yourself."

"Please return soon."

She clings to me.

"I will my love."

Our lips bid a goodbye kiss, and I leave to travel the outlying farmland. After quizzing some of the countryside residents about Wade, Tamba and I return to Middleton Barony.

I inform Henry of the recent development.

"Do you think the governor will be receptive to the ladies' petition of pardon? The respite period only prolongs the inevitable."

"I don't know, Adam. When I held the position, the subject of pardon never arose. This matter requires deep thought, and he will be reluctant to overturn the court. The Governor must temper the jury ruling with his own personal convictions. Rest assured he would also weigh any political ramifications. Of course, if cowed by anything, it will be the wrath of women socialites. However, undue pressure could be an irritant. The governor can be difficult as you know."

"Henry, this situation is most frustrating. I do not know what else to do."

"Her fate is now in the hands of the powers to be. Just pray and be there for her."

"Thanks, I appreciate your remarks."

"I only wish my words offered more."

Frustrated and tired, I retire early.

The next morning several clergy call on Lavinia for spiritual counseling. The devout Baptist Reverend Doctor Richard Furman patiently pastors her. The subject of repentance is difficult for her to accept since she continues to maintain her innocence. Her focus even in prayer is of a pardon. Several church ladies, including Mistress Matilda Wightman, Mistress Magdalene Brown, and Miss Selina Smith also visit for salvation of her soul.

The governor, aware of the ladies pardoning petition, appears reluctant to take it under advisement. So far, he seems to sidestep the issue regardless of their persistence. I hope the dedicated socialites open his mind to temper the ruling with compassion. If he weighs the verdict relative to the facts-of-record, common sense dictates a less harsh punishment.

As the fourteen days of the execution reprieve commence, I visit Lavinia daily and scout the outlying area for clues about Wade.

14

Lurking Danger

On Saturday, the fifth of February, I join Henry in the dining room. The respite period continues to dwindle with no word from the governor.

"Adam the grain was delivered to Savannah, and everyone is safe on Shiloh. Your mother requested this letter be given to you."

He slides a sealed paper across the table and resumes reading.

"Thank you, that is good to hear."

I slowly open the note, hoping for no new negative news.

January 25, 1820

My Dear Son,

Henry's slave captain called upon us to ascertain our welfare. I insisted he wait before departing, so to write this letter.

The city fire was devastating, and thank God we remained afar. It seems to have started at Mister Boon's livery stable behind Mrs. Platt's boarding house on Franklin Square.

Since there has been no rain for quite some time, the town structures were dry and vulnerable. The shooting flames lit up the night sky and burned for hours.

Many cities and states have come to our aid with money and provisions along with private donations. Please extend my thanks to Henry for his concern and generosity. The City of Charleston also donated a sizable amount of money.

New York contributed funds for the indigent, but stipulated there was to be no prejudice toward persons of color. Mayor Charlton and our council, rightfully insulted, promptly returned over ten thousand dollars. I declare, do those Northerners think we are incapable of serving our own citizenry? We continue to assist the homeless and destitute families. Some of the displaced house servants are boarding with our slave families.

I hope for more information leading to Wade, and the appeal for Lavinia granted her a new trial. Know everyone here is all right, and your father is returning home next month.

As always, convey my warmest regards to Henry and Mary Helen. Care for yourself, and I pray for your safe return.

Your devoted loving parent,
Mother

"Henry, Mother sends her sincere appreciation for the grain provision, and extends warmest regards to you and Mary Helen."

"I only wish we could do more. A fire of that magnitude crushes the life out of a city. Fortunately, there were few, if any, deaths."

"She also wrote of Father's return home next month."

"Did he find a cure?"

"Mother made no mention."

"I hope so, Adam."

"I know. This has been a heavy burden on Father and especially upsetting for Mother."

Hearing from Mother is reassuring of everyone's safety, and I am glad to know of Father's scheduled arrival home.

"Henry, Sheriff Cleary mentioned this being horse race week."

"Yes, the city overflows with wagerers. It is a boost for the lodging and eatery merchants, not to mention the taverns."

"Whereabouts is the race course?"

"It's called Washington Course, located west of Rutledge Avenue and just south of Lowndes Grove. It's a full mile track, and the races commence at one o'clock. Actually, in about five and one-half hours," he remarks, glancing at his timepiece before resuming, "Our Charleston Jockey Club is the managing sponsor and a member of a statewide track consortium. I'm not much of a gambler, but if you would like to go we shall."

"No, I am not a wagerer either. Sheriff Cleary cited the two week stay of execution being a ploy to avoid disrupting the races."

"The governor is highly political, and I tend to agree. His merciful gesture is surely an appeasement, disguised for his own benefit. Of course, he'll be in church on the Sabbath. I only wish people could be forthright and dispense with the facades."

"Not on this earth."

"I know, Adam, only in heaven."

As Lavinia's impending execution date nears, my stomach sickens constantly. I partake in a daily elixir of Seidlitz Powders. Henry senses my heightened anxieties and is most considerate. The ongoing quest for Wade has also become equally discouraging. Tamba and I canvassed all of the farm families on the outskirts of town, but to no avail.

* * *

On Wednesday, February sixteenth, two days before the gallows, I visit Lavinia in the morning. My private time with her is difficult. A quiet desperation fills the air mixed with lingering hope. I assure her the governor has been petitioned for a pardon, and we can only wait.

As I leave the confinement room, a feeling of helplessness follows. While passing the sheriff and Rufus in the corridor, I can tell preparations for the execution are being discussed. Lavinia's fate is now in the hands of God and the governor.

While walking to the wagon, I observe Tamba waving a piece of paper.

"What is it?"

"Mass Adam, a colluh boy gave me this and ran."

He hands me a folded sketch of Wade, and I read the backside aloud.

Be known Wade Shiloh is being ransomed for five thousand dollars. Place money in satchel, and deposit in rowboat at city end of Ashley River Bridge. Light the boat lantern, and set the vessel adrift at midnight on hanging day.

A note inside a bottle beside the lantern will tell of his whereabouts. So to know we have him, remember the war battle at Autosse. If no payment, he'll be hanged at sea. Any double-cross, instant death!

"Tamba, he must be alive! Wait, while I tell the sheriff!"

I hasten back inside the vestibule.

"Sheriff, read this! It was just delivered to Tamba by a boy Negro!"

He presses on his pockets fumbling for his spectacles.

"Well according to this, he could very well be alive. They must be pirates of sort, although whoever printed this note appears to be well educated. I don't recall a ransom since Blackbeard plundered Charleston years ago. We actually have a band of sea bandits jailed now. It's a gamble you know. He may already be dead, or they don't have him at all."

"Only Wade would know about our presence on the battlefield of Autosse. I have to think he is with the living. Remember the dock man? Maybe he did see Wade in Barbados."

"A distinct possibility."

"Sheriff, how do you think we should proceed?"

"Well, I can try to trick them into an ambush, but it would be difficult on the water at night."

"I'll just take my chances, Sheriff. If a trap is sensed they might kill him."

"It doesn't give you much time to come up with the money by midnight Friday. That's only thirty-six hours from now."

"I know."

"Adam, I'll be here if you need me. Keep me posted, and be careful old friend."

"I will. Thanks, Sheriff."

I quickly leave for the wagon.

"Tamba, head back to Middleton Barony. I must speak with Henry right away."

"Yaas, Mass Adam."

With a whistle and tug, he hurries Gabriel and Nicodemus onward. We arrive at the big house, and I request Jessie to alert Henry of my presence. Momentarily, she directs me to the study where he is performing paperwork.

"Henry, thanks for seeing me on such abrupt notice."

"I hope it is good news."

"Yes and no."

I hand him the ransom note.

"I see what you mean. Did you discuss this with Sheriff Cleary?"

"Yes, he says it is a roll of the dice."

"I don't see where you have much choice."

"My sentiment completely."

"Adam, I know you do not have this tidy sum of money in your possession. There isn't much time, so let's proceed to the bank immediately," he urges, standing from his chair.

"Jessie, Jessie!"

She scurries into the room.

"Have the carriage brought around right away."

"Yaas, suh."

"Please have Tamba meet us there."

"Yaas, suh, Mis'tuh Shiloh."

"Henry, I will sign a promissory note and reimburse you promptly upon returning to Savannah."

"There is no need for a contract. The handshake of friendship is binding enough."

We firmly grip hands.

"Thank you, Henry. I know Mother and Father are most indebted, as am I."

We quickly head to the carriage, and arrive at the Second Bank of the United States on Broad Street.

"I'll return shortly, Adam."

I gaze upward to the building's gable and again notice the adorned gold leaf eagle. About twenty minutes later Henry returns with an old satchel in hand.

"I knew you needed a carrying case so everything is here. They're slower counters than I thought," he jests, opening the leather bag for inspection.

"I cannot thank you enough, Henry."

"Just pray Wade is found alive."

On the way back to Middleton Barony, we discuss the tenuous situation of dealing with pirates. Henry indicates the cutthroats have upheld most past ransoms when receiving payment. Of course, the threats are duly fulfilled for noncompliance.

"Adam, would you like me to store the money tonight for safekeeping?"

"Please, I will pick it up tomorrow."

"Are you hungry?"

"Actually, my stomach feels queasy."

"I'll have Jessie bring you a belated dinner. Hopefully, you'll feel like eating then."

"Thank you, Henry."

I go to my quarters, and a few hours later Jessie serves a hot plate of food. My insides are still bothersome, so I only nibble on the cooling meal. The combination of a tired mind and comfortable high-backed mahogany readily cradles me asleep.

I sluggishly awake to the annoying glare of sunlight. My neck is slightly stiff from the sleeping position. I stretch to loosen my tightened limbs. After bathing, I join Henry for breakfast this execution eve, Thursday, February seventeenth.

"Good morning, Henry."

He looks up from his newspaper.

"Adam, good morning. I have heard no mention of a pardon, but it is typically granted last minute."

"I know. It is very agonizing."

"Today and tomorrow will be quite stressful for you. I hope for the best. Do be careful tonight, delivering the ransom."

"I will."

"And be sure to stay in town this evening. It will be too dangerous to return here at that late hour. Know I will be by your side tomorrow at the gallows."

"Thank you. I appreciate all you have done."

"Jessie, please bring the handled bag from my study."

"Yaas, suh."

"By the way, can you have Tamba drop off four bags of rice to Bill Bull the grocer? In the heat of everything yesterday, I forgot a shipment was promised."

"Most certainly. I will have him make the delivery during my visit with Lavinia. Thanks again for everything, Henry."

"I am happy to be of help."

"Thank you, Jessie. Adam, I pray for Wade's well-being."

He hands me the satchel.

"Likewise, Henry."

I return to the south flanker and Tamba awaits me.

"My stomach is still upset. I will lie down awhile and meet you at the stables later."

"Yaas, Mass Adam. I'll brush dah horses."

Last night my sleep was restless and tormented with horrendous dreams. I remember the hangman's noose choking the life out of me, and black crows plucking out my eyes. I lie down exhausted, and wake up early afternoon. I head to the stables. Tamba, himself tired, is resting on a pile of hay.

"I brushed and fed dah horses, Mass Adam."

"Good, store this satchel under the wagon seat. We must also deliver rice to Mister Bull's store for Henry."

"Yaas, Mass Adam."

After Tamba tosses the bags of grain into the fodder-filled wagon bed, we ride into town. My stomach remains squeamish as I mull over the ransom note. On the way, we discuss the looming unknowns.

"I do not know whether Wade will be delivered dead or alive. Nor do I know if Lavinia is to receive a pardon. Leave me at the City Jail and ride around the corner to the Poor House coffin manufactory. I must prepare for the worse if returning to Shiloh with a lifeless brother. Purchase a casket of proper size. Here is payment."

"Yaas, Mass Adam."

He places the money in his pocket with a sad face.

We arrive at the prison yard around dusk. Tamba proceeds to the coffin manufactory on Mazyck Street and to Mister Bull's grocery.

Meanwhile, I enter the vestibule and observe Rufus speaking with a gentleman. Aware of my arrival, he gestures me to approach.

"She is in the confinement room with the Reverend Doctor Furman. He just arrived, so they'll be awhile."

"I will wait. Thank you, Rufus."

I glance at the unknown person and start to walk away.

"Oh, Adam, have you met John Blake White?"

"My pleasure, sir. I am Adam Shiloh of Savannah."

We exchange handshakes.

"I heard about your stay with Henry. Any luck finding your brother?"

"Not yet, sir. Thank you for your concern."

Although a stranger, he appears truly considerate.

"Mister White is an attorney and also a proponent of penal reform and criminal rehabilitation," Rufus interjects.

"That I am. We cannot continue with severe punishment, substituting ourselves as the Almighty. Only he can pass judgment on life and death. I believe many wrongdoers can be rehabilitated and become assets of society."

"Sir, I very much agree."

"I am documenting another inequity of man, strongly opposing tomorrow's execution," Mister White affirms.

"Hello Coroner, right on time," Rufus blurts.

I turn around to see Jervis walking toward us.

"Hello, Rufus, Mister White."

He finally recognizes me in the dim light exclaiming, "Why Adam, I didn't expect your presence."

"Neither did I yours."

"Come with me, Jervis. I will show you the preparations. Mister White, Adam, please join us."

Rufus motions, and we follow his swinging handheld lantern. He stops and unlocks a door, leading us into a large chamber.

He lifts the burning wick overhead to illuminate the dismal space. I see stacked coffins and executioner tools of trade, including rope, a spade, pickax, an unassembled gibbet, and other small implements. Rufus examines the parts for the gallows, verifying completeness and fit. He ensures there will be no issue for morning assembly.

"Rufus, where is the execution scheduled to take place?"

"At the suburbs of Meeting Street Road on the city's War of 1812 fortification lines, Mister White. We'd use the jail yard contraption, but it only handles one soul at a time. Besides, we need an open public area. An unusually large crowd is expected."

Rufus turns to shine the light on a pile of caskets.

"Coroner, note your pick for proper sizing."

"Well, each is tall like Adam."

He hesitates and glances between the coffins and myself. I am surprised he did not ask me to lay aside the stack.

"Rufus, these two will do."

"We'll deliver them in the morning."

"Why thank you. Good night, everyone."

Jervis leaves, tipping his hat with the normal unnerving smile. We continue following the swaying flame down a dark corridor to a remote corner cell.

We stand in front of an unbarred door, and Rufus repeatedly calls out for someone. Finally, a voice from within utters unintelligible words. The jailer unfastens the lock. I observe a grotesque figure sprawled on the gloomy floor. His garments are tattered and unwashed, cladding an emaciated, haggard being. I behold an image most unimaginable, groaning and growling like a beast.

Slowly rising to stand erect, his pale face mutters, "Thus am I served, whenever you want my work. But give me something to drink. I must have drink, and I will be contented."

"The sheriff wanted me to check on you. You shall have your fill of liquor after completing tomorrow's task," Rufus stresses, and signals us to leave.

The wretched being returns a ghastly smile, and the door is rebolted.

"That apparition of a human is the executioner," Rufus tells us, shaking his head in disgust.

"This is how the Jack Ketch lives?"

"Adam, we have to secure him in quarters before an execution to ensure sobriety. The sheriff ordered him incarcerated two days ago for tomorrow's repulsive job. After the gruesome task, his reward is the exchange of departing spirits for those of consumption. While clutching bottles of whiskey, he'll pace the floor celebrating. The miserable oddity will drink until unable to stand, mumbling and laughing between gulps."

"Rufus, the hangman receives no visitors?"

"The departing souls are his only company, Mister White. He cares for their afterlife journey with a twisted sense of responsibility. Shunned by society, he has no family or friends. He is merely a pensioner of the sheriff. His work earns food, lodging, and alcohol. However repugnant, the outcast is harmless, unless operating the gallows. There he exudes the pride of a craftsman."

"These pathetic surroundings and lost souls within reaffirm my convictions for reform. Good night to everyone."

Mister White leaves obviously appalled, and Rufus is summoned upstairs. I resume my wait for Lavinia outside the confinement room, while she remains in spiritual consultation with the Reverend Doctor Furman. As I stand in thought, I cannot help but overhear their conversation.

"I do not understand. My life must end because of unjust pretense, and the Lord shall forgive the instigators. How can this be?"

"Lavinia, he is a loving and forgiving God to all. Remember, he also was unjustly accused, sentenced, and executed. Repent in your heart for any sins, and the gates of heaven shall open."

"How can I express remorse if I am innocent of these alleged acts?"

"None of us are without sin. Our past ways of error deserve contrition. Whatever reasons bring us to death are through the hands of fate. We must prepare ourselves for the moment. Yours my child is tomorrow. May the Almighty have mercy on your soul."

"Thoughts are easily spoken when no noose chokes the words. Leave me to myself!"

As the reverend exits the room cell, we pass one another and exchange somber looks.

This may be my last private moment with Lavinia. She realizes the day of execution is upon her, but maintains hope for a pardon. Today, her expressions are few and filled with regret and sorrow. I caress the familiar soft hand, which feels thinner and trembles.

"Adam, promise me you'll mail this letter to Mama and my sister Olivia."

"Consider it done."

"Know that I harbor ill feelings toward everyone except you, Sheriff Cleary, Rufus, and the attending clergy. All others are cursed into damnation. I cannot be a hypocrite and profess godly beliefs. Where is He to rectify this injustice? Whenever I pass into the spirit world, even if Satan's, it will offer more comfort than this earthly life."

"Lavinia, we can only hope for a final hour pardon. I pray for your soul. Know you will forever remain in my heart and thoughts. I am grateful for our time together, and only wish more could be done to free you."

"Hold me, Adam. I'm afraid."

We hug tight, and she weeps beyond consolation. My tears wet her hair.

"I want you for my wife, even for a moment. Tomorrow, know we are married in spirit. I will love you always."

My voice quavers, joined by teary-eyed sniffles.

"I will wear my white gown, signifying the purity of our love. The eternal bond of our hearts shall remain united, as chained together on my necklace. I shall love you in death as I do in life."

Sadly, I realize this could be the last memory of her dimpled smile. We exchange a final kiss and embrace, knowing our love withstands all. As I leave, my vision is blurred from emotion, but she beams with inner peace.

Tamba awaits me outside. He has delivered Mister Bull's grain and purchased the coffin. It is buried beneath the wagon bed hay. I regain my composure, and we ride to the Ashley River Bridge. The midnight ransom hour approaches as Tamba and I hike along the riverbed. He carries the satchel while I shine a lantern about the waterfront.

"There, Mass Adam!"

He points to a small boat banked nearby. Hearing a rustle in the brush, I promptly blow out the flame. We stand silently behind two adjacent trees, and I draw Equalizer from my boot. As a shadowy figure passes, I touch the stubby barrel to the nape of a neck.

"Do not flinch!"

I cock the pistol hammer, and Tamba steps forward.

"Adam, it's me," whispers the sheriff.

"What are you doing here?"

"I just wanted to make sure an old friend was all right."

"I am obliged, Sheriff. We just spotted the rowboat."

"Tamba, relight the wick."

"Yaas, Mass Adam."

The three of us trudge through thicket to the shoreline. An unlit hanging lantern and bottle lie inside the boat, just as the ransom note indicated.

We break the glass bottle against the hull, and a piece of paper falls to the ground. I shine our flickering flame on the message and read it aloud.

Wade shall resurrect from the dead on hanging day.

"What in God's sake is that suppose to mean?"

"Adam, these pirate types are cunning, and often speak in riddles."

"Tamba, place the money in the boat, and light their lantern."

"Yaas, Mass Adam."

We push the craft adrift, and watch until the shimmering light fades from sight.

"Extra deputies will be in town tomorrow. They'll be alert to suspicious activity and looking for Wade. For now, you better get some rest."

"Thanks, Sheriff. You are right. Nothing more can be done this evening."

"Where are you staying tonight? It's too late for a journey to Henry's."

"We will find accommodations in town. I did not think to make reservations earlier."

"At this hour, many of the family hostels are closed, and the hotels are still full from race week. You and Tamba can bunk at my place or in a witness cell at the City Jail."

"I guess we can survive a night with Rufus. We must be there tomorrow anyway."

"Fine, I'll ride over and let you in. There's no sense waking Rufus or his family."

We meet the sheriff in the prison yard, still hearing chatter from some late night patrons. The building and grounds are even more ominous at dark. Sheriff Cleary has a key to the vestibule, and shows us to our sleeping quarters. We bid each other good night.

Lavinia is one floor above me, and I sense her presence. A strange feeling of both anguish and comfort besets me. I fall asleep quickly from a long and stressful day, realizing dawn will bring my most punishing tomorrow.

15

Steps to Eternity

I awake to the smell of food cooking and step into the corridor. Tamba is talking with Rufus as I approach them.

"Adam, good mornin'."

"Good morning, Rufus."

"Tamba informed me of your stay last night. It's not the Planter's Hotel, but we do our best."

"I was so tired, I could have slept standing up."

"I'm glad we could help out."

"Did you sleep, Tamba?"

"Not good, Mass Adam."

"I did for part of the night. We will be here all morning, so rest in the wagon later."

"Yaas, Mass Adam."

Several men pass us carrying gallows sections and implements to be loaded onto a supply wagon.

"I hope a pardon comes through today."

"I do too, Rufus."

"Well, I have to go check on our long term guests, but I'll have some breakfast sent for the two of you. Oh, did you want to see Lavinia?"

"I do, but her private time this morning along with words from the reverend are of utmost importance. I pray for our conversation this evening."

After eating on china of forged tin, Tamba naps in the wagon. Sheriff Cleary and Mister White arrive. I am also officially introduced to the Reverend Doctor Furman before he ministers to Lavinia once more. The morning passes quickly through discussion and observation of prison routines.

"Any word, Sheriff?"

"I'm sorry Adam, but the court order forces me to start this dreadful journey."

I frown, nodding my head.

"Rufus, bring the prisoners down."

"Right away, Sheriff."

My timepiece reads fifteen minutes until one. The now sober hangman emerges from his locked quarters, and outstretches ropes along the floor corridor. He is arranging the slipknots and nooses, tugging to ensure precision. A coach inside the vestibule awaits the prisoners instead of the regular transport wagon.

All conversation suddenly ceases. I look up to see Lavinia stepping down the stairs. Attired in a laced white gown and veiled hat, she appears as a princess bride. The executioner approaches her and she shrieks. Undeterred by her reaction, he binds Lavinia's wrists behind her. She resists him and squirms to no avail. The hangman seemingly takes possession of her and husband John, fulfilling a duty of deliverance. I can only stand by helplessly and hide my emotions.

The Reverend Doctor Furman and the executioner accompany Lavinia and John inside the coach. I observe the pastor trying to console her, but she maintains an empty stare. Lavinia appears oblivious to his words. Then I notice the hangman positioned opposite her and ogling. Being sober, he must be intrigued to have a client so lovely.

Finally, the sheriff motions to ride the road of no return. The weather is sunny and comfortably warm with a pleasant breeze, which seems unfitting for such a gruesome ordeal.

Deputies and a company of cavalry lead the traveling entourage. The coach is guarded as if they were royalty. Sheriff Cleary and his new successor, Sheriff Deliesseline, flank each side of the coach. Tamba and I follow in our wagon. I am sickened inside, wishing to awake from a cruel nightmare.

The sound of clattering horses and chirping songbirds break the uneasy silence. Occasionally, reverent whispers and weeping emanate from the coach. The wheels of injustice creak along the final turns toward the executioner's noose, and our entourage pulls behind the wooden gallows structure. Here the coroner waits in a funeral carriage with his preselected coffins.

The Courier publicized the execution as being between twelve and four o'clock, but bystanders are overflowing into the streets by one-thirty. I still hold hope for a pardon, praying that only the dangling necklace will hang from her neck. Tamba and I spot Henry standing at the foot of the scaffold and join him.

"Is there any word on Lavinia?"

"None, Henry."

"And Wade?"

"Nothing so far."

"Adam, I am so sorry."

He rests his hand on my shoulder.

Within moments Lavinia appears from the coach. She reluctantly walks with a lawmen escort toward the ghastly apparatus. Onlookers strain their necks for a glimpse of the convicted woman, while the hangman makes final preparation for his appalling deed. The spectators buzz with anticipation as the execution time nears.

People of all ages and social status are in attendance. I observe dainty ladies with parasols and coonskin-capped ruffians. I overhear judgmental comments from educated elite and ignorant riffraff alike. Children are even serving warm apple cider to quench the public's cold-blooded thirst.

"Adam, her beauty is no myth," Henry remarks, seeing her the first time.

"I know. She is a goddess on earth."

Already standing on the platform, John Fisher hangs his head in prayer. At the bottom of the steps to eternity, Lavinia vehemently refuses to climb onto the scaffold floor. Successor Sheriff Deliesseline and deputies physically drag her up the stairs.

"May the Almighty send Governor Geddes into eternal damnation!" she screams. "I shall haunt him and Charleston forever!"

Then John expresses a desire to address the masses. He says Sheriff Cleary called him by name, prompting a false identification by Mister Peoples. He begs forgiveness for injuries to anyone by his hand, and professes his blood is on Sheriff Cleary's hand.

Suddenly, Sheriff Deliesseline, standing on the top gallows step, is presented with a document. The curiosity seekers fall silent as he unfolds and reads the note. Could this be the governor's pardon? I feel my heart pounding through my chest. Lavinia smiles and exclaims a cry of joy. She walks across the scaffold toward me, but the hangman gently guides her back.

Sheriff Deliesseline folds the paper and announces, "There is no pardon, nor a drop of hope."

I am absolutely devastated. I do not know whether I can bear the next few moments of life. I look at Lavinia, but her glaring eyes focus on Sheriff Deliesseline. Her stare seems to pierce his very soul.

I look up to see the executioner climbing the hanging post. He is tugging on the ropes to make sure all are tightly secured. Lavinia's noose sways in the breeze above her head, forming a halo from hell. With her eyes closed she whispers in prayer. Now she seems to have accepted the inevitable.

The hangman descends to the platform, and slips one of the knotted nooses around John's neck. Next he approaches Lavinia.

"Please, raise my veil."

The hooded executioner pauses, honoring her wish. Then he carefully places the noose over her head, and slips the knot to her throat. She gazes at the swarm of people, focusing lastly upon my eyes.

I read her lips that form the words, "I love you."

My head nods, while whispering, "I love you, too."

The shrouded hangman proceeds to cover John's head with a black cap. Turning to Lavinia, he appears reluctant to perform a regretful deed. Her eyes fill with tears and her body trembles. The bystanders remain quiet.

"Lavinia, the buried bodies! Did you kill them?" a lone voice interrupts.

Everyone focuses on her. An eerie smile crosses her face. Our eyes engage, and even now the puzzling look prevails.

"Murderess!" another person yells, as grumbles of agreement rumble throughout the crowd.

Lavinia remains speechless, still displaying the mysterious expression. Without hesitation, the crude executioner's fingers become like those of a skilled seamstress. He gently lifts and pulls down her delicate veil fabric.

Slightly after two o'clock, calm again besets the throng of people.

"Lavinia! Proclaim your innocence!" someone else shouts out.

Seconds later, the hangman grasps the trapdoor lever and focuses upon Sheriff Deliesseline. I bite my lip and feel a sense of weakness overcome my legs. I cannot bear this.

The new sheriff signals the executioner with a nod. My eyes shutter as both platforms plummet with a resounding thump. I hear Lavinia cry a hideous shriek, which sends shivers down my spine. The still crowd gasps. I am numb and wobbly, staring at her swaying body. As my eyes fill with emotion, a tear slips down my cheek. I wipe it away, and Henry presses his arm across my shoulders. Shocked and distraught, I say a silent prayer.

I watch Lavinia's body sway in the breeze. She departed instantly without struggle. The death she feared was painlessly quick compared to her last lingering year of agony. John dangles in the air grappling with death for several minutes before succumbing. I believe the hangman comforted her passing through instantaneous death, but he deviously knotted John's noose otherwise.

I notice the executioner has a slight smile erupt on his face. He appears to pride himself on another successful performance. Such a wretched job can only bring satisfaction to a demented mind.

A satisfied public promptly disbands and resumes daily activities. The executions seem to be regarded as nothing more than an afternoon tea social.

"I am so sorry, Adam. You have my deepest condolences."

"Thank you, Henry."

"I'm sorry, Mass Adam."

I look at Tamba and nod. His comforting arm weighs across my shoulders like the heavy sorrow I feel. Henry offers consoling remarks, as we walk toward his carriage through the dispersing crowd.

"No matter what sins Lavinia committed, she remains a child of God. The Almighty is filled with forgiveness and love."

"Henry, I cannot bear to have her buried as an indigent in the cold and desolate potter's field. May I lay her to rest at the plantation gardens? I would be eternally grateful. The resting place will be unmarked and unknown to all. She will lie beneath a bed of flowers. The vibrant earthly blooms will epitomize her heavenly beauty forever."

Henry stops and smiles, placing his hand atop my shoulder.

"Adam, the location is to your choosing. May we all know the peace through death never found in life. I shall see you at the big house when your task is complete."

"Thank you, Henry."

While walking back to the gallows, sidestepping the horde of exiting spectators, a passerby stops me.

"Aren't you the person seeking his brother?"

"Yes, do I know you?"

"Don't you recall? I am the Planter's Hotel clerk."

"Oh yes, of course."

"There is the woman who escorted your brother."

He points toward the front of the scattering mob.

"Where? What is she wearing?"

"Why, the white gown, sir. The one hanging."

"That is impossible."

"Her features are identical, but she does appear thinner."

"Surely you are mistaken."

"Sir, unless a twin, she is the woman. Only now she wears no wig."

He walks away leaving me stunned.

"Mass Adam, you all right?"

"Tamba, how can all this be?"

His head shakes in disbelief.

I will ponder the clerk's comment later. At this instant, I hastily devise a plan with Tamba to deceive the hangman and coroner.

"Now go, Tamba. Wait by the wagon."

"Yaas, suh, Mass Adam."

Minutes later, only Sheriff Cleary, the executioner, and coroner remain. The newly appointed sheriff was summoned away. Sheriff Cleary pulls me aside.

"Adam, my sincere sympathy. I let Sheriff Deliesseline give the command. I just couldn't do it. Now I'm going into town looking for any sign of Wade."

"Thank you, Sheriff. I will join you later."

I step atop the scaffold with a lump in my throat, as an eerie stillness blankets the empty grounds. Jervis the coroner is holding Lavinia's body while the hangman cuts the rope.

"Why, Adam, are you reconsidering my need for an assistant?"

"No, Coroner, just helping where possible."

After the severed rope falls, I remove the noose from her neck. Jervis and I carry her down the steps, resting her in one of his coffins.

"One down, one to go."

His grim humor has no end.

"Coroner, I will secure the lid on this one."

"Why, thank you, Adam. I'll work with the executioner to remove the other body."

I signal Tamba nearby, and he dashes over with two fifty-pound rice sacks. I hand him Lavinia's body, and he hides her beneath our wagon bed of hay. I throw both grain bags in the coroner's coffin and hurriedly nail on the cover.

The coroner and hangman return with John's corpse. After nailing his casket closed, they place both coffins in the funeral carriage.

"Thank you again, Adam. Would you like to view Potter's Field?"

"Not today."

They go their way while Jervis hums another funeral dirge.

"Time to leave, Tamba."

"Yaas, Mass Adam."

"It is good the grocer, Mister Bull, only needed two sacks of Henry's rice."

"Quick thinkin', Mass Adam."

We hasten toward Middleton Barony, and I point Tamba to a floral garden.

"This is the location. Pull over."

"Yaas, Mass Adam."

We stop and carefully remove Lavinia's body from the wagon bed.

While kneeling and holding her, I brush the hay from her hair and clothes. I raise her veil and look into her deep dark eyes. My hand gently closes her eyelids forever. As tears stream down my face, I pull her close for a long final embrace. Carefully, we lay her body in the casket previously purchased with Wade in mind.

I hold that familiar soft hand, now cold, and observe the other clutched tightly. When loosening her fingers, I notice writing paper folded around a small object. I unwrap it and stare stupefied.

"Oh my God! It is the arrowhead belonging to Wade!"

Tamba looks at me shocked.

"I know, Tamba. I do not understand either."

I read the note.

> *Adam My Love,*
>
> *I will love you in death as I did in life. I tried to save your brother and beg your forgiveness. Know our spirits are forever wed.*
>
> *My eternal love,*
> *Lavinia Marguerite Shiloh*

"Mass Adam, what does it say?"

My hand drops to my side. Momentarily, I remain speechless, kneeling over her body.

"I am not sure what it means."

How did she become involved with Wade's disappearance? My mind struggles with unanswered torment as we dig the burial site, first removing the planted flora.

I hold her hand a final time and pause in thought. Even in death, her beauty has a radiant presence. Around her neck hangs her cherished necklace of conjoining hearts. I switch her emerald keepsake to her left ring finger and cross her hands. I reach over and snip off a long-stemmed crimson rose she so pleasured. After a kiss for eternity, I shroud her face with the veil. I look at her a final time and lay the flower beside her. Slowly I nail on the coffin lid. Tears roll down my face with each angry hammer blow.

Tamba and I strap two ropes under each end of the casket. From opposite sides, we slowly lower the wooden box. Careful not to draw attention to the gravesite, we level the dirt and replant the blooming flora.

While kneeling over Lavinia's final resting place, I bow my head and speak my last farewell. A lone tear zigzags down my cheek.

> *Lavinia, as I promised, you shall smell the fragrance of flora gardens each day. May the merciful Almighty forgive and bless you. Know I shall always love you. May you rest in peace through the end of time.*

I look up to the glorious wood nymph sculpture she so admired. The statue serves as a most fitting headstone as beauty besets beauty.

I will never know the unspoken shame of her past, only her love and struggle for happiness. Like the enigmatic expression of the wood nymph, Lavinia's departing smile will forever cast a mystery over her deeds.

"Tamba, we must return and seek Wade. I pray we will not need another coffin."

It is late afternoon when we ride toward town. Threatening clouds form overhead. As we pass the gallows, the foreboding contraption still stands. We stop, and I climb the steps to eternity. Drizzling rain falls from a darkened sky while thunder rumbles. With Lavinia dead and no sign of Wade, I raise my hands toward the heavens.

"Why, God? Why? First my brother, now my love!" I scream angrily, falling to my knees amid a lightning lit sky.

Thinking a muffled voice speaks "Little Brother," I turn around to no one.

My mind feels crazed.

Again I believe to hear the subdued words "Little Brother."

"Tamba, come quickly. Tell me I am not going insane."

He steps atop the scaffold and listens intently.

Once more, I think I hear a weak voice utter, "Little Brother."

I look at Tamba and he grins.

"I am not crazy!"

"Under dah floor, Mass Adam!"

"Go and pull the lever, Tamba!"

The trapdoors drop.

I look into the dark abyss beneath the wooden skirted platform, and a strained voice peeps, "Over here, Little Brother."

"Wade, my God it is you! Tamba, he's down here!"

I drop into the opening, finding Wade tied and partially gagged. After uncovering his mouth and cutting the constraints, I drag him toward the daylight.

"Tamba, pull him up!"

"Yaas, suh, Mass Adam!"

His colossus arms hoist Wade and me atop like rag dolls. Thinking of the pirates' riddle, his body is literally resurrected from the gallows dead.

"Wade, are you all right?"

"You reached me sooner on the battlefield of Autosse."

He collapses in my arms.

"Tamba, help put him in the wagon, and we must hasten to town for a physician."

"Yaas, Mass Adam."

*   *   *

Doctor Samuel Wilson examines an unresponsive Wade, using smelling salts to help him regain consciousness. He cleans Wade's abrasions and prescribes liquids and rest for dehydration and exhaustion. Tamba and I lift him into the wagon bed.

"Wade, we are going to Middleton Barony so you may convalesce. Drink this water and lay down."

On the way through town Sheriff Cleary is standing in front of McCrady's Pub.

"Tamba, slow down as we pass the sheriff."

"Yaas, Mass Adam."

"Sheriff, we found Wade!"

"Hallelujah! Is he all right?"

"Beaten and bruised, but he will live. We just came from Doc Wilson's place and on our way to Henry's. We will stop by your office in the morning," I holler.

"Good, I want to know what happened," he yells, as we pass by him.

After reaching the south flanker, Tamba and I help Wade stumble inside. Without delay, he falls asleep, and I immediately go to inform Henry.

"I am pleased for Wade's well-being. Although the good Lord took Lavinia this day, he gave you a blessing with Wade."

"Henry, I buried Lavinia where the ...."

He interrupts me before I can finish.

"There is no need to divulge the whereabouts. Rest assured, as long as Middleton Barony exists, she shall rest in peace. This is a private matter of the heart. Know you may visit anytime."

"I cannot thank you enough."

He reciprocates my solid grip.

"Jessie will prepare an extra hearty breakfast tomorrow. Wade will probably eat enough for two."

"That he will. See you in the morning, Henry."

I check on Wade and hear his infernal snoring. Secretly, I rejoice.

Never before have I experienced such a combination of diverse emotions. Although I feel misled by Lavinia's omission of knowledge regarding Wade, I am elated to find my brother safe. At the same time, I am devastated with her passing. However, I know Mother will be relieved and overjoyed with the news about Wade. I compose a quick letter before retiring.

February 18, 1820

Dear Mother,

Today is one of the saddest yet happiest days of my life. I agonize over the death of Lavinia, but joyfully inform you of Wade's safe recovery. We shall journey home from Middleton Barony tomorrow, arriving near the time you receive this mail. All will be explained then.

Your loving son,
Adam

The next morning Wade awakes still shaken. After a refreshing hot bath he changes into an extra set of my clothes. Then we begin our walk to meet Henry for breakfast. As he limps down the second floor stairway, we engage in conversation.

"Wade, you look and smell better already."

"Thanks, Little Brother," he says smiling.

"I thought you dropped the *little* part?"

"I do when you don't take so long to save me."

We chuckle.

"Wade, tell me what the hell went on."

"Well, after arriving in Charleston I went to King Street and negotiated a contract for the harvest. It was race day so I tried my luck at the Washington Course. While there I became acquainted with a lovely lady. At the conclusion of the races and several libations, she agreed to supper. We met at the Planter's Hotel tavern, and before long food became forgotten. I decided to register and represent her as my wife. When we entered the room two men from the hallway barged in from behind. I was robbed at pistol point, and one of them ripped off my leather-strapped arrowhead."

He pauses at the bottom step landing, rubbing the back of his neck.

"Adam, can we rest a spell?"

"Sure."

I help him sit in one of the high-backed mahogany chairs in the parlor.

"What happened then?"

"Well, they roughed me up, and led me down the hotel's back stairway. Outside they bound, gagged, and threw me on a wagon. We arrived at the harbor, and I thought the fish awaited me for sure. Instead, they dragged me aboard the bowels of a ship where I was locked up. I had been sold to a crew of pirates. About six weeks later we voyaged from Charleston to the Caribbean. Captain George Clark commanded the ship. It was named Louisa and flew the Buenos Aires flag."

"My God, Wade, you were in town when I first arrived. Did you make a stop in Barbados?"

"We docked there briefly. Why?"

"Never mind, was there any chance to escape?"

"I tried to, but it almost cost me my life. Actually it was in Barbados. I banded with other slaves, and we fought our way off the ship."

"*Other* slaves? What are you saying?"

"There's a lot to tell you about my captivity. I never felt less human in all my life."

His head drooped as he bit his lower lip.

"Are you all right?"

"Yes, I'm fine, Adam."

"What did they do to you?"

"The pirates impressed me into service as a cook by day and confined me at night. They even tried to resell me once, but ironically the old war gimp prevented the barter."

"No, I asked what they *did* to you."

"I don't want to talk about that."

He squirms in his seat and rubs his forehead.

"But you almost escaped?"

"Yes, sir. I befriended a slave lady, and we devised a plan. It almost worked. I fought side by side with the Negroes, just like we did at Autosse. I made it ashore along with most of the other slaves, but a few died fighting for our freedom."

Wade hesitates. I can tell by his crackling voice the memories are upsetting to him.

"What about your friend?"

"She was recaptured along with the rest of us. The locals in Barbados had a strong alliance with some of the crew and gave us up. All of our lives were even more of a living hell after being returned to bondage, especially Zazu."

"Zazu?"

"My lady friend."

"Is she still on the ship?"

"I have to free her!"

He tries to stand up and topples back into the chair.

"Wade, you're in no condition to free anyone. We will talk with Sheriff Cleary this afternoon. I am sorry to hear about your terrible hardship."

"I never want to go through it again. Murder, beatings, torture, and rape were normal occurrences. I was thankful for each day of living. They also plundered any ship they felt capable of overpowering, enslaving men, women, and children."

"So how long have you have been in port since your return?"

"They sailed back in December. The captain and some of the mates were recently jailed here, and charged with crimes on the high seas. After they were arrested, I overheard the remaining crew speak about a sketch and ransom. One of the cutthroats told me to tell a private tale only known to family. I told them about the Battle of Autosse, and they made me print the ransom note."

"Why you?"

"For God's sake, Adam, I didn't ask. I'm guessing the derelicts weren't very literate. What's the difference?"

"The Sheriff thought it was written by an intelligent person. Oh well, his mistake."

"Adam, you can kiss where the sun doesn't shine."

We both laugh.

"Are you ready to walk some more?"

"Yep, I'm hungry."

He grabs my arm and pulls himself up. I open the front door, and we amble along toward the big house.

"Wade, all of this could have been avoided if you learned to control yourself."

"Hell, I was just out to have some fun."

"Some fun? You have been missing one year to the month. You know Mother will want a full accounting of the time."

"I know," he replies sighing.

"So what happened after you docked in Charleston?"

"Well, I overheard the scalawags talking about releasing me. You know, when I was originally kidnapped and still in Charleston, I remember the captain instructing one of his henchmen. He told him to inform an inquiring party that I already perished. I figured it was you trying to have me freed."

"Was one of the pirates a tall, bald mulatto with a bushy mustache?"

"He was a mean sort. How do you know him?"

"I saw him at the town marketplace."

Recalling my observation of him with Lavinia, I now realize the meaning of her departing note.

"Go ahead, Wade. You were saying."

"Well, in the middle of the night yesterday I was bound, blindfolded, and gagged. They threw me in a wagon and rode awhile. The next thing I recollect is hearing crowd noise and trapdoors giving way. I managed to peek out the blindfold, and saw some daylight and dangling feet. My God, Adam, one was a woman. What on earth did she do?"

I look at Wade with a blank stare.

We finally reach the foot of the big house tower, and I hand him the arrowhead. He is flabbergasted.

"How did you get this?"

"From a mutual friend."

"Wade, what was the woman's name?"

"She went by Marguerite."

"Did she have a last name?"

"I don't believe I asked."

"You are an unadulterated letch."

"Not any more, Adam."

"Right, like I believe that."

He just looks up and mumbles, "More steps."

"Can you make it?"

"After what I've been through, hell yeah!"

"The lady Marguerite. Tell me again what she looked like."

"Well, she was about our height, extremely pretty, voluptuous, with a gorgeous smile."

"Was the hair long to mid back?"

"No, it was shoulder length with blonde lockets."

"So it was a wig?"

"I believe so."

"Her smile, did she have dimples?"

"Yeah, yeah she did. Do you know this woman?"

"I thought I did. Now I know I do."

We pause climbing the steps, and he looks at me puzzled. I grin.

"The two men who accosted you at the hotel. Did they have names?"

"I recollect her saying, 'John', and he called the other hoodlum Hayward. Do you know them too?"

"I will explain all during our journey home. You know Mother has been worried sick."

"Is everything on the home front all right? How is Father?"

"Everyone is fine."

I choose not to speak of the town fire just yet.

"How was my release possible?"

"About five thousand dollars worth, thanks to Mister Middleton. Father will be thrilled with this debt."

"I guess we can tell him together."

"Wade, I'll tell Mother, and you tell Father."

We both tighten our lips, not able to hold back a laugh.

"Adam, what brought you to the gallows?"

"It is a long story. Like I said, the tale will be told on our ride home. Right now, you are in store for a tremendous meal."

Jessie greets us at the entrance, and we make our way into the dining room. Henry stands elated.

"Wade, it's so good to see you safe and sound!"

"Thank you, sir. It's good to be back."

"Jessie, hot tea for Wade and Adam."

He motions with his usual cup gesture.

"Yaas, suh."

Wade explains the events to Henry, and we thank him dearly for his assistance and generosity. I assure him of a speedy return to repay the ransom loan.

"Adam, I have new flora for your mother on the downstairs tower landing. Also be sure to convey best wishes to your father."

"That I will, Henry. Thanks again for everything."

We bid gratitude filled farewells, sharing vigorous handshakes and pats on the back.

Tamba places Mother's flowers in the wagon bed, and we climb aboard. With a whistle and jerk on the reins, Gabriel and Nicodemus trot onward. We turn and flail our hats goodbye, as Henry along with family and Jessie wave from the steps.

16

Haunting Love

On the way to our beloved Shiloh and Savannah, we roll by the harbor before stopping at the sheriff's office a last time.

"That's where the ship dropped anchor."

"They are long gone, Wade."

"But I have to find Zazu!"

"First you must regain your strength."

"You don't understand. She will be grossly abused and exploited more than ever."

"There is nothing that can be done for now. I want you to meet Sheriff Cleary. Perhaps he can assist in some way. He and Henry were instrumental helping find you."

"You're right. I should be thrilled to be alive, but feel empty inside."

"You have been through a lot. Give things time."

"My mental scars will never heal."

"Perhaps not. Just remember, Father would say, 'Your adversity has made you a better person.' "

"I can only hope. Tamba, wait!"

"Yaas, Mass Wade."

"What is it?"

"Adam, something caught my eye down that pier. I'll be right back."

"I will go with you."

"No, no, I'll be fine."

Wade hobbles down the long boarded walkway while Tamba and I look on. I can hear him calling for someone. He finally gimps back, clutching something in his arms.

"Who is that?"

"This is Lucy."

He is snuggling and making over her as if a long, lost friend.

"Meow," the Calico responds, and purrs.

"A cat, Wade?"

"No, Adam, far more than a mere kitty. I was dehumanized until she restored my sense of love and compassion."

"Love and compassion? You mean lust and indifference? I apologize, Wade, but those spoken words are not normal, coming from you."

"People change, Adam."

Tamba and I look at one another confused. We both know his past distain of felines, and have never heard him speak with a soft side. Hopefully an epiphany has also changed his infernal snoring.

We resume our ride to the courthouse. Tamba watches Lucy while Wade and I enter. Upon opening the sheriff's door, Daisy springs from the chair, approaching me like clockwork. She sniffs the feet of a new friend as Wade pets her.

"Adam!" Sheriff Cleary greets.

"Sheriff, his story is unbelievable."

"Wade, I'm really glad we found you. With all your posted sketches, you could run for politics."

Everybody laughs as we exchange firm grips with the sheriff.

"By the way, one of our recent arrests turned out to be George Clark. I recognized the name from Rufus' lodging registry, and the blacksmith identified him as the horse thief. It seems Mister Clark is actually a wanted pirate captain, along with a number of his crew. Rufus has them under lock and key. I'll arrest the remainder of his mates, if I can find them."

"Sheriff, we rode by the harbor on the way here, and his ship pulled anchor."

"How do you know about his vessel, Adam?"

"My brother will explain all."

Wade describes his abduction ordeal and voyage to the Caribbean. The sheriff listens intently, performing his own sailing to the spittoon. I fill in Wade's narration regarding Lavinia's involvement. Sheriff Cleary is amazed he survived the calamity.

"After they got the ransom money, I suppose they didn't need their convicted captain or crew mates."

"You're right, Sheriff. So much for honor among thieves. I'm just glad I lived to tell the story."

"We are deeply indebted and cannot thank you enough. You're always welcome at Shiloh."

"Thank you, Adam. Charleston is a better city, and I'm a better lawman having known you."

"I also want to thank you, Sheriff," Wade interjects.

"Just glad you're all right."

"Sheriff, I need to locate a person I befriended during my captivity, but she set sail with Captain Clarke's thugs."

"I'm notifying the military about the sea bandits. Hopefully one of our schooners will outmaneuver it, so we can arrest the remaining crew. What is her name?"

"Zazu."

"I'll keep you posted on any development, Wade."

"Please do."

We all shake hands during our expressed farewells.

Before leaving town, we stop by the post office to mail Mother's final letter. Postmaster Bacot is pleased to hear of Wade's finding and removes the posted sketch. I notice another person's drawing, thinking he is also missing. However, Sheriff Cleary thought the display of wanted outlaws might also prove beneficial.

Leaving town, we travel Meeting Street Road, passing the Six Mile House ruins. Only the weathered road sign speaks its existence. I tell my brother this desolate ground is where my incredible venture started.

"Tamba, halt!"

"Yaas, Mass Wade."

Wade slowly climbs off the wagon toward the signpost. He grabs hold of it and struggles to remove the sunken relic. Tamba looks at me grinning, and I nod.

"Mass Wade, I'll do it."

He jumps from the wagon.

Tamba wraps the post within his massive arms. Then he bends his knees and plants his footing solidly on the grass. He grunts once and unearths it with ease.

"Tamba, you get stronger with age."

"Yaas, suh, Mass Wade."

He smiles proudly and tosses the sign in the wagon.

"Little Brother, this is your memento."

"Thanks, Wade."

"You're surely welcome, Brother."

"What happened to *little*?"

"You just graduated, again."

I resume the story of Six Mile House and our common distraction with Lavinia. Although her pretense undoubtedly led to Wade's misfortune, she tried to free him because of our love. Lavinia died regretfully, feeling responsible for Wade's presumed death by pirates. Knowing this, I am more convinced than ever of her honorable intentions. She was an unfortunate victim of intimidation and abuse, misguided by fear. During our time together, true love and friendship blossomed, something that she never before experienced.

The trip home is filled with conversation, and I tell Wade about the great Savannah fire. He is disheartened. However, my thoughts lament foremost over Lavinia. Before we know it, the strong sentries standing guard appear, and we creak along under nature's canopy.

When approaching the big house, Mother runs toward us crying and screaming, "They're home! Thank God, they're home!"

Fatu dashes from the entrance door holding Gumbu. Jeremy and Sanie come running from the secret garden, chased by a barking Colossus.

"Look, Sanie, a kitty-cat!" Jeremy shouts.

"Here, Tamba. Please put her in my room, safe from Colossus."

"Yaas, Mass Wade."

Tamba and I once more look at one another in disbelief. Wade is not known for rendering polite requests.

We all leap from the wagon, enjoying loving embraces from our families. Mother is so excited to see Wade she becomes faint. We sit and fan her on the portico, but not before she reddens Wade's forehead with kisses.

"Mother, you received our letter?"

"Yes, it arrived yesterday."

She catches her breath while holding Wade's hand.

"Were you fighting Indians, Wade?" Jeremy asks.

"No, I was fighting ships of pirates on the seven seas."

"Feeding ships of pirates is more accurate," I mumble to Tamba, and we laugh.

"Tell us, Wade! Tell us!"

"After dinner boys, not now."

"Come on Sanie, let's find some swords!"

The boys run to play with an excited Colossus trailing.

"Mother, Henry sent you new flora."

"I'll get it, Mass Adam."

"Tamba, place it by the garden entrance. I will plant it tomorrow, but do water it," Mother yells.

"Yaas, ma'am."

"Oh Wade, we missed you so much. Thank God you're alive. Tell me what happened."

He informs Mother of his misfortune and capture by pirates, careful to omit any upsetting details. After supper we return to the portico, and he imparts another embellished version to Jeremy and Sanie. The boys are intrigued listening to a swashbuckling story. Of course, the twisted plot credits Wade as the hero with Tamba and I having incidental involvement.

"Adam, come with me," Mother requests, while Wade continues to entertain the boys.

"Yes, Mother."

We walk into her secret garden, and she questions me regarding Lavinia. I talk about our friendship, feeling she would not understand or condone the extent of our real relationship.

Arriving at the gate temple, we sit at a small table. She looks at me calmly and smiles.

"Adam, a mother knows when her son is in love. I'm so sorry for her passing."

She reaches out and pats my hand.

Feeling emotion overcome me, I glance at her and simply nod my head. I should have known her intuition prevails. She stands up and walks behind my chair. Leaning over, she hugs my shoulders and kisses my temple.

Mother empathizes over Lavinia's death, citing such punishment as barbaric, unjust, and unchristian. She mentions Pennsylvania abolished capital punishment for most criminal cases years ago, substituting solitary confinement. Mother credits the Quaker religious influence for the penal reform.

While strolling toward the big house, we stop to pay homage to her crucifixion statue. She grabs my hand and we kneel. I bow my head in prayer, and we deliver reverent whispers.

After everybody retires for the evening, I remain on the portico, smoking one of my delectables. Chirping crickets and a cool night breeze join my thoughts, as Tamba approaches.

"Mass Adam, I forgot to return dis."

He hands over my undelivered note, intended to introduce Lavinia to Mother.

"Thank you."

"I'm sorry, Mass Adam."

"I know, just pray she has found peace. Sleep well, Tamba."

"Good night, Mass Adam."

As he walks away, I gaze to the stars and ponder our existence and afterlife. Does she see me as I stand here?

Will I meet her in death? On the way to bed I place the letter keepsake in the study strongbox.

Before long the plantation was operating as normal, and Father again arrived home from England. To our dismay, Doctor Parkinson's remedies proved no cure. Father, Tamba, and I travel to Middleton Barony the subsequent month to repay the ransom loan. Wade opts to remain home citing enough absence already.

*   *   *

Once we arrive, Henry and Father reminisce past times, joking and laughing like I have never seen before. Both know the years are dwindling and acknowledge the preciousness of time. I watch them recapture a youthful vigor if only through stories. Their lifelong friendship is quite admirable.

I visit the wood nymph statue every day. Knowing Lavinia is at rest in a peaceful setting helps soothe my soul. Hopefully, prison and judicial reforms are on the horizon. Perhaps proof of guilt beyond doubt and humane punishment will someday prevail.

Tamba and I venture to town to visit Sheriff Cleary. Although once more a deputy, he still can be found in the same office. Like Grandfather with Charles Town versus Charleston, I insist on calling him Sheriff.

"Tamba, come greet the sheriff after securing the wagon."

"Yaas, Mass Adam."

I open the door, and Daisy again leaps from the chair seeking my affection.

"Adam, good to see you old friend," the sheriff exclaims, after wiping his mouth from a successful spittoon sailing.

"Sheriff, I miss our daily visits."

Our hands engage a firm handshake.

"Are you in town awhile?"

"We return to Shiloh in a couple of days. Father is visiting with Henry."

The door again opens as Tamba stoops to clear the entryway.

"Tamba, greetings!"

"Hello, Mis'tuh Sheriff Cleary."

Strangely, Daisy remains in the chair, staring at Tamba while wagging her tail. The four-legged creature appears intimidated by the towering man. Tamba, a gentle soul with animals, kneels to coax the apprehensive dog. Eventually, she warms and another friendship is seeded.

"Adam, this visit calls for celebration."

The sheriff opens his desk drawer, and removes a bottle of whiskey with three glasses. I normally never imbibe before evening hours. However, refusing the hospitality of such a special friend would be rude. Tamba is thankful for the gesture but never partakes in alcohol. Of course, if Wade the raconteur were here, the bottle would be emptied by a full afternoon of hot air.

"Adam, I published a statement disavowing John Fisher's final words. I assured the public of no impropriety concerning Fisher's identification by the waggoner, John Peoples."

"I doubt if anyone believed him."

"Well, if nothing else it made me feel better. How's Wade doing?"

"He is doing well, but seems like a different person in many ways."

"Adam, his ordeal would surely make a man think. It appears he was real intent on locating Zazu when he was here last."

"I know, Sheriff. It is almost an obsession."

"Well, remind him I'll help any way possible, but so far I haven't heard anything from our military."

After good conversation and many laughs, we prepare to leave.

"I cannot thank you enough for your help and concern this past year. You are always welcome at Shiloh."

"That's what friends are for, Adam. I'll pay you a visit soon."

"By the way, Rufus seems to be on edge lately. He asked if you would stop by when you were in town."

"Sure, we will ride over before heading back to Henry's."

"Adam, farewell old friend."

"Stay safe, Sheriff."

Our hands grasp firmly with the strength of friendship.

"Good day, Tamba."

"Goodbye, Mis'tuh Sheriff Cleary."

In an unusual gesture the sheriff extends his hand. Both men smile as the sheriff's hand disappears within Tamba's massive grip.

Tamba and I depart to the City Jail as our wagon wheels bounce along the familiar uneven pavers.

*   *   *

"Good day, Rufus."

"Adam, I'm so glad you're back. Greetings, Tamba."

"Hello, Mis'tuh Rufus."

"Sheriff Cleary said you wanted to see me."

"Yes, I need to talk to you in private."

"You can speak freely in Tamba's presence. Is there a problem?"

"In a manner of speaking. There have been strange sounds originating from this ground floor. I heard them echoing down the hallway toward my quarters. Even the ghastly hangman in his drunken state has questioned me about them," he explains nervously.

"What is this noise?"

"It's an awful shriek and footsteps pacing the corridor."

"Perhaps, an agonizing cat's cry has captured your imagination."

"No, not a feline or other animal can mimic what I heard. It chills your spine I tell you."

"Rufus, what time does this occur?"

"Only during the wee morning hours of Friday."

"When did these events begin?"

"A week after Lavinia met her Maker, the following Friday and each one since. Remember, she vowed to haunt the governor and Charleston forever, seeking revenge!"

"I am sure there is a plausible explanation. Besides, fear not for yourself. She was thankful for your kind concern."

"Adam, I know it is her."

"Pray tell how."

"I make no mention, fearing I'll be thought a lunatic."

"We shall tell no one."

He pauses, whispering, "I have seen her apparition."

"A specter, what are you saying?"

"It's true. The first night a terrible scream awakened me around two o'clock in the morning. Seconds later, I heard steps in the hall pass my door. With a lantern in one hand and pistol in the other, I went to investigate. While I crept along the corridor wall, the sound of distant walking was joined by the thump of a closing door."

He hesitates, and wipes his sweaty brow on his shirtsleeve.

"Here," I offer, handing him a handkerchief.

"Adam, as I neared the vestibule, the confinement room entryway was shut. I know it was open when I retired, but no one else was in sight. I rarely use this room, unless for private discussion. As a matter of fact, it hasn't been occupied since you last met with Lavinia. Anyway, I caught a glimpse of movement within the room. It dashed past the barred window," he goes on to say, motioning with a quivering hand.

"Are you sure the guards were not playing a trick?"

"No one can enter this floor past ten o'clock at night. I personally lock the stairwell and outside entrance doors. Sheriff Cleary has the only other key. I've done it for years as a safety precaution for my spouse."

"What exactly do you think you observed?"

"What I saw from the corner of my eye was no prank. An image rushed by the window bars wearing a white garment. That's when I became really scared and cocked the hammer on my gun. As I sneaked closer to the door, my hands and knees were trembling. Finally, I got up enough nerve to peer through the iron bars and point my shaking pistol."

He takes a breath and pauses, raking jittery fingers through his hair. I glance at Tamba, who is listening intently. Never witnessing Rufus in this state, my skepticism turns to concern.

"You are doing fine, Rufus. Continue."

"Adam, I swear it was her. She stood bent over weeping, having her back toward me. When her upset voice sounded your name, I gasped for air. Then she vanished before my eyes!"

He squirms in his seat, breathing rapidly and perspiring profusely.

"Rufus, calm yourself, and take slow deep breaths."

"I'm all right," he tells me, trying to compose himself.

"Are you sure your senses were not afflicted from liquid spirits that evening?"

"The only liquid afflicting me was that of my wet trousers. Besides, I never drink alcohol, fearing the wrath of my wife."

"I know you to be a hard working honorable man, but this story is difficult to swallow."

"Believe me, Adam. Lodge tonight, and see for yourself. Tomorrow brings another foreboding Friday morning."

"Has this tale repeated itself?"

"She only appeared once to me, but others have heard the screams and footsteps. I told them it is simply late night arrests for drunkenness, not wanting to cause panic. Since my encounter, I lock myself in quarters and do not come out until daybreak."

"So be it. I will prove your imagination got the best of you."

"I have two empty witness cells on this floor where you and Tamba may sleep. I'll bid you goodnight when I lock the entranceways later."

"Fine, Rufus."

He points to our sleeping arrangements and walks away, rubbing the back of his neck.

"Tamba, we will remain here this evening."

He gives me an uneasy look with wide-open eyes.

"Mass Adam, can I sleep outside in dah wagon?"

"You do not believe his preposterous story. Do you?"

"I feel better not sleepin' inside, Mass Adam."

"Very well."

It is ironic observing an otherwise fearless mammoth man, restless with the thought of a ghostly presence. Although I do recall that Sierra Leoneans strongly believe superstitions that revolve around the spirit world.

The sunset brings nightfall and a full moon. Rufus walks through the candlelit hallway and vestibule areas, locking all access doors to the ground level.

"Adam, I only need to bolt the vestibule double doors leading to the jail yard, and all is secure."

"I'll go now, Mass Adam."

"Sleep well, Tamba."

"You're not staying?"

"Yaas, Mis'tuh Rufus, in dah wagon outside."

"Can't say I blame you. Good evening to both of you. The candles will burn until midnight. I placed a lantern in your cell, Adam."

"Thank you."

As the midnight hour approaches, the burning hallway flames flutter. Finally, the candlewicks melt away, as does the building inmate chatter. I walk through the vestibule past the confinement room, and retire to a nearby cell. I lay on a bed of straw restless and thinking about the story Rufus told us. I close my eyes but only doze for short periods of time.

*   *   *

Suddenly, I hear walking in the corridor. As my eyes adjust to the darkness, I light the lantern and ease into the hallway. Holding the shimmering light overhead with Equalizer in my other hand, I see nothing. The footsteps persist toward the vestibule becoming more distant. I follow, treading cautiously. Halfway down the hall, a hideous shriek startles me and sends shivers down my spine.

"Dear, Lord," I utter.

I become spooked, only hearing this sound once before.

As I approach the confinement room with its barred window door, my heart palpitates.

"Addddam. Addddam," a muffled voice chants.

All at once, a flash of light sweeps past the opened doorway.

"Can it be?" I ask myself.

I lean forward in the entrance and shine my lantern, but see nothing. I inch my way inside. Out of nowhere a burst of cold air smothers my flame. Standing in total darkness and quivering, I turn around to leave. At that second, another frigid blast whips the door closed.

"Lavinia, my love. It is Adam."

I find myself talking to no one, but the strange feeling of anguish and comfort again besets me. All of a sudden I feel familiar soft fingers brush down my hand that is clenching Equalizer. Startled, I drop the miniature pistol.

"Addddam, I'm here."

I turn around, but my terrified eyes see nothing. I dash to open the door. Once in the corridor, I slam the solid oak behind me, breathing rapidly.

"Addddam, I love you."

Frightened, I lean against the door with sweaty palms, looking at the corridor floor.

"Addddam, I love you."

With wide-open eyes, I peer through the barred window, beholding a ghostly image of Lavinia. She stands in her white gown with her face veiled. As she gestures for an embrace, I open my arms. I stare with my mouth agape and heartbeat racing as she walks toward me.

"I love you too, Lavinia!"

She approaches me closer, and another gust of air ruffles her loose-fitting gown and lifts her hair. Then she starts to walk away. I grasp the cold window bars, watching her leave. She turns and waves goodbye.

*   *   *

"I love you too, Lavinia! I love you too, Lavinia!" I awake talking and gasping for air. My heart is pounding, and I am sweating profusely.

"She was so real," I tell myself, catching my breath.

I head to the vestibule. The double doors are open. Tamba stands outside talking with Rufus. As I pass by the confinement room, I hesitate. I step inside and walk around, assuring myself it was but a dream.

The room where we confided, shared tears, and made love does hold her presence. I can almost smell the fragrance of her hair. Last night's vision, words, and touch seemed so genuine. Sometimes the mind can outsmart itself. I turn to leave and step on a hard object. Stooping down, I brush away the straw and Equalizer appears.

"My, God," I mutter, shaken to the core.

Was I sleepwalking? Or was Lavinia actually here?
Once outside, Tamba and Rufus simply look at me.

"I do not know what to say, Rufus."

"Say nothing. Believe what you may."

"Tamba, I will never again question your beliefs in the supernatural."

"Yaas, Mass Adam."

Dream or not, my mind refuses to fully honor the reality of a ghostly existence. We bid Rufus farewell and return to Middleton Barony, never speaking of the incident. I tell Father and Henry our stay in town that evening was by invitation to see an old Charlestonian friend.

* * *

Father, Tamba, and I set out to Shiloh after a most enjoyable visit with Henry. Shortly thereafter, Sheriff Cleary wrote that pirate Captain George Clark was convicted of crimes on the high seas. He was sentenced the following month and hanged from a United States schooner. The horizontal yardarm fronting the mast, which mounts the square sails, swung the noose. The hanging transpired in Charleston harbor. Wade expressed no pity for him and applauded the execution setting as quite befitting.

Later the sheriff told us that Hayward was hanged in early August and Roberts pled guilty of assault. The cropped ear only served a prison term of one year and was fined one thousand dollars. I cannot help but feel the justice system lacked in rendering fair and equitable punishment. Sheriff Cleary also indicated Jervis the coroner continues to pursue an assistant, and still inquires to my status. Sheriff Cleary and I continue to correspond, and periodically visit one another. His tobacco stained bachelorhood remains untainted.

Rufus did not personally witness any more sightings after my last visit. However, he and the guards swear to unidentified footsteps and ghastly screams in the middle of night. I never returned to the City Jail. Perhaps a ghostly presence serves as her legacy, keeping her memory alive forever.

Father took ill in August this year from a Savannah fever outbreak and was treated by Doctor Waring. In a weakened state he succumbed to the illness and was buried in our family plot at Colonial Cemetery. Mother was devastated and Henry deeply saddened. The scourge lasted between May and November, claiming over six hundred and fifty lives. About one tenth of our population was lost including two physicians.

After Father's passing, Mother never recaptured her spirited self. She grieved his death and that of several fever stricken friends. Sorrow followed her every step, even negating the solace afforded from her secret garden. Wade and I care for a mentally ailing Mother and assist rearing Jeremy.

Later this year Congress again addressed the pending statehood admission for Missouri. Basically, slavery is not permitted in any territory north of Missouri's southern border. Missouri itself was permitted to enter as a slave state.

Congress further reacted to end the illegal international African slave trade. Any such trade is now an act of piracy and punishable by death. I foresee this Missouri Compromise accentuating a physical and philosophical divide in our great nation. The soul of our country cannot continue to serve two masters.

The American Society for Colonizing the Free People of Color in the United States also began the process of emigrating free people of color to Africa. The first voyages proved difficult due to the African native chiefs' unwillingness to sell land. President Monroe ultimately sent a convincing military convoy escort, securing a territory purchase for colonization. Although many Negroes opposed the idea, thousands of black colonists eventually returned to the soil of their roots.

The divide deepens between our free and slave states. I also recognize a resurgence of hope for freedom within the most dispirited slaves. I continue to anguish over this issue, knowing their marked freedom will someday erase Grandfather's Shiloh.

Wade has not yet found matrimony, and imbibes no less than usual. He is cautious of every new lady, especially those of blonde persuasion. He continues to sleep with Lucy by his side. She has adapted well to the family, barring Colossus. Wade shows reluctance discussing his bondage ordeals, and I have learned not to pry. I witness a level of respect and compassion from him as never before, especially toward the slaves. The military has not located Captain Clarke's pirate ship, so he is chartering a vessel to find Zazu. Although I empathize with his frustration, I cannot help but feel poetic justice is being served upon him.

Vandi miraculously remains spry and lucid. His story of the African slave traders continues to intrigue the youngsters. Most importantly, the tale is imparted for future generations to be retold and never forgotten.

I freed and discharged Tamba, Fatu, and their heirs from service, but they chose to remain on Shiloh. He is now the head overseer.

Jeremy and Sanie continue to share the foundation of our upbringing. The enduring bond between Tamba and me is a testament to the *gold, frankincense,* and *myrrh* of life.

I think often of Father, forever cherishing his love and guidance. I miss him deeply.

Henry remains a close and dear family friend, and his gardens become more breathtaking with each visit. His slaves continually embellish the grounds and maintain its pastoral setting. The enigmatic wood nymph, graced with perpetual flora, forever epitomizes Lavinia's life and death as beauty besets beauty. With each visit to her final resting place, I still honor our love with a single crimson rose.

*   *   *

Friday, February 18, 1821

Still sitting at Father's desk, I shutter from a smashing lightning bolt. It seemingly awakens my reminiscent trance. I stand and step to the window by way of a small puddle. Rain continues to drip beneath the sill as blustery wind vibrates the whistling sash. Now slightly after two o'clock, the anniversary of Lavinia's passing is marked.

In deep thought, amid ground-shaking thunder and pelting rain, my hand slowly reaches out. I touch the tattered Six Mile House road sign hanging on the wall. Emotion overcomes me. I glance at the letter a final time, and ponder what might have been. Then I sigh and crumble my wishful written words, finally accepting fate's reply.

My love for Lavinia forever haunts me. I cannot deny the passion and bond we shared. My soul remains spellbound by her heavenly beauty. Our love weathered life's tribulations, transcending into death. She will live in my thoughts and forever in my heart.

As I leave Father's study, the door is unbolted only to be relocked. I pause and picture Lavinia grasping the cold window bars, watching me leave. While walking away, I turn and wave goodbye.